The
Goodness
of
Unicorns

What Other People Are Saying...

"WEAVING TOGETHER FAMILIAR FANTASTICAL creatures with elements of vibrant faith, *The Goodness of Unicorns* is such a sweet story that reminds us of the value of family and that our worth goes far deeper than our outward abilities. With the onset of battle between kingdoms and within hearts, I eagerly await the next installment of *The Tritonia Chronicles*."

-Tabitha Caplinger
Author of Realm Award and Carol Award finalist novel, *The Wayward*

"THE GOODNESS OF UNICORNS is a tale of two sisters that combines the whimsy of *The Wingfeather Saga* with the sweetness of *Little Women*. Filled with spiritual truth, lighthearted moments, and magical gifts, this story is a pure delight that readers will fall in love with again and again."

-Mariposa Aristeo
Author of *Sons of Day and Night*

"THE GOODNESS OF UNICORNS is an endearing story that showcases deep unconditional sisterly love, finding joy amidst chronic illness, and doing the right thing even when it's dangerous. Kayla E. Green weaves a story appropriate for all ages without shying away from real-world struggles."

-Anne J. Hill
Author of *What Darkness Fears*

"FILLED WITH HEART. HOPE, and goodness, this fantasy is a fresh addition to the genre. It's perfect for anyone who loves a quest, the power of faith, and strong family ties."

-Moriah Chavis
Author of *The Curious Case of the Midnight Specter* and *Heart of the Sea*

"THE GOODNESS OF UNICORNS beautifully blends faith, courage, and wonder into an unforgettable tale. This enchanting story reminds us that true strength comes from within and hope can light even the darkest paths. A magical read you won't want to put down!"

-Jen Weaver, Patient Leader & Advocate with RA
Author of *So, You're Newly Diagnosed*
Creator & host of *My Spoonie Sisters*

"A UNIQUE STORY THAT touches on a variety of themes! While Rowan is thrust into court politics and ancient prophecy, Blythe's quieter journey is just as powerful. Living with chronic pain and often overlooked, Blythe's voice is a tender and raw mirror to so many who feel unseen. Her storyline is a brilliant counterbalance, showing that bravery doesn't always look like riding into battle. Sometimes, it looks like holding on when everything hurts. With beautifully written characters, a richly imagined world, and emotionally grounded stakes, this story is a must-read for fans of fantasy. It speaks not just to young adults but also to anyone who's ever wondered if their pain or imperfections disqualify them from making a difference."

-Readers' Favorite 5-Star Review

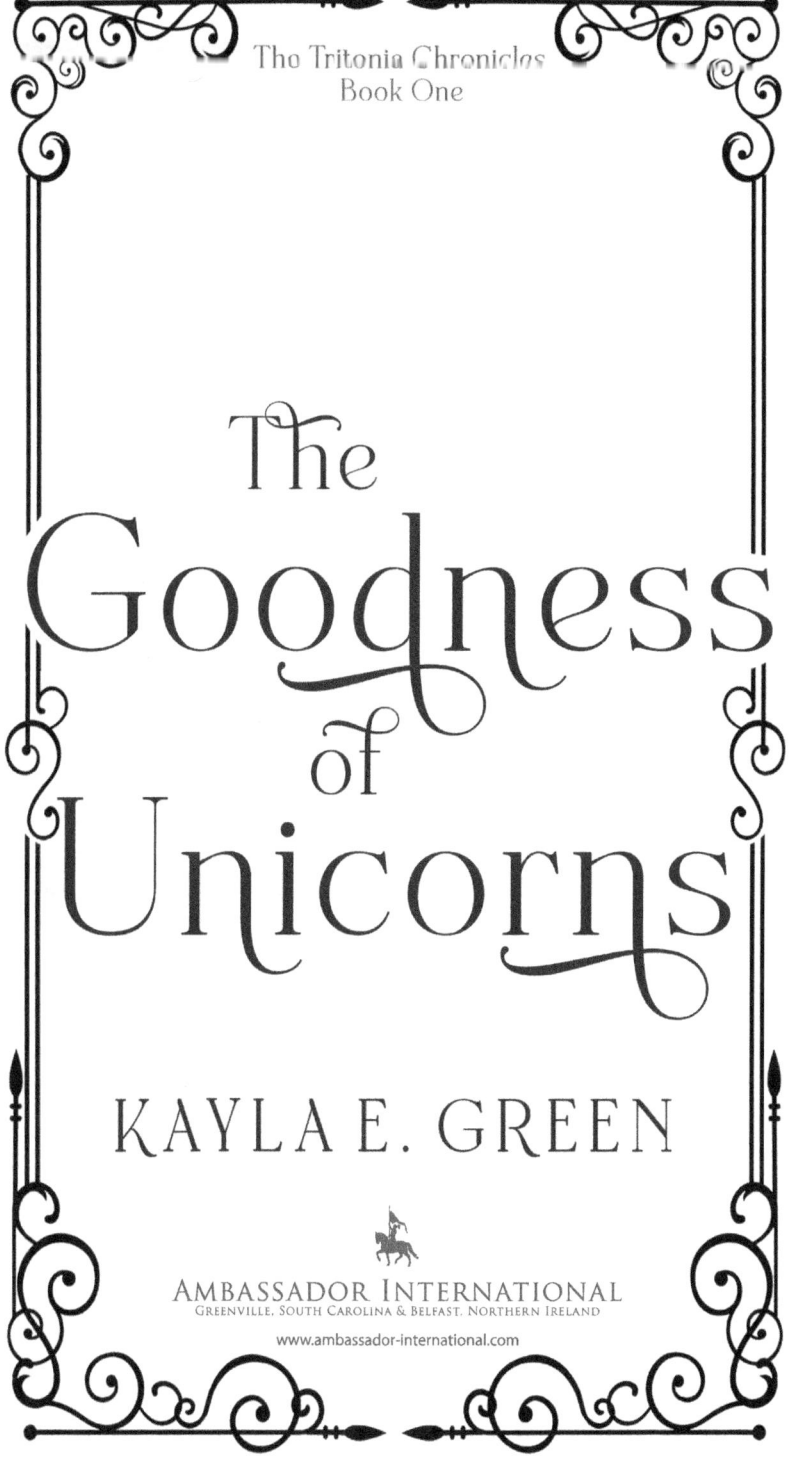

The Tritonia Chronicles
Book One

The
Goodness
of
Unicorns

KAYLA E. GREEN

AMBASSADOR INTERNATIONAL
GREENVILLE, SOUTH CAROLINA & BELFAST, NORTHERN IRELAND

www.ambassador-international.com

The Goodness of Unicorns

The Tritonia Chronicles, Book 1

©2025 by Kayla E. Green

All rights reserved

ISBN: 978-1-64960-882-6, hardcover
ISBN: 978-1-64960-602-0, paperback
eISBN: 978-1-64960-653-2

Cover design by Emilie Hendrix
Interior typesetting by Dentelle Design
Edited by Sydney Witbeck

AMBASSADOR INTERNATIONAL
Emerald House
411 University Ridge, Suite B14
Greenville, SC 29601
United States
www.ambassador-international.com

AMBASSADOR BOOKS
The Mount
2 Woodstock Link
Belfast, BT6 8DD
Northern Ireland, United Kingdom
www.ambassadormedia.co.uk

The colophon is a trademark of Ambassador, a Christian publishing company.

For my twin sister and first friend, Kari:

My world, and the world at large, is brighter with you in it.

May everyone who reads this find the strength in their own journeys to embrace the beacon of hope God has placed in their hearts for both themselves and those around them.

"But in your hearts revere Christ as Lord. Always be prepared to give an answer to everyone who asks you to give the reason for the hope that you have. But do this with gentleness and respect."
-1 Peter 3:15

Prologue
The Almost Queen

"WHAT IF I TRIP OR fall—or worse?" asked the young servant girl as her eyes widened. "What if I spill water on Sir Elias, and he arrests me?"

"Sir Elias is a loud, boisterous man, but he's sensible," Linnea offered while holding back a smile for fear the girl would think she was mocking her. "He won't arrest a maiden for a simple accident." She placed a gentle hand on the thin girl's shoulder. "Nora, you are sweet and trustworthy. It's an honor to be the cupbearer of the king."

Nora's face blanched. "Maybe Mrs. Ginty should send someone else."

"Do you see this plant, Nora?" Linnea softly touched the orange-tinged green leaves of an herb with bell-shaped purple petals. The tall, flowering plant nearly reached her waist. "This is a *Medirorum Mundatium*, better known as the Healing Bell."

Nora fidgeted with the frayed edges of her apron. "Forgive me, milady, but I don't know a lot about flowers."

Lines crinkled at the outer corners of Linnea's eyes as she swept an arm around the room lit only by candlelight. "There are no windows. One might think the Healing Bell should not be here. But there's purpose beyond what is visible on the surface. You can worry and fret that it will wither or trust that it will thrive. Do you understand what I'm trying to say, Nora?"

Nora cast her green eyes down. Linnea offered a hand to her young companion.

"You are capable of more than you know. You are a strong, and you shouldn't let—"

The large wooden door was thrown open. A broad-shouldered young man adorned in a silver tunic with a green sash and the Obsilvian crest barged in with a scowling Wisterian soldier at his heels. The soldier spoke, but the traveler's voice drowned him out.

"Milady, are you lost?" The newcomer asked as he scanned the king's advisory hall, his eyes landing on Linnea. His roguish, sharp accent was harsh. "I think the acting troupe is performing in the main dining room for courtiers and female guests," he added with a sneer that Linnea felt was not intended to be subtle.

"An acting troupe?" Linnea responded with a smile. She turned toward the man who stood on the other side of the council table in the center of the room. She lightly touched the golden brooch on her shoulder as she continued speaking. "I'm sure my brother will love to attend their show later. He is a lover of drama."

The visitor pulled out a chair. The reflective green stone on the signet ring on his thumb caught Linnea's eye before he casually turned it to where the gem faced his palm. He said, "You'd best fetch him before the king finds a woman eavesdropping on the business of men."

"Sir Hamlin, you are a visitor to Wisteria, so I will forgive your ignorance only once." The king's youthful yet strong voice preceded his entrance, causing Hamlin to rise to his feet again. "Not only is Lady Linnea my sister; but she is also my most trusted advisor, aside from the diatomist, and she serves as royal regent in my absence." The king eyed Hamlin. "You're younger than I expected. Have you had only fifteen naming anniversaries?"

Hamlin's jaw clenched. "Twenty." He scratched his thin, close-cut black beard, a token style of the kingdom of Obsilvia, before he nodded. "My apologies. It seems I failed to do my part in preparing adequately for this meeting as your guest, King Isak." He turned to Linnea and smiled warmly. "If the city of Tulium proves to be half as beautiful as you, Lady Linnea, then my travels will have been well worth it."

Linnea smiled in return, hoping her growing disdain was well hidden as she stepped to the seat to the king's right. Shortly after King Isak entered, the royal diatomist, Dendro; the royal finance officer, Lirk; and the chief army commander, Elias, joined them around the short, oblong table.

"I trust your travels over the Dimidi Sea were well with Verimor's provision?" Dendro's raspy voice questioned after polite introductions were made. He leaned over the table and crossed his arms, which were engulfed by his long, wide sleeves.

Hamlin nodded. "Yes, my travels both by sea and on horseback were quite good. Your kingdom's territories are quite hospitable and welcoming to travelers. Someone unknowing of the Wisterian desire to earn approval from their perceived deity might interpret your people's kindness as something to approach with apprehension. But every encounter has been most pleasant."

"*Perceived deity?*" echoed Dendro with a sputter. His eyebrows were raised over his low-perched, gold-rimmed glasses. "The Caranaithian dynasty is young; but surely, they have not strayed away from the very cornerstone of the world's creation!"

Hamlin waved his hand, dismissing the objection. "The Caranaithian royal family are, by necessity, modern people who seek out truth that rigid tradition and unwavering loyalty to mere lore tries to hide from the masses. Nevertheless, King Tramein believes that a truce can be achieved between Wisteria and Obsilvia."

"Ha!" The ruddy-faced Elias snorted. "Tramein, led by only his own whim with no regard for Divine authority, sends an obnoxious fool to meet with King Isak in hopes of appeasement?" He slammed his fist down as his voice grew louder. "Preposterous!"

Hamlin leaned back in his chair just as Nora stepped forward with cups and a pitcher of water. With a clatter, the tray she held hit the tabletop; but Hamlin's quick reflexes steadied the water pitcher. He helped the blushing girl right the turned cups before she poured water into each one with shaking hands. Linnea tried to offer her a comforting smile from across the table, but Nora never looked up as the cups were filled.

"The ongoing war, which we all know was first waged by Tramein's grandfather," Lirk's flat, tired voice droned in Linnea's ears while she watched Nora with concern, "is at an impasse primarily because of the natural borders between both kingdoms."

"Is it?" Hamlin asked as his expression turned to exaggerated awe. He cupped his palm around his chin. "Now, I am only from

Obsilvia, and I clearly am not adequately prepared for our meeting. However, if memory serves me well, there are both mountains and a sea creating a divide between the two kingdoms." Hamlin took a deep inhale as Nora placed the final cup in front of him before retreating to the corner of the room. "However—and correct me if I'm mistaken—there is also a territory within the Dimidi Sea that Wisteria insists they have a right to rule over?"

Elias slammed his fist against the dark wood of the table once again. His chainmail clanked as his whole body shook with the movement. "The Dimidi Isles have always been outside of any kingdom's rule!"

"That's *almost* true." Hamlin placed emphasis on the second word and let his eyes meet Linnea's. "Those lands were meant to fall under Obsilvian authority, and Obsilvia would have been successful had it not been for Wisterian trespassers who convinced the people of the Isles to rebel. Your people's need to interfere was unfounded and only added to the distrust between our nations. Such a pity, truly."

King Isak reached for his cup with a sigh; but Linnea put her hand out, stopping him. Etiquette dictated that no one could drink before the king started, so all other cups remained untouched. She cleared her throat and wrapped her fingers around the stem of her brother's gem-studded goblet.

"My people only desired for the Dimidi Isles to keep the independence they have always had. And the real pity, Sir Hamlin," Linnea said as she stood, "is that King Tramein, as well as the entire Caranaithian royal family, did not send an honorable man to pursue a peace agreement."

As she talked, she moved slowly sideways toward the Healing Bell, her eyes never leaving Hamlin's face. "In fact, my good sir, you have made it quite clear your intentions are far from pure as you have insulted my own person directly as well as spewed clear blasphemy against Verimor."

Linnea watched Hamlin's face grow dark as she tipped the cup and let the water fall into the plant's soil.

Hamlin laughed, but the sound was stiff. "I promise any insult was not intentional. But it seems I will have to let my king know that a truce was not even *almost* obtained." He stood and turned to leave.

Linnea stepped quickly toward him with her hand extended. "Now, I must insist that you don't hurry off." She placed a hand on his arm. "I may only be a woman interjecting into the affairs of men, but it does seem you have more to tell about who you are and why you were sent. In fact, with that symbol on your signet ring, you don't appear to be a royal ambassador at all."

"Four serpents converging into one?" Elias snatched Hamlin's hand, bending the Obsilvian ambassador's wrist at an unnatural angle. The subdued man winced and gritted his teeth. "What does this mean?" Instead of answering the knight, Hamlin spit at him.

Elias dropped the man's arm with a snarl while Dendro raised his pointer finger and shouted, "The leaves—the Healing Bell's leaves are turning black!"

"Sir Elias, arrest him!" King Isak ordered among the mangled shouts of the other men.

Hamlin twisted Linnea's arm and pulled a small dagger from his belt, which had been tucked away out of sight. He pulled her against him and held the weapon against her porcelain skin. "You think you're clever, don't you?" Hamlin hissed in Linnea's ear. Louder, he seethed, "There is no Verimor or any Divine power, but the only thing prompting my question of that fact is that you were indeed *rightfully* kept from the throne!"

"Do something, Sir Elias, now!" yelled Isak as the blade pricked Linnea's neck just enough to draw blood.

She didn't flinch, treating the attack as no more than an insect bite. "When it comes to the label 'almost,' we are one and the same," Linnea whispered. "For you didn't achieve your goal here today." In repetitively swift movements, she retrieved a hidden knife in her brooch, cut Hamlin's arm, and broke away from his grasp.

The man fell to his knees with a wide-eyed expression.

"Oh, Sir Hamlin, do not fret. I know a mere woman who believes lore as truth should not be among men; and she certainly should not have the intellectual capacity to understand poisons or poison-detecting flora, let alone carry a poison-dipped blade on her person that causes long-term consequences. But here I am."

Elias, with the help of the soldier who stood guard outside the room since Isak's arrival, hoisted Hamlin to his feet.

"Lock the would-be murderer away until next steps are arranged," said a tight-lipped and tense King Isak.

As the men went to cross the threshold with their prisoner, Linnea leaned over the immobilized Hamlin. She boldly declared, "May you, and all of Obsilvia, know your assassination plot turned into an *almost* success because of the *almost* queen."

Chapter One
Your Eyes

"**I**'LL GET THEM!" ROWAN'S GOLDEN-AMBER cheeks, framed by wavy locks of brown hair, flushed as she frantically chased after four rolling tangerines on the ground. Securing them in her hands, the girl stood up and placed them back in their bin. "Mr. Oxeye, I didn't mean to bump into your table and encourage these runaway citruses."

"Don't worry, Rowan," said the tall man with graying hair standing beside the fruit stand. He resituated the same fruit she had touched, making a uniform row. "We just want to make sure the tangerines are arranged in a way that will *appeal* to customers." Mr. Oxeye chuckled at his own words. His son, Bane, who stood next to him, laughed as well.

Rowan shifted back on her feet and tugged at the long sleeves of her orange dress. "Oh, I don't think you have to worry about customers not liking the fruit. Everyone knows Mrs. Oxeye's family orchards have the best produce in the kingdom of Wisteria."

Bane stifled a laugh. "Pops said '*appeal*,' but it was a play on the fruit having *a peel*. Get it?"

Shaking her head, Rowan linked arms with Bane once again. "See you and Mrs. Oxeye at dinner tonight," she called to Bane's father. Mr. Oxeye chuckled and waved as Rowan and Bane turned away.

"This is for you, but I'll give it to you when we stop for our treat after the library." Bane tucked the little bag into his own pants pocket.

"If this promise you do break"—Rowan thought a bit—"then a . . . *bite of lemon* you shall take."

"Eww! You know I hate lemons. They're too sour." Bane grimaced.

"Then you'd best keep your promise," Rowan smiled triumphantly.

The pair walked together through the bustling cobbled streets of the local town market in Aconite, a small, subdued territory tucked away by the coast of the kingdom of Wisteria.

"Don't you think it's strange?" Rowan asked, her gaze shifting from passerby to passerby as they strolled.

"How you often have an inner monologue and then pull me in as if I know what you're talking about?" Bane raised one eyebrow.

Rowan giggled.

"What I meant is all this." She gestured around with her free hand. "These people each have their own life and their own story. Some faces I know by name, some by sight; and yet I still feel like I see new people on each trip to the market at the week's end. There are so many stories in the world that we'll never know."

Bane shrugged nonchalantly. "Seems like with all the books you read, your head would be tired of stories. I honestly don't know how you read like you do."

"Like I've said for years, reading is beautiful." She paused as they turned the corner toward the Magna Library. "You just haven't found the right book yet."

"All books include people; and I have met the right person for me, thank you very much."

Rowan stopped walking. She looked at Bane with a tilt of her head, her heart beating quicker. "What do you mean?"

Bane's fair complexion burned red. Rowan felt her own cheeks heat, and she wasn't sure if it was because of Bane's words or his reaction to her question.

Her friend cleared his throat and pointed to a vendor near the library's entrance. "Look! Flower crowns! Let's get one for you to take back to Blythe."

Rowan froze. Despite the smile on her lips, her muscles tensed. Bane released her arm and placed a hand on her shoulder. "Your sister is strong. She *will* get better. Soon, she'll be out and about with us, just like old times."

Rowan simply nodded before moving closer to the merchant. "Excuse me, ma'am, how much is it for one of these?"

"Two coppers, please," the blonde woman replied. Her hair was swept atop her head in a full, towering, braided bun.

Rowan pulled the needed copper coins from her brown messenger bag, and Bane waved at the woman. "Ida, right? I met you in the jeweler's shop a while back with my father. I didn't know you worked with the florist, too."

Ida smiled sweetly. "It's important to keep busy and offer a working hand whenever you can." She handed Rowan a crown made of bright marigolds that sat on a small rolling cart.

Rowan's hands gingerly grasped the floral wreath. Before Ida released her own grip, she whispered, "May these gold blooms be a reflection of the light of goodness Verimor extends to you and all of His children."

"Thank you," Rowan said softly, perplexed by the goosebumps prickling down her arms.

Bane stepped forward and took the crown. He placed it on Rowan's head. "Might as well wear it until we get back home."

"You don't think I look silly?" Her nose crinkled. "I mean, am I too old for things like this now?"

"Rowan, you look beautiful." Bane looked in Rowan's brown eyes for a moment, then quickly shifted his gaze. He cleared his throat. "And who says there is an age limit on fun?" He motioned her up the stone steps into the library with a wave of his hand.

She turned back to where the flower merchant was, but the woman had apparently been swept away into the busy crowd. Rowan rotated again and directed her gaze upward. Even though she had been to the library countless times, multi-colored, stained-glass windows above the library's door never ceased to amaze her. Two panels showed different illustrations of important messengers of Verimor found in the ancient text, the *Book of Verimor*: a unicorn in front of the sun and a phoenix rising from flames.

Rowan heard a small cough behind her. She looked over her shoulder and found Bane staring at her with a half-smile.

"Sorry, the windows always distract me," she said before stepping inside the stone building.

"No need to apologize," Bane said, his footsteps echoing hers on the stone. "I imagine we all get caught up in our thoughts when it comes to Verimor and what lies ahead in life from time to time."

Rowan let her fingertips lightly touch the leather spines peeking out at her from their place on the wall as she slowly strolled down the main aisle. Every inch of wall space held book-covered shelves. "Just like there are so many people in the world today we will never know, think about all the stories before us we will never hear." Her voice dropped in volume as she added to herself, "I wish Verimor would send one of His unicorns to help heal Blythe."

"Rowan, I love your crown." Miss Thistle, the head librarian, waved from where she stood behind a large, wooden desk. She was a short woman, who had white hair despite only being in her mid-thirties. Her hair was almost as long as she was tall, but she wore it swooped up in a large bun on the back of her head.

"Celebrating something special today?" Miss Thistle asked.

"It's her sixteenth naming anniversary," explained Bane.

"Oh, happy day to you! I pray Verimor grants you with lots of wishes on this very important day." Miss Thistle pushed open a short door and walked from behind the desk to a shelf a few aisles from Rowan. She climbed a ladder and pulled down a small book. "Do you know why wishes are given on the sixteenth naming anniversary?" she asked while thumbing through the pages. Her thin, golden-framed glasses perched so close to the tip of her nose that Rowan wondered how they didn't fall off her face all together.

Rowan straightened her shoulders as she recited:

"To show His love to all His kin,

Verimor gives wishes when the sixteenth year begins.

Every heart's request is granted,

For every single seed unplanted, giving us all a life fully blessed."

Miss Thistle nodded. "Beautifully recited! Now, most Wisterian children have heard that rhyme, but do you know the *truth* behind it?"

"The unicorn Cressida visited Liam, the boy who would grow up to be the first king of Wisteria, when he was sixteen and gave him a somni melon. She told him that each seed would give him a gift from Verimor," explained Rowan.

"Someone knows her history. Well done!" Miss Thistle looked in the book she was holding and read, "Young Liam opened the pale green somni melon, a gift from the guide sent by Verimor, and found four seeds. Through the seeds, he received the following blessings: deliverance from a plague that struck his household, a promised land for followers of Verimor, liberation from his enemies with peace during his reign, and the assurance that Verimor would never stop loving anyone who believed in Him—including Liam." She slid a ribbon bookmark between the pages and closed the book. "I think Blythe will enjoy this one. It's an academic exploration of the role of unicorns as messengers of Verimor, protectors of His children, and defenders of light."

"I'm sure she will like it," Rowan agreed with a nod.

Bane shook his head. "I don't understand how either of you Tritonia girls read so much, and I definitely don't get how an *academic exploration* is interesting to anyone."

Rowan sighed. "Miss Thistle, do you have any books for Bane? I need to prove to him that he will love reading once he finds the right book."

"Of course, I can offer suggestions," said Miss Thistle with a beaming smile. "The first place to start in finding a book you will like is by finding topics you like. What do you enjoy, Bane?"

The boy gave a stilted laugh and rubbed the back of his neck. "It's not that I dislike reading. I just can't devour book after book like Rowan and Blythe do."

"He likes watching the boats by the docks, building things with his hands, riding horses, and—" A sharp pain in Rowan's temples throbbed violently, making her forget what she was saying. Dizzy and hurting, she swayed on her feet.

"What's wrong?" Bane quickly steadied her.

Rowan exhaled a shaky breath. The pain subsided almost as quickly as it developed. "I felt like I was spinning for a minute, but I'm okay now."

Bane left his arm around Rowan's shoulders. His brow furrowed as he studied her face.

"Have you eaten today?" inquired Miss Thistle. "Maybe if you get something on your stomach, it will help."

"Yes, some food will probably do me good." Rowan smiled at Bane. "I'm fine, really."

Slowly, Bane let go of his hold on Rowan.

"If it happens again, you have to tell me, so we can go see my mother."

"There's no reason to bother your mother. I don't need a healer. I—"

"If this promise you do break, then a . . . drink of dandelion tea you shall take," interrupted Bane.

"Eww, you know I hate that bitter mess. Yes, I'll tell you if my head starts hurting again. I promise." Rowan faced Miss Thistle and gestured to the book still in the librarian's hands. "Thank you for thinking of Blythe. Hopefully, she will be able to visit you in person soon. I know she misses the library."

Miss Thistle pulled a quill from behind her ear, licked the tip, made a quick note in her large librarian's ledger, and handed it to Rowan. "Tell Blythe hello for me. Oh, and I do wish you a happy naming anniversary."

Rowan thanked her once again as she tucked the book in the leather bag hanging over her shoulder. Bane and Rowan exited the library and found themselves back on the cobblestone street. They walked a bit and turned left at the corner toward Mrs. Bredon's tea shop, which was less than a block away.

The sweet aromas of chocolate, cinnamon, and fresh-baked pastries greeted Rowan as she pushed open the wooden door. The animated laughter and multitude of conversations from a crowd of patrons was a stark contrast to the empty quiet of the Magna Library.

"Rowan, why don't you go find us a place to sit, and I'll go buy us something to eat?"

"Okay." Rowan opened her bag. "Here, let me give you some coins."

Bane shook his head and said, "My treat." Before Rowan could protest, he turned and got in the long line. Rowan maneuvered through the crowded shop. Her forehead creased as she concentrated fervently on not bumping into anyone while squeezing through the narrow spaces. All the tables and the corner booths were occupied, so Rowan made her way to the pair of large doors at the back and walked outside.

There was much more space between the rectangular tables outside than the round tables inside the shop. The added distance between patrons also made it seem less stuffy and overwhelming. Two tables were available; and she selected the one closest to the fountain in the center, which had three marble tiers shaped like large leaves. Water pooled in each layer before babbling down to the large basin at the bottom. Rowan listened intently to the sound of the moving water. The *tinkle* of the thin stream awakened memories she had that were tied to the beach.

"Rowan!" A short child of six years with sun-kissed brown hair eagerly called. "Look!"

"What is it?" Rowan, eight years old, asked her younger sister as she crouched down next to Blythe at the edge of a tidal pool. "Oh, that's a jelly snail!"

Rowan bent down to get a closer look at the oblong, slug-like animal. Its body was transparent blue with white spots, reminiscent of the night sky, tucked under a white conch shell. The skin on its face pulsated like it was being moved by ocean currents.

"You're so smart!" Blythe announced. "But he looks scared. Is he scared of us?"

"He might be. Let's leave him alone." Rowan stood up.

"Wait. I think he's stuck." Blythe picked up a stone, freeing one of the jelly snail's tentacle-like arms. A raspy sound emanated from its body, and it started to move toward the ocean.

Tears pricked the younger girl's eyes. "I saved him, but he yelled at me and ran away!"

Rowan grabbed hold of Blythe's hand. "Maybe he didn't know you had saved him."

"Well, I wished he loved me, but . . . but" Blythe sniffed. "I'd save him again and again." She wiped her nose on her arm and blurted out, "Race you to the big boulder!" Blythe broke into a run, pulling Rowan along the sandy beach as they both giggled.

Soon, that memory blurred into another scene in Rowan's mind. It was the same spot, seven years later . . .

"Look! It's a bunch of baby jelly snails. They must have just hatched." Rowan turned to Blythe. "Remember that one jelly snail you saved when we were little?"

Blythe wrinkled her nose as she tried to recall the memory. "No, I don't. But let's make sure no gulls get any of these babies before they make it to the water!" Blythe took off running, her brown waves of hair bouncing against her back.

Rowan joined her sister in twirling and dancing around the baby jelly snails, keeping the birds away.

"Go, little jellies! Go, go!" the girls cheered in unison.

As the last snail splashed into the waves, the girls jumped up and down. But then Blythe collapsed.

"Blythe! What's wrong? Did you hurt your ankle?" Rowan knelt by her sister, whose face was contorted in pain.

"My legs. Something's wrong with my legs!"

"What's wrong?" Bane's voice snatched Rowan from her mind. She turned toward him, trying to let go of that terrifying day.

"Is it your head again?"

"What? No, I—"

He reached out and softly wiped a thumb across her cheek, drying tears Rowan hadn't realized were falling down her face.

She let out a long breath. "I was thinking about last summer when Blythe first got . . . sick." Rowan bit her lip as she tried to organize her thoughts. "What did you wish for?"

Bane sat opposite Rowan. The food he'd brought over lay on the tabletop between them. He wrapped his hands around one of the warm cups of tea. Rowan glanced at the two sticky buns with melted cream cheese dripping down their cinnamon and pecan-filled sides. She looked back at Bane, waiting for him to answer. He ran a hand through his black hair, which had a touch of white in the front.

"You mean what did I wish for on my sixteenth naming anniversary?"

Rowan nodded. "I know it's rude to ask. And you only got one seed in your somni melon, so you only got one wish. But I need to know—did it come true?" She reached out and touched Bane's hands as silent tears continued to fall. "I know the most wishes anyone gets is four. I don't know if I'll get that many, but I'm going to use any wishes Verimor gives for Blythe."

Bane shook his head. "We all want Blythe to get better and stronger. We want to see her walking without pain again. But, Rowan, you know the wish isn't guaranteed, right?"

She pulled back, clenching her fists. "No! Cressida gave blessings to Liam, and Verimor gives us wishes, too." Her voice became louder and harsher with each word. "He makes sure our wishes come true. He has to! He . . . " Rowan's voice caught on a sob. She wrapped her arms around herself, trying to slow her breathing.

Bane reached back out to Rowan, but she slouched down in her chair. She asked with a shaky voice, "How do you know the wishes aren't guaranteed? Did yours not come true?"

"At this time, no, my wish hasn't come true."

"But there's still time, yes?" She leaned back toward him. "You can't say your wish is definitely not going to happen."

Bane sat back and crossed his arms. "Rowan, the wishes tradition is based on the *Book of Verimor*. But unlike the blessings that were given to Liam, it's just a game we play for fun. It's a way to start conversations about the truth, but the act itself is not true. Yes, I *hope* my wish will come true. But that doesn't mean it will." He reached back out to Rowan. "You can't put all your hope in the naming anniversary wishes and then lose your faith if Blythe doesn't get better."

"You don't think she's getting better?" Every muscle in Rowan's body tensed. Her nostrils flared repeatedly, and she shook slightly as she tried to hold back more tears and her growing frustration.

"I don't know." Bane ran both hands through his hair again. "I want her to get well. I pray Verimor heals her, but wishes and prayers are two different things. And like the clerics say, our plans are not necessarily Verimor's plans."

Rowan stood up. "I'm using my wishes for Blythe. You'll see . . . " The world spun around her. Swirls of green and gray blurred her vision as a sharp pain shot through her head from temple to temple.

"Rowan!" Bane's voice sounded distant like he was underwater. Rowan squeezed her eyes shut. She felt herself falling from her chair but couldn't stop. She lay there, completely still for a few seconds, until the world around her stabilized. Rowan slowly opened her eyes. A gasp escaped her lips.

The world was drained of color.

"What's happening?" Her voice was unsteady. It sounded distant to her own ears, as if she was talking underwater. Her head still ached, and her hand shook as she raised it to her ringing ears. Then her gaze jumped from the sky to the fountain to random onlookers. Bane's voice pulled her focus. Rowan looked at him, only seeing her best friend in shades of gray. Her stomach grew queasy, and she felt like retching. Terror squeezed her heart and threatened to steal the air in her lungs.

"Your eyes . . . " Bane whispered as his own eyes widened.

Rowan closed her eyes tight. She shook her head, hoping to restore color in her vision, hoping to not need to find out what Bane saw. Opening her eyes, she still only saw colorless hues. She whispered, "What's wrong with my eyes, Bane?"

"They're not brown anymore. Rowan . . . they're magenta!"

Chapter Two
Dysfunction

LINNEA ABSENTLY STROKED HER NECK, the pads of her fingers finding a scab. She sat on a velvet stool while Mrs. Ginty, the head lady's maid, stood to her back. There was a large dresser with an elegant mirror in front of them both. Morning sunlight flooded through the open curtains which showed a glass door leading to a terrace.

"Milady, you shouldn't pick at it, or the scarring will be worse," Mrs. Ginty chided. "Here." The older woman was in her sixties with graying red hair. She slathered a thick ointment on the spot.

Linnea coughed at the nearly overpowering scent of roses that flooded the room. "If I had known the Obsilvian ambassador pricking me with a knife would result in your torture by that foul flower, I would have been quicker." She coughed. "Really, Nanny Helene, I think you found something with such a strong smell on purpose."

The maid snorted, tucking away a smile at the term of endearment now only used in private. Linnea was no longer a child, after all. "Well, you're a bit too old for a time out like in your nursery, eh?"

"Times were simpler back then." Linnea sighed. She took a cotton wrap from the top of the dresser and placed it over her neck in attempts to smother the odor. "Back before Father started training me to become the monarch."

Mrs. Ginty rested a pale hand with its underlying blue veins on Linnea's fair head. "You would have been a worthy queen, Linnea."

Linnea shook her head. "I fought so hard to break away from the weight of leading the nation, especially from being the first Wisterian queen. Even with Verimor's nudging to forge ahead."

"Verimor still led you right where He needed you, eh?" The older woman clicked her tongue. "Even if no one will remember your name in history, only the king's."

Linnea smiled softly. "Neither my name nor any Wisterian ruler's name is the one that needs remembering. Only Verimor. I need to remember that when it seems . . . "

A series of sharp knocks on the other side of the bedchamber door caused Linnea to stop talking. Both women turned. Mrs. Ginty's flat shoes echoed on the marble floor as she walked over to meet the visitor. It was Oren, Dendro's pupil.

"Happy day, Mrs. Ginty. I have been sent to escort Lady Linnea to Diatomist Dendro in the gardens for their weekly breakfast. Is she ready?"

"Happy day, Oren," the maidservant greeted.

Linnea stood and joined the others at the doorway. Her face was somber. "Has something happened? It's not typical for Dendro to send someone to accompany me around the castle grounds. Though I mean no offense to you as his apprentice, by any means."

Oren raised a closed fist in front of his torso. His knuckles were white from his grip around whatever was between his fingers and palm. The boy, who Linnea surmised had only had sixteen naming anniversaries, kept his voice steady. "There's no imminent threat."

"But?" Linnea pressed.

"But . . . " The diatomist's apprentice cleared his throat. "There has been a development." He extended his hand toward Linnea. She opened her palm, and cool metal found her skin.

"The would-be assassin's ring?"

Oren responded with a small grunt. He stepped back to allow Linnea to enter the hallway. Oren took the ring back and fell in stride with the king's right hand. "Upon examination, I found it was cursed—marked by the shadows of a dysfunction."

Linnea's steps faltered. She placed her arms out to balance herself and caught a whiff of something strong, acidic like vinegar. "The dysfunction has been cleansed?" She posed it as a question, even though the biting smell confirmed her suspicion.

"Yes, milady. All traces of darkness were removed, but . . . " He paused, taking a lengthy inhale. "There were traces of a blessing's light on the document which were unable to be restored. So the source is unknown."

Linnea stopped and glared at Oren. Her voice dropped dangerously low. "A blessing? How can you say there is no imminent danger when the enemy clearly has one of Verimor's messengers or the last oracle in their claws?"

A muscle in Oren's jaw twitched noticeably. Linnea closed her eyes and took a sharp inhale. She released the air slowly and held out her hand. The young apprentice dropped the ring in her open palm. "Has any information been learned about this symbol?"

"Under the head diatomist's orders, scribes used hawks to send letters to all the surrounding cathedrals. I am not aware of any new knowledge at this time."

Chapter Three
Snake In The Garden

LINNEA RUSHED FORWARD. THE HEM of her dark blue dress ruffling behind her ankles. A gentle winter breeze, common in the mountainous region of Wisteria, enhanced the fabric's movement. She spotted the yellow-orange robes of the royal diatomist sitting at a round table a few yards into the gardens and near her greenhouse of plants. The table was already set for breakfast.

"Why didn't you alert me sooner?" Linnea's raised voice carried over the soft wind. Dendro looked up and smiled. His facial features did not falter when Linnea placed the prisoner's ring on the tabletop in front of him. The saucer under her teacup rattled with the force. "You should have told me immediately instead of sending your student to tell me there is nothing to fear."

"Oren said there was nothing to fear?" Dendro raised one gray-streaked eyebrow.

"He said there was no imminent threat right before I learned about the ring." Linnea rubbed her forehead and sat in the chair next to the diatomist, perching on the edge as if to illustrate her anxiety.

"Perhaps the boy's understanding of 'imminent' is that of 'immediate' rather than . . . "

"It is not the time for semantic games, Dendro." Linnea rested her hands neatly on her knees in front of her. "I know you enjoy words, but we do not have time to dawdle."

The diatomist chuckled. "You know, my friend, I do love that: 'dawdle.' Now there is a word with a fascinating etymology of its origin." He waved one hand while reaching the other for a cup of hot tea. "Had I not been called to religious pursuits, I am certain I would have been an academic, studying language. But that is neither here nor there."

"The ring was cursed. Is Hamlin under the influence of darkness himself? How deep do the shadows of evil reach in Obsilvia, Dendro?" Linnea wrung her hands together, still standing.

"Quiet time with Verimor is needed so that we may feel His direction rather than react to our emotions." Dendro never discussed anything of importance until they had eaten. He pulled items from a serving tray and arranged each of their settings. It was the same each week.

Linnea released her growing frustration with a long sigh. She sat back in her chair, watching as Dendro stood and poured her a cup of tea and added a spoonful of honey to it. Dendro placed a boiled egg on a small stand and then put a plate with sausages, berries, and a little bowl of yogurt in front of both of their places at the table. He bowed his head and was silent, another part of the routine of their breakfast meetings. Linnea closed her eyes.

Verimor, help me follow You, even when fear gets in the way.

Although she felt more level-headed now, Linnea's stomach still objected with waves of nausea. She picked the shell away from her egg slowly, but she abandoned it once half of the shell was removed. Linnea nibbled on a strawberry, then gave up on the food altogether, focusing on her tea instead.

Her gaze wandered over the castle garden. The vibrant green grass combined with the menagerie of topiaries and the blooming flowers lining walking paths defied the cold dryness of winter—a possibility because of the diatomists and their divinely sanctioned ability to work with elements of nature.

Goosebumps prickled on Linnea's arms, despite the long sleeves of her dress. The increasing wind sent a chill down her spine and cooled the rising heat within her. Though not part of the regular rhythm of breakfast, Linnea stood. She walked closer to a nearby oak tree that stood behind the table on the opposite side from her greenhouse.

The loose tendrils of hair that framed her face tickled her cheeks in the breeze. She cocked her head to the side. "Do you hear that rattling sound?" Stepping forward, her foot caught on an exposed portion of the large tree's root. She dipped forward. Something whizzed past her left ear and pierced the tree's bark with a loud thud. Linnea scrambled to her feet and stared at the tree.

An arrow with a piece of parchment. Fear bubbled in her queasy stomach. On the paper was an ink sketching of a snake with four heads conjoined with one body. Crude lettering spelled out, "We have eyes everywhere."

"Guards!" Armed knights scattered at particular spots across the gardens rushed toward Linnea. "There's an enemy among us."

She snatched the parchment. It tore nearly in half, and the arrow remained in place.

Dendro moved to Linnea's side. "Drop it. I sense dysfunction." Linnea's face drained of all traces of color. The parchment floated down; but before it could land on the lush grass, Dendro asked the wind to blow it in his direction. Grasping a cloth napkin, the royal diatomist caught the ripped paper but did not let it make contact with his skin. He folded the fabric over the parchment and placed it in the deep pocket inside the arm of his robe. "No one touch the arrow either."

"Search the area, the castle, everywhere! No one enters or leaves until we have found the person responsible for this," Linnea ordered. The knights scattered quickly. The king's sister and right hand turned to Dendro. "Will you accompany me to the dungeons and tell me what you know?" Though phrased as such, it was not a question.

⁓❧⁓

"What I don't understand, Dendro, is how there is a traitor in our midst! And if I hadn't tripped . . . " Linnea shuddered while walking swiftly beside Dendro. The two entered the castle entryway from the garden and hurried through the main floor. "That dysfunction could be infecting my bloodstream right now had I survived the arrow. Verimor only knows if it was meant to curse the body, the mind, or the heart."

"There are certainly more questions than answers, but it is imperative that we use all resources provided by Verimor to take action," said Dendro. "Hamlin is one such resource, as is this parchment. I have a working theory, and I will have Oren assist me in figuring out what this dysfunction was meant to do to its victim."

Linnea and Dendro descended the main staircase to the lower floor. "I must apologize to Oren for being so short with him earlier. He told me the signet ring harbored the darkness of dysfunction." She pointed toward the parchment with her elbow as she held her dress to keep from tripping on the steps.

"I know you struggle with patience, Linnea; but even in times of stress, it's important to listen for guidance."

Linnea stopped at the top of the staircase leading to the dungeon. A guard stood at attention on either side of the banisters. "I think you can agree that this may be the most stressful time of our nation's entire history. Time is of the essence."

"I do agree. Yet"—Dendro paused while resuming his steps downward—"there is only so much that can be done until we have more information."

"You mentioned a working theory. What can you tell me about the ring?" Linnea and Dendro descended the final three steps, finding themselves in front of the locked dungeon door. Outside it, a guard stood at attention. Linnea crossed her arms and leaned slightly toward Dendro. She fought against the urge to tap her foot while mentally scolding herself for the fact the head diatomist was correct in his assessment of her impatience.

"The ring not only held a dysfunction, but the jewelry itself was altered from its original form." Dendro's gray green eyes flashed to the guard and back. "I will share more when we meet with the king."

Linnea nodded and turned to the guard. "Sir Bert, Diatomist Dendro and myself are here to see the Obsilvian prisoner."

"Hammy? He's been asking for you," replied Bert rather casually.

Linnea raised her eyebrows. "*Hammy* has been asking for me?"

Bert's cheeks reddened above his dark beard. "I . . . I give nicknames to those locked up." He straightened his posture, his spine so taut, he looked as if he was a child insisting that he was taller than his older brother. Bert cleared his throat, removed the key ring from his belt next to his sheathed sword, and unlocked the door. "Lady Linnea, Apprentice Oren is questioning the Obsilvian right now."

The hinges creaked, though there were no visible signs of rust. The dark, damp, slender hallway allowed the three of them to only walk comfortably in a single-file line.

When they stood in front of an iron-barred cell door, Bert selected a second key. "Oren, Lady Linnea and Royal Diatomist Dendro are here to speak with the prisoner." He stepped back, offering a low bow to the new arrivals.

Linnea noted absently how the man seemed to be overcompensating for his initial discourteous and inappropriate tone. Her mind cleared of anything except the threat Obsilvia posed and how much greater and darker it was than she had ever imagined.

"Hamlin . . ."

"I knew you wouldn't stay away." Hamlin, wrists chained and linked to shackles around his ankles, sat on the stone ground in the middle of the small, square space. "Is your *Verimor* not forthcoming with answers you seek?"

"What does the four-headed serpent represent?" Linnea asked, refusing to reply to his attempts at provocation.

Hamlin laughed. "You steal my ring after poisoning me and now expect me to just hand over any information just like *that*." He snapped his fingers and then clicked his tongue. "Milady, I think you're confused."

"Looking at your drooping cheeks and the curling of your arm toward your body, I'm gathering you don't have the ability to stand—and you must have a limp. The nectar of the *Pars Sicarius* . . . " Linnea stopped, shocked that Hamlin stated the name of the plant with her.

"Based on the paralytic effect and the most likely permanent damage to my muscles, I could only assume you used one of the most fatal flowers in the world. Did you know there is an Obsilvian legend that says a snake once consumed the *Pars Sicarius*? The poison resulted in him growing three additional heads."

Linnea's stomach churned watching the smirk plastered on the prisoner's face. She looked to her left in both diatomists' direction. "The symbol has something to do with death." Her eyes narrowed as she returned her gaze to the seated prisoner, his expression that of a mischievous child. "Or, more specifically, murder."

Hamlin leaned forward and touched his nose with the pointer finger on the side that was not pulled to his body. "That's *almost true*! How fitting for the woman who was almost queen."

"You brought my past up when we first met. Why are you obsessed with the fact that I was almost the ruling monarch?" Linnea couldn't push back her genuine curiosity.

Hamlin raised one corner of his upper lip contemptuously. "Wisteria may refuse to accept religion is an archaic practice meant only to self-soothe humans who rely too much on emotion. However, they did one thing right when they prevented a woman from sitting on the throne." He spat on the ground in front of him, spittle staying on his lips.

"It is no secret Obsilvia views women as second-class citizens." Dendro took a small step forward when addressing Hamlin. "But Verimor tell us differently—the last known phoenix was a woman. Do we dare ask what your king, Tramein, wants with her? Why would you need the phoenix if religion is folly in your minds?"

"Phoenix?" Hamlin snorted air from his nose as he exhaled. "Like Obsilvia has time for your Wisterian fairytales."

"He refuses to give any information to help me learn more about the ring and the dysfunction placed on it." Oren's firm voice reminded Linnea he, too, was in the cell.

"He's shared enough." Linnea's mind whirled with a chaotic mixture of Obsilvian legend, four-headed serpents, and poisonous plants. Furthermore, this would-be assassin sent to steal her brother's life didn't seem to know everything Tramein was involved with. Darkness would consume Hamlin and his king completely, as well as all goodness in the world, if nothing was done to fan Verimor's light.

"What's this?" Linnea squinted in the growing candlelight as she exited the dungeon and saw Thaddeus' familiar form.

Two more knights followed, carrying a man who didn't appear to be a day older than his twentieth naming anniversary. His body was prone. One man held his legs, and another held his arms. His swollen eye, split lip, and the blood pooling down his chin and on his neck spoke volumes of a large scuffle.

"Milady, we found the traitor."

"Dendro and I will question him at once. We need Commander Elias summoned immediately."

"You won't get anything from him," Thaddeus said, his voice tense. "When we were searching the servants' quarters, he ran. Before we apprehended him, he cut out his own tongue."

Chapter Four
The Walk Home

ROWAN COVERED HER EYES WITH her hands. The mutterings of a growing crowd reverberated in her ears.

"Rowan." Bane's voice was stern yet comforting. "I'm going to take you to my mother."

Rowan nodded, noticing the marigold crown was looped around Bane's wrist. "I'll—"

Bane's arms wrapped around her and lifted her off the ground. She opened her eyes. "Bane, you'll hurt yourself! I'm too heavy . . . "

"I've got you, Rowan."

Tears streamed down her face as she looked at the black-and-white version of her best friend. Where his heart would be in his chest, she saw tendrils of gray shadows and swirls of white light.

She stared at the smoky phenomena, her forehead furrowing as she processed what she was seeing. Her heartbeat quickened with every passing second until she felt as though it would break through her ribcage.

As Rowan looked at the light and shadows swirling together, faded images began moving. She saw herself laughing while being chased on the beach with the tang of a salty breeze in the air. She saw herself bandaging Bane's knee. Rowan tilted her head, recalling that same memory of when Bane had fallen years ago first trying to mount a horse, and she insisted on helping him.

Rowan raised her eyebrows. Her chest constricted with her epiphany. She was looking into Bane's memories. She inhaled a loud breath and couldn't keep her mouth from falling open. None of this made any sense.

The light within Bane vibrated slightly, pulsating white warmth as she continued to watch. After a moment, she closed her eyes. These new sensations—losing the ability to see normally while gaining some surreal vision when she looked at her best friend—were too much. The thought of using a somni seed to wish for time to rewind and this strangeness to never have happened flashed though her mind. She immediately felt tightness in her stomach. She wouldn't take a wish she had planned to use for her sister and waste it on herself.

A sigh escaped Rowan's lips, and the sound of Bane's footsteps grew harsher as he left cobblestone streets and turned onto the gravel path toward their homes. She whispered, "Bane, I can walk the rest of the way."

"It's fine." His voice was strained, but his breathing remained steady.

Rowan pushed against Bane with her hands, careful not to touch the gray shadows and light on his chest. "No, really. Put me down."

Bane stopped and carefully set Rowan on her feet. She wobbled slightly, and his brows furrowed. "We are almost home. I don't mind carrying you the rest of the way. What if you fall again?"

Leaning against him for support, Rowan shook her head slowly. "I appreciate that, but I can't ask you to keep carrying me. I should be strong enough on my own."

In a voice so low that Rowan questioned if he'd even spoken, Bane said, "But you don't have to be."

As they walked in silence, Rowan looked around, soaking in the grayscale world around her. Everything—the round, puffy clouds in the sky, the towering trees on the path's eastern border, the flower crown now in Bane's hands—lacked color.

Another sigh escaped Rowan's lips as the scattered houses came into view, but this time there was some relief behind the unconscious action. The Tritonia family cottage was the first on the left, and Rowan just wanted the comfort of home.

"Rowan, we need to go see my mother," Bane said, gently touching her elbow. "I'm really worried about you."

"I feel like a giant knotted ball of yarn on the inside, and all I want is to see my sister," Rowan blurted with more edge to her voice than she intended. Bane's gaze dropped to the ground, and Rowan quickly added in a softer tone, "Not that I don't want to see you, too. Why don't you bring your mother over before dinner? I'm sure my parents will want her to see if she can help with . . ." Rowan's voice cracked as she motioned to her eyes.

She blinked back tears when she saw moisture reflected back at her in Bane's eyes. Rowan only remembered him crying once since his tenth naming anniversary, and she didn't want to see him break down—especially over her.

"Bane, I'm going to be okay," she offered half-heartedly.

"Promise." Bane said as Rowan touched his shoulder and turned. "You have to be okay. If this promise you do break . . . "

Rowan stopped and turned to look at Bane as he paused.

He inhaled and audibly released the breath. "Then a *sliced tomato* you shall take."

She snorted. "Tomato slices are so *slimy*. You know I can't stand how they feel!"

"Then you'd best keep your promise." The left corner of Bane's mouth tilted upward before he stepped up and placed the slightly crumpled flower crown on Rowan's head. "Or you'll have to eat a very slimy tomato."

Rowan felt his eyes linger on her own as his hand tucked a wave of her brown hair behind her ear. Bane pulled away and turned, sprinting toward his family home down the dirt path next to her own home. Rowan shook her head to herself, a small smile touching her lips, and then walked up to her front door.

Chapter Five
Questions

ROWAN LET THE BROWN LEATHER bag slide off her shoulder and hit the floor by her feet. She leaned back against the wooden door after it closed behind her. The delicious aroma of garlic herb bread baking in the kitchen caused her stomach to growl in anticipation. She hadn't eaten since breakfast at first light.

"You're back early," said Blythe, although her face didn't leave the book on her lap. Rowan watched as her sister's hand hovered in the air, holding a goose feather as she mentally found a stopping point. Blythe slid the feather in and closed the book. As she looked up, her eyes widened; and she caught her breath. However, Rowan held her sister's gaze steadily as she soaked in the black-and-white scene before her.

Blythe's warm brunette hair, pulled back in a cleanly woven bun, was now void of color. The crocheted blanket that sat over her legs looked like a pale afterthought of the beautiful scene of fishing boats by the docks that it illustrated. Rowan's eyes settled on Blythe's heart. Just like with Bane, a swath of white light with gray shadows looked back at Rowan.

Rowan cleared her throat, but Blythe said nothing. Rowan crossed her arms and walked across the small room to sit beside Blythe on the tattered, old cushions. Rowan placed her hand beside her with her palm up. Her younger sister interlaced their fingers.

"Do you want to talk about it? Or do you just want to sit?" Blythe asked.

Rowan blinked back tears before they could fall. She sniffed. "Bane is getting Mrs. Oxeye to come over to look at my eyes before dinner."

Blythe nodded, and it encouraged Rowan to continue. "I got a very bad headache; I fell; and now I . . . I can only see gray. There's no color." She focused on steadying her quivering bottom lip. "And Bane says my eyes are magenta, and I have no idea what's going on or what it means, and I . . . I . . . " Rowan collapsed into herself, sobbing so hard, her entire upper body shook.

Blythe stroked her sister's back, humming a gentle tune, but said nothing.

"What in the name of the Admiral Ocean is wrong?" The girls' mother rushed into the sitting room, wiping her hands on her apron. She knelt by Rowan, and Rowan turned to lean her head against her mother's shoulder.

"Shhh," soothed her mother. "You're safe. When you are ready, tell me what's wrong. Breathe in . . . and breathe out. That's it. Again."

After some guided breaths, Rowan sat up straight, her eyes shut tight. Slowly, she opened them.

Rowan's mother gasped, and she covered her heart with her hand. "What happened? Are you hurt?" She closely examined her

daughter's face, removing Rowan's flower crown and then tilting her head, pushing her eyebrows up, and looking at her neck.

Rowan picked at her cuticles as she recounted what happened, each word coming out a little steadier than the last. Her mother's eyes never wavered from Rowan's face as she asked, "Does your head still hurt?"

"No." Rowan looked around her. "But I can't see right. There's no color."

"Blessings be to Verimor." Her mother kissed her bent index finger and held up in front of her, her head bowed slightly. "At least you aren't in pain like Blythe. It'll be okay." She tilted her head and sniffed. "The stew is bubbling over!" She bolted away, yelling over her shoulder, "I'll be right back. We'll get through this!"

Rowan recoiled back into herself, wrapping her own arms around her shoulders.

"She didn't mean it that way, you know," Blythe said softly.

With a shrug, Rowan said, "She's right. This is nothing compared to what you go through daily."

Blythe shook her head. "I don't think she was trying to make light of what's happening. I think she's relieved you aren't physically hurting. I am, too. But"—she tapped her leather-bound book absentmindedly while she spoke—"just because your pain isn't the same as mine doesn't mean it's any less hurtful."

Rowan giggled through her tear-stained face.

"What?" Blythe asked, her head tilted slightly.

"I don't know. Sometimes, you sound more like one of the clerics instead of my little sister."

Blythe touched Rowan's shoulder. "I'm sorry. I didn't mean to not sound honest or authentic. I just—"

"No need to apologize." Rowan grabbed and squeezed her sister's hand. "I know you spend a lot of time with the local clerics when they visit. And you read even more than I do. I shouldn't be surprised when you say profound things. You're a wise, old soul, Blythe."

Rowan could tell her sister's cheeks flushed because they darkened slightly. Blythe said softly, "I wouldn't say that."

They sat in a moment of comfortable silence before Blythe asked, "What do you want to do?"

Rowan rubbed her forehead. "I want to find out what this colorless vision means." Her fingers slipped into her long hair. "But I've never heard of such a thing!" She sighed in exasperation as she leaned back heavily on the loveseat.

Blythe simply said, "Everything happens for a reason. Perhaps . . . " She paused in thought.

Rowan looked up and watched as her younger sister cupped her own chin and crinkled her nose. "We can assume that there's a purpose in you losing your vision."

Rowan snorted, ready to disagree, but Blythe didn't let her interrupt.

"Maybe the answer can be found in the teachings of Verimor?"

"That . . . " Rowan stopped mid-thought as she processed Blythe's suggestion. She nodded once. "That actually makes sense. Turning toward Verimor for guidance, I mean."

Blythe straightened, visibly invigorated by Rowan's agreement. "The *Days of the Beginning* has several instances of people receiving unique gifts and blessings from Verimor. Hand me my cane, please." Rowan's eyes darted to the light in her sister's chest. She felt as if it had brightened with Blythe's energized demeanor.

Rowan averted her eyes and stood. "I don't know that this can be classified as a *blessing*." Her shoulders slouched as she walked to the bookshelf tucked in the corner of the room. Books filled each of the three short shelves and perched in large stacks on the very top. Piles on the floor also leaned on either side of the wooden piece of furniture. Though it might look chaotic to a random observer, the Tritonia family organized the books alphabetically by title. Rowan knelt. "Just tell me what titles you think will be helpful, and I'll grab them."

"The *Book of Verimor*, of course. The family copy is in the kitchen from breakfast, but there should be another copy on the shelf. Also, grab *Interpretations of Histories Recorded from the Days of the Beginning* by the former Arch-cleric Sage. And I should have a copy of *Understanding Important Women from the Book of Verimor and Their Legacies*."

"Oh, Miss Thistle sent you a book, too. I don't know if it will necessarily help, but I should give it to you before I forget."

After taking a minute to locate the requested titles, Rowan grabbed the third and final book and deposited the volumes next to Blythe on the loveseat. As she walked back to the door and picked up her bag, there was a knock.

Rowan opened the wooden door. "Hi, Bane, Mrs. Oxeye. Thank you both for coming over." She smiled, although it didn't reach her eyes, and stepped aside so they could enter. As the guests moved forward, Rowan realized they weren't alone.

"Cleric Jimson," she added, dipping her head slightly. "Please come in." Rowan flinched as his eyes widened upon seeing her. She assumed it was her new eye color that caused his reaction.

"Happy Naming Anniversary, Rowan. It seems that this will be one to remember," he said warmly in his deep yet gracious voice. "Blythe, it's so good to see you. And, Maryam, always a pleasure," he added as the girls' mother joined everyone in the sitting room.

"Cleric Jimson, likewise. Please, have a seat." Rowan's mother gestured to the mismatched chairs across from Blythe and the loveseat while she set down a plate of freshly sliced bread, goat cheese, and fruit. "And please enjoy a bite to eat, but don't overfill because dinner will be ready soon. We will be having cabbage stew and fish with my black pepper and parsley butter sauce."

"They're my favorite dishes," Rowan added, feeling unsure what to think about Cleric Jimson's presence as she sat beside Blythe once again. He visited Blythe and the family regularly. However, he usually came in the morning hours, and Rowan had never been the reason for his visit.

The adults exchanged polite small talk. Rowan slowly looked from person to person, noticing the differences between the area of light in front of each one. If her gaze lingered too long on one person's light and shadows made of gray shades, images started to form.

Rowan let her gaze land on her mother. Despite her pleasant demeanor, the images in the light before her heart illustrated an anxious scene. Her mother, wet hair plastered to her face, was yelling at a midwife, asking if her baby was okay—somehow

Rowan knew her mother's worry for her on her first naming anniversary equaled the worry she felt today. She leaned forward, hoping to see more.

"Right, Rowan?"

Rowan looked at Blythe. She felt her cheeks grow warm. "I'm sorry. I was lost in my own thoughts." Her eyes flitted to her mother, then landed at her own hands in her lap.

Blythe laid a comforting hand on Rowan's arm. "I was just explaining how we were thinking that this might be a blessing from Verimor."

Bane stood and handed a cup to Rowan. "Drink this. My mother said this is a tea blend that has been known to help with vision loss."

"This isn't exactly vision loss, so I don't know if it will do anything. But a warm drink might be soothing, nonetheless," Mrs. Oxeye offered, her voice lyrical and gentle.

Scents of cinnamon hit Rowan as she took a sip of the drink. As the warm liquid trickled down her throat, she felt the muscles relax throughout her tense body.

"I think you girls have the right idea trying to find answers with some research," Cleric Jimson said with a nod. "In truth, I've never seen anything like this in my lifetime. But it is vaguely familiar to the story of Dinah in the *Book of Verimor*."

Rowan's nose wrinkled. "I'm not sure I know about her."

The religious man leaned forward and clasped his hands together. "Dinah is mentioned very briefly in chapter thirty-seven as being blessed with a gift called Sight. She used this gift to aid Liam's son Cillian in preserving the throne of Wisteria; however, if my memory serves me well, there are no details in what exactly the Sight was nor how she used it."

"So, there's nothing really that says *this*"—Rowan motioned to her eyes—"is actually the same as Dinah's Sight?"

"It's just a theory," replied Cleric Jimson as he sat back in the chair.

Blythe's fingers flipped through a small-print version of the *Book of Verimor*. "Hmm, according to this index, it looks like there are three verses that mention Dinah. It says her Sight was bestowed on her by Verimor through one of His unicorns."

Rowan's mind raced.

"That rules out Sight. I mean, this couldn't possibly be a unicorn blessing."

"Rowan, breathe," her mother counseled. "I can tell you are getting yourself worked up again because your nostrils are flaring."

Rowan bit the inside of her cheek to keep her muddled thoughts inside. She let each of her fingertips touch the pad of her thumb methodically. A noise came from the back of the house.

"Maryam, everything smells delicious," Rowan's father called out. "Oak and I are going to wash up."

Rowan heard shuffling as her father and Mr. Oxeye moved about.

Cleric Jimson stood. "I'll let you all enjoy your dinner."

"You're more than welcome to stay," Rowan's mother said, standing, too.

"I won't impose on Rowan's naming anniversary celebration any longer. I will send a hawk with a message to Royal Diatomist Dendro, and I will be in touch with what he suggests."

Rowan's body moved automatically as she stood to show respect while the cleric took his leave. She felt numb as she helped set the table and took her place at dinner. Her mind asked the same questions on repeat.

Why would the Royal Diatomist Dendro, the highest religious leader in the entire kingdom, be concerned about my colorless vision? Surely, he won't be. But . . . what if he is?

Chapter Six
The Somni Melon

ROWAN CLEANED HER HANDS ON her cloth napkin, sitting back in her chair at the kitchen table.

"Mama, that was delicious."

She was exhausted, and an uneasy feeling still gnawed at the back of her mind. However, Rowan felt better now that she'd finally eaten. She said a silent prayer of thanks that everyone was attempting to act normal before questioning if ignoring the issue was wise.

Rowan's father stood up and grabbed a small box wrapped in brown paper hiding in the corner behind him. He set the package in front of her and returned to his seat at the head of the table. "Rowan, you love with all your heart; you are intelligent; and you spread light wherever you go. Your mother and I are so proud of you. No matter what happens in life, I hope you always remember to take root wherever Verimor sends you, allowing your gifts to blossom to their fullest potential. He is the One Who will set your paths straight."

He motioned for Rowan to open the paper. Her heart raced in her chest. This was it. She knew the yellow-green somni melon was within the wrapped box, even if she couldn't see the color in her current circumstances. Rowan tugged on the string and carefully unveiled the fruit.

She imagined she could hear her heart beating in her chest as her fingertips traced the rough texture on the melon's surface and followed the lighter swirls on the skin of the fruit with her fingertips. Her eyes flickered to her right where Blythe was sitting. Rowan believed she could see the fatigue in her younger sister's eyes.

Rowan gritted her teeth and picked up the small knife next to her plate. Silently, she prayed, *Verimor, please grant me however many wishes I need to heal Blythe.*

The blade sliced easily through the thick outer layer of the somni melon. Roughly the size of a large onion, the fruit easily turned within Rowan's grasp. Juice that smelled of tangy citrus dripped around the opening. It covered Rowan's fingers and fell in splotches on the wooden tabletop. Slowly, she pulled back the skin and revealed fruit that she knew was normally bright yellow with swirls of green inside. Though gray to her gaze, there was a clear darker line, which revealed where the two halves of the melon met.

Rowan placed each hand on one half. She closed her eyes and twisted her hands as she pulled the fruit halves apart. Sticky pulp lingered as juice dripped, and the fruit created a slight slurping noise. Rowan opened her eyes. She felt like her heart might stop.

There were no seeds in her somni melon.

Rowan sat back. Each piece of the melon rolled slightly upward, allowing everyone at the table to see.

"Have you ever seen a somni melon without even *one* seed?" Bane asked.

The chattering around Rowan seemed to fade into distant humming. She stood up shakily, accidentally knocking her chair down.

"Sorry, I'm so clumsy." Rowan's words were barely louder than a whisper as she righted her chair. "Mama, I'm going to start cleaning dishes."

"It's your naming anniversary. I can—"

"No, please," Rowan interrupted her mother. "Would anyone like some tea? I'm going to start the kettle, too." She turned around with a strained smile on her face.

Pans clattered as Rowan started carrying items to the wash basin. "It looks like we are running low on water," she said as she looked in the water pails under the basin at her feet. "I'll start the kettle and then go out and get more water and—"

A sharp inhale paired with leaking tears stopped Rowan from finishing her thoughts. She felt an arm wrap around her shoulder and found that Blythe was standing next to her.

"Blythe, you need to rest. Everything is fine. Bane was right. Wishes and prayers are different, so what does it matter if I didn't get any wish—" Her voice caught on a sob. Rowan wiped her face and nose with her hands.

Her sister leaned her head against Rowan's shoulder as tears continued to drip down the younger sister's nose. Blythe's own tears mixed with Rowan's.

"Don't cry, Blythe. See? I'm fine." She forced a tight smile, but Blythe didn't move her head to look at her sister directly.

"Rowan, it's okay to not be okay. You wanted wishes and didn't get any." Tears rolled onto Rowan's shoulder, but she didn't pay attention to the dampness. "You can cry."

"Why are you crying, Blythe?"

"I don't like seeing you upset . . . but a selfish part of me wants life to be as easy as making wishes. Wishes for everything to be like they were and—" Blythe hiccupped, and Rowan turned and pulled her into a tight hug.

They held each other and cried together.

Chapter Seven
Advising The King

DAMP SOIL SQUISHED BETWEEN LINNEA'S fingers, dirtying her typically clean, manicured hands. It lifted her spirits, though, along with the humidity of her garden room—a small greenhouse in the garden that was solely hers to tend to. Mrs. Ginty had long stopped asking Linnea to wear gloves while caring for her beloved plants. The older servant simply pursed her lips and muttered, "Again?" each night she cleaned Linnea's nails.

Meow.

Linnea turned her head to find a small cat in the arms of her brother. "Isak! I didn't even hear someone walk in." She stood, wiping her hands on her apron.

"I suppose this is one of your cats?" Isak held the long-haired gray cat, who purred so loudly in his arms that Linnea could hear it standing a few feet away.

Linnea laughed. "One of my cats?"

"You are the person who convinced Father to not only issue a decree that cats couldn't be killed on castle property but also that the milk should be put out regularly for hungry felines. Are you denying this fine fellow?" The cat continued to purr as Isak scratched under its chin.

"I could never deny sweet Smokey." Linnea walked up to her brother as the cat opened its eyes, meowing seemingly in response to hearing its name. She petted the cat's soft head with gentle strokes. Then she sat on a small, metal stool near a round wooden worktable. "It's been quite a while since you joined me in here."

Isak placed Smokey on the center of the table and sat upon one of two open stools. Smokey sniffed at a trowel on the table and jumped down. Linnea's gaze shifted from the cat to her younger brother. In her garden room, without his crown, he simply was Isak. He cleared his throat, and the forlorn expression which emphasized the premature worry wrinkles around his eyes and across his forehead shattered Linnea's daydream of simpler times that never were. Simple was rarely possible when leading people who were—like everyone else—emotional and fickle beings. Linnea knew she was the same. Each day, she worked to become better and fulfill her duties toward Verimor and Wisteria.

"What do you need from me?" Linnea's question broke the silence that had settled.

"Your wisdom." Isak leaned forward, placing his clasped hands on the table in front of him. "I spoke with both Dendro and his apprentice. I have their advice; I know what Sir Elias will want to do; and now I need the opinion of the person I trust the most."

Linnea's brow furrowed slightly. An anxious bubble grew in her chest, threatening to pop if he uttered the word "war."

"I know you are aware that Dendro believes the dysfunction on the ring was the dark twisting of a blessing from a phoenix," she said. "Obsilvia is becoming more and more threatening by the day. We currently have one prisoner dying of infection from cutting out his own tongue rather than provide us with any information. Verimor only knows why he refuses anything from us that may help his fever and pain. He won't last much longer. And then we have another prisoner in custody for attempting to take your life. Surely, we will receive a demand for his release any day. As I do not want to overreach, what precisely would like my opinion on?"

"Obsilvia clearly wants war, but Tramein does not wish to declare it himself. He wants the rest of the world to see Wisteria as the aggressor. What's the best move: to wage war to defend ourselves, our people, our faith at the risk of turning other countries against us and away from Verimor? Perhaps the thought of war might even incite rebellion among our own people. Or should we continue to fight this underhanded onslaught in order to prove that we cannot be bullied into doing an enemy's bidding?"

Linnea interlaced her fingers and brought them to her chin. "I have done my best to advise you over the years."

"I know, and I hope you realize how much I appreciate your guidance."

Linnea shook her head even as a smile tugged at the corners of her mouth. "If the last few days have revealed anything, it is that I am easily shaken with the threat Obsilvia poses—not just to Wisteria, but to you." Standing, Linnea walked to a rectangular bench against the closest wall behind her. She leaned and picked up a watering pot. She motioned with her head for Isak to follow her as she moved to make her way around the greenhouse.

"Dendro is a good man, as you know. He has been more of a grandfather to us, not just a royal diatomist." Linnea poured water over the lush vegetation where vibrant blooms of all colors peeked between the green leaves.

"Are you advising me to seek out Dendro's council again?" Isak questioned.

Linnea continued to pour, slowly moving down the row. "No. I'm advising you to seek Verimor's council like Dendro has always modeled for us." She set the nearly drained watering pot down. "He may not tell you with words, but Verimor will put the right thing on your heart."

Isak's lips quirked as if he wanted to grin, but he held it back. "What has Verimor put on your heart to tell me?"

"First, you need to follow up with the scribes about the Obsilvian legend I asked them to search the library archives for. My directive only carries so far. Second, there needs to be a plan of action to find out exactly what Tramein is after. Is it simply adding the Dimidi Isles to his kingdom? To invade Wisteria? Hamlin, the traitor we haven't found, and the symbol suggest that this is bigger than land and resources for trade." Linnea stopped and bit her lip.

Isak crossed his arms. "We can't forget the dysfunctions."

"Exactly. Dysfunctions only exist as a corruption of blessings. And it makes me shudder to think of the evil required for such dark power." Linnea shuddered. "Hamlin won't reveal more than what he wants us to know."

"King Isak?" A man's voice called from the closed glass door of Linnea's garden room. She recognized him as one of Isak's most trusted guards, Thaddeus. "The royal diatomist's apprentice is here looking for you."

Linnea picked up the watering pot and returned it to its place while Isak left to join Thaddeus and Oren. She took off her apron and hung it on a nail to the side of the rectangular table. She walked through the threshold. The cold air felt exceptionally chilled with the sweat on the back of her neck from the humidity and warmth of the greenhouse.

The air was as tense as it was dry. Linnea caught Isak's eye when she walked up to the men. "A diatomist scribe from the falconry tower received a letter from Aconite. Dendro wants us to meet him in the reading room there at once."

"Aconite? Nothing ever happens in that little coastal town. Unless . . . " Linnea's eyes narrowed as she processed possibilities. "Has Sir Elias been concerned about an attack by way of the Admiral Ocean?"

"An attack by sea would be disadvantageous for Obsilvia because of how long they would need to be at sea to reach our western coast. The news is nothing like that," said Oren, standing in robes of green, a mark of his apprenticeship. Linnea knew Dendro planned to have the young man take his place when he was no longer able to continue the role of Royal Diatomist. Oren bowed his head and then looked at Linnea directly. "However, it is something the king needs to see to make a decision on how to proceed."

෩

There were three separate floors to ascend before reaching the winding staircase that led to the falconry tower. They were the living quarters for the castle's groundkeepers, scribes, and animal marshals. The tower itself sat above a large structure in the inner section of the castle. Linnea imagined her ribs constricting her lungs as she stepped from the final stairs to the top.

Two guards were patrolling the perimeter of the falconry. Dendro stood next to a marshal in the center. His gray moustache twitched as he saw Linnea and the others approach. "My king, Cleric Jimson of the cathedral in Aconite has sent word of something that is nothing short of a miracle." His excitement was palpable as he shook an open scroll in front of him. "One of Verimor's messengers has blessed a young girl with Sight—this is the way we defeat Obsilvia and the darkness they are so adamant to spread!"

"Thanks be to Verimor," Linnea whispered as she watched her brother take the letter. His blue eyes darted quickly back and forth as he absorbed the contents.

"This girl, Rowan, must come to Tulium at once," Oren said, his face turning from King Isak to Dendro. His mentor nodded his head emphatically and agreed, "Yes, yes, yes!"

The king cradled his chin with his forefinger and thumb. "The cleric says she just had her sixteenth naming anniversary." His eyes flitted to Linnea. "It seems she and her family are very distressed by not knowing the answers to her situation. Will Rowan want to help if her parents even allow her to travel here?"

"I do not mean to speak out of turn," said Oren. "But you are the king. Your word is final."

Isak pursed his lips in contemplation. "I can't justify making a girl—a mere child, really—leave her home to be used in a war.

Because Wisteria *is* going to war with Obsilvia." A heavy silence settled briefly, though no one was wholly surprised with the king's words. "Dendro and Oren, are you both sure this girl was blessed by a unicorn?"

"I am positive," the royal diatomist said. His apprentice nodded once in agreement. Oren added, "Sending for the girl will prevent more distress for her and her family. She would be better protected here than there, sitting as an easy target for Tramein."

Isak's jaw tensed. "If she has been giving the unicorn blessing of Sight, then the threat of dysfunction by darkness exists. If memory serves me well of your lessons, Dendro, Sight can fan the flame of cleansing light; but if used for evil, it has the potential to spread shadows until all goodness is extinguished in the hearts of all."

Dendro's moustache seemed to droop somberly with the rest of his face. "The burden she's been given to carry is heavy. But we cannot leave her to do it alone or leave her at risk to being used by Tramein."

"Why would a unicorn not bless someone older and wiser with more experience? Surely, the girl will be terrified to leave her loved ones and be thrust into the heart of both physical and spiritual warfare." Isak extended his hand in front of him as he held the letter.

Linnea put a hand on her brother's arm. "Verimor equips those He calls." She pulled her hand back. "I'll go myself to speak with . . . " Linnea moved to look over the letter herself before finishing her thought. "Rowan and her family."

"It's settled then." Isak handed the letter back to Dendro. "Burn the letter. Send word to Aconite's cathedral that Rowan is being summoned to the castle by royal order." He held up his hand and looked between Dendro, Oren, and Linnea. His guard had long ago fallen back to the lone entrance. "No one outside of us must know yet that we are bringing her here. I do not want any trouble while Linnea and Rowan are outside the protection of the castle."

Chapter Eight
Road to Aconite

THE WINTER WIND BLEW WISPS of blonde hair around Linnea's face, but the fur-lined coat over her traveling cloak kept the rest of her body unaware of the air's frigid chill. She stood by the tree near her greenhouse. The scar on the bark made by the enemy arrow was a silent reminder that someone who could not be trusted had been with them in the castle. Sir Elias had been questioning and interrogating everyone behind the scenes since the capture and death of the traitor. No evidence had been found of additional enemies internally.

"Lady Linnea, I was surprised by your invitation to meet you here before you depart." Oren bowed respectfully when she turned to face him. She greeted him with a soft but authentic smile.

"Oren, there has been something weighing heavy on my mind since our encounter before breakfast earlier this week." She inhaled sharply, then released the air slowly. "I try to stay levelheaded, but stopping an attempt on my brother's life was a surreal experience. I let my emotions take over. Because of that, the following day, I spoke to you as if you were a confused child and not the young man training to one day be the head diatomist in service of Wisteria. I hope you can accept my apology."

Oren's tense shoulders relaxed. "I appreciate the sentiment, milady, but it is unnecessary. I wish you safe travels." He turned.

"That's not all. Could I have a few more minutes of your time, please?" Linnea waited for Oren to resume facing her. Something in his eyes flashed. Linnea thought she saw gray tendrils in his irises; but after he blinked, they returned to their normal green color. She coughed to clear her throat. "Dendro thinks very highly of you. You will be taking a more active role moving forward. You are an apprentice, but you are also skilled to do more than be an assistant collecting people and delivering messages and the like."

Linnea paused briefly, and Oren's shoulders rose. His chest puffed slightly at her words. "There is much work to be done in the coming days. When I return with Rowan, you will be assigned to assist her with her Sight. Dendro will be talking with you on the specifics, but I wanted to take the time to tell you myself first." She took a small step forward. "Be careful. We do not know who can be trusted outside of the king's council. Rowan and her blessing of Sight will be vital in determining the outcome of this war."

"I'm aware." The boy sighed. An exhaustion seemed to overtake him that made him look as old as Dendro. "Those who can be trusted and those who cannot will soon be rooted out."

"I pray so." Linnea walked away, heading toward the stables. Oren said nothing more, but she heard his heavy tread of his footsteps as he paced in the opposite direction. Linnea absently hoped she could hold herself together to make sure the girl they were bringing into this mess was safe and felt supported—just as

Mrs. Ginty had been there for Linnea when her mother passed when Isak was only three years old.

The carriage bounced forward on the uneven terrain. Outside of the castle grounds, Tulium was draped with a thick blanket of snow. A rotation of guardsmen had worked to clear the snowfall in order to allow the horses and carriage wheels to have a clear path until the frosty obstacle thinned in the increasing temperatures. They had only stopped for twenty minutes around midday since leaving after first light. Judging by the sun's position when peering through the curtained window, Linnea surmised there was approximately one hour until sunset.

The carriage stopped as if Linnea's thoughts signaled the party to halt. "Milady," the driver called while opening the door, "we are going to stop and set up camp for the night."

"Very good, I'm ready to stretch my legs. Thank you, Mr. Ginty." Linnea accepted his weathered hand.

"I will never tell you what to do, milady, but you are welcome to call me George," he said with a smile. "I know you still call my wife Nanny Helene more often than not."

Linnea joined him in a short bout of laughter. "Yes, I do, but I do try to uphold decorum when in public."

Mr. Ginty was already walking to the smaller carriage behind them before Linnea finished her sentence. She waited and watched. The man, who was broad shouldered with strong looking arms, placed his hands on his wife's sturdy middle when she placed a foot on the step beside the carriage door. He picked her up and

twirled her around as if she was as light as a paper doll. Mrs. Ginty laughed with her head thrown back. When her feet touched the ground, she smoothed her husband's vest. Her eyes flickered to find Linnea staring unabashedly, and Mrs. Ginty's face darkened to the same shade her ginger locks must have been in her younger years. She took a step back, picking out a piece of lint from Mr. Ginty's shoulder. Observing two people so obviously in love and watching the way their faces lit up in each other's arms made Linnea's heart smile.

"Lady Linnea? Your tent is ready if you would like some privacy while we get the fire ready for Mrs. Ginty to warm the soup," said a knight with brown hair peeking from beneath his chainmail hood. A scar, which started near his lip, ran across his cheek to his left earlobe.

"Thank you." Linnea followed the man, her gaze landing on the back of his head.

"Here you are, milady." He reached for the fabric opening of the tent that was taller than they were, but something grabbed his attention behind Linnea. The tent flap fell from his fingers. He pointed slowly, never fully extending his arm. "Do you see that?"

Turning, Linnea saw a white horse with a long, white tail and matching mane. A pink-tinted horn protruded from the animal's forehead. "A unicorn." The word escaped her lips in an awed whisper.

"What do—" Before the knight could finish, a blinding white light flashed. Linnea held her hands to cover her face. When the glimmering beam faded, Linnea dropped her hands slowly and blinked.

In the place of the horned horse stood a woman. Her golden curls were wrapped in a beautiful towering bun on top of her head. Her dress was a translucent pale pink. "Linnea, I have a message from Elodi."

The knight fell to his knees, his palms together in front of him. "Verimor, to see one of your messengers with my own eyes!" His words became rushed, muttering as he continued to pray.

Linnea stepped up at the mention of the name of Verimor's prophetess. She softly placed a hand on the woman's upper arm. "Is she safe?" Linnea asked as she twisted her head side to side.

Two knights a few feet away were gawking, but the rest of the camp seemed preoccupied.

"Tell me in here," she said, pulling the woman into the tent behind her. The grim look on the visitor's face made Linnea's stomach churn and her heart ache.

"Elodi says she knows you may not understand, but her part in the story is over . . . "

"No," Linnea cut her off. She grabbed the woman's hands in her own and aggressively shook her own head.

"Your story, however, is not," the woman pressed on. She pulled Linnea's hands to her chin, prompting Linnea to lift her tearful eyes to her. "I know you wanted to see your friend again."

"It's been so long—*years*—I didn't know the last time I saw her would be . . . " A sob bubbled in place of words.

"She said to tell you, 'Everything happens for a reason, and beauty can be born from what is broken.'"

"Is that all?" Linnea choked out between cascading tears and sharp breaths.

"There was more:

> *'The snake in the garden is close to your king.*
> *Of the serpent's evil, the trapped rat will sing,*
> *But darkness lurks in hearts well masked.*
> *Take heed that eyes do not pick up wicked tasks.*
> *So another's dark choices can be proved wrong,*
> *With the help of a blessing, the phoenix passes on.'"*

Linnea repeated the prophecy several times to herself to commit it to memory. Voices outside the tent pulled her attention away for a brief moment. She felt the woman drop her hands. "I'm sorry she wasn't able to deliver these words. I have to go. We will see each other again."

"Wait . . . " Linnea raised her hand, but in the woman's place was a unicorn. Then another brief flash of light came before she found herself alone in the tent once more. Movement at the tent opening caused her to look.

"Milady, please ask the unicorn to speak to us," the knight from earlier said as he peeked through.

"Cassian, you can't go into her tent without permission!" A gruff voice shouted as the knight was jerked back.

"It's . . . it's all right." Linnea wiped her face with her cloak and stepped out. It looked like everyone was there waiting for something. She looked at Cassian but addressed the crowd. "Verimor's messenger is no longer here."

A few mutterings erupted. A bearded fellow who looked familiar crossed his arms and smirked. "Cassian, I knew you were lying. There's not been a unicorn sighting recorded since the *Book of Verimor* was written!"

"Bert, a unicorn was here!" Cassian looked to Linnea with arms outstretched and his wide eyes begging for support.

"She was indeed here but no longer. We will not discuss the matter anymore." The crowd disassembled, and Linnea stepped toward Cassian and Bert. "Bert, I thought you were guarding the dungeon. Is it common for Sir Elias to reassign posts frequently?"

Bert shrugged and then rubbed the back of his neck, his chainmail only covering his torso under his shirt. "No, milady, but I go wherever he sends me."

Linnea offered a simple nod to let him know he was free to go. Cassian stepped directly in front of her. "It is a sign that Verimor and His light will prevail." He kissed a curved finger and raised it to the sky.

"There you are!" Mrs. Ginty called, walking toward her. "What was all that chaos? Never mind for the moment. Here is some dinner. I needed to make sure you got a share before those men act like they've not eaten for days."

Linnea took the bowl without offering a word of thanks or explanation.

"Linnea, what's wrong?" Mrs. Ginty's jovial expression was replaced with a crease-marked forehead and pinched lips.

"The last prophet of Verimor—Elodi, the phoenix—is . . . " Linnea struggled with the last word. "She's . . . she's dead."

Chapter Nine
Morning Coffee

"ROWAN, ARE YOU AWAKE?" BLYTHE whispered. Their shared room was still mostly dark as the sun was just peeking through the single window. She looked and watched the gentle rise and fall of her sister's chest under the frayed handmade quilt.

With aching muscles and stiff limbs, Blythe pulled herself to the edge of the bed she shared with her sister. She grabbed her wooden cane leaned against the wall and determinedly pulled herself to stand.

Her left knee shook in protest. Blythe closed her eyes and pursed her lips together. Part of her wanted to wake Rowan to ask for help, but she also wanted to be self-sufficient. She *needed* to be okay. Her older sister already had enough going on without worrying so much about her.

Moving slowly, Blythe slipped out of her nightdress and pulled on her pale blue frock; it was one of her three options. She paused to look at the faded yellow nightgown that had fallen beside her clothing trunk and held in a tired sigh. She shook her head slightly, fighting the feeling of defeat because she knew she couldn't bend down and get back to her feet on her own.

Blythe took a deep breath, trying to stay quiet. She decided she would clean up later. Using her cane to hold the weight her left side didn't want to support, Blythe carefully moved to the doorway, trying to limit the *thump* her cane made on the rough wood floors. She looked one more time at Rowan.

Verimor, she prayed silently, *please give Rowan the peace she needs to be okay.*

Leaving the door slightly cracked behind her, Blythe made her way down the narrow hallway toward the kitchen, the center of their humble home.

The comforting scent of coffee enveloped Blythe as her cane creaked on the floorboards. "Happy day, Baba," Blythe said cheerfully.

Her father returned both her smile and her greeting as he poured the contents of the kettle into two mugs that were already on the wooden counter. Picking up both cups, Blythe's father turned to meet her at the table.

"It has been a long time since I was up early enough to join you for your pre-breakfast coffee." Blythe inhaled the sweet scent of her beverage. "I thought you preferred your coffee without chocolate?"

Her father took a sip. "I know you prefer yours with chocolate. It's how I make the first batch every day."

Blythe let her hand touch and squeeze her baba's rough fingers that rested on the table. "It's been months since I sat with you in the morning," she said quietly.

"That doesn't matter," he said with a shrug. "I'll be here every morning with an extra cup for you waiting for whenever you can join. But don't fret if you don't make it. I'll just have extra coffee for my lunch." He winked, causing the wrinkles around his blue-gray eyes to crease.

Taking a sip of her warm drink, Blythe looked at her father. His hair had long ago migrated from the top of his head to his chin. There, he had a wiry beard that Mama described as "salt-and-peppered." His tan skin was darkened further by many days working in the sun with other fishermen.

"Baba, are you happy?"

"Why wouldn't I be happy?" Her father's bushy black and white eyebrows pulled together.

"Because you have a crippled daughter." Blythe stared into her coffee.

She feared if she looked at her father the tears would fall as freely as they did last night. When she felt the weight of her father's arms around her, the tears came anyway.

"Blythe, you know I'm not always good with words. That's your mother's area. But if I have ever said anything that has made you think I'm not happy—and especially because of your health—then *I* have failed *you*."

Sniffling, Blythe patted her father's arm and looked up at him. "Sometimes, I feel so helpless. I hate physically hurting. But even more than that, I hate to see the people I love hurting because I'm in pain."

Her father kissed her forehead. "You can't control how others around you feel. That's not your burden to carry." He returned to his seat but kept a hand extended toward Blythe. "Aside from your worries about other people, are *you* happy, Blythe?"

Blythe inhaled a shaky breath. "I mean, I love when we all eat together and share morning prayers. I like when the clerics visit and when I am able to read books." She laughed gently. "I like when you and Mama dance and Rowan and I sing. I think some of my favorite times have been when you help me outside, and we sit around the fire in the evenings. The best singing and dancing happens by the fire on cool autumn nights." She sat up straighter. "I can honestly say I'm happy."

"But?"

Blythe smiled. Leave it to Baba to know she was holding back. "I just wish, especially on days my legs hurt too bad to walk at all, that I could still *move*." She sighed. "I would love to go to the library in person again."

Her father sat back in his chair. He ran his calloused fingers through his beard in thought. "You know, I might have a solution. I don't know why I haven't thought of it before."

"You physically can't carry me to the library." Blythe laughed as she considered what her father might be implying. "I mean, you are strong, Baba. But that's a *long* walk, and I'm not a little child anymore!"

"No, you aren't a little child anymore. But you'll always be my little girl." Baba smiled, and Blythe felt she saw his eyes twinkle. Blythe started to ask what his solution was when her mother walked into the small kitchen.

"Happy day, you two," Blythe's mother said in a sing-song voice. She grabbed a basket out of the cupboard. "I'm going to see if the chickens have any eggs this morning. Matthias, Blythe, do either of you want—"

A knock sounded on the front door of the little cottage.

"My, it's a bit early for visitors, don't you think?" asked Maryam.

"It might be Bane checking on Rowan," offered Blythe as her father stood up. She heard his heavy footsteps move through the short hall and into the sitting room. The front door opened. The small space allowed the conversation to be heard.

"Cleric Jimson, please come in," her father's strong voice welcomed.

"I apologize for the early hour, but I have news. A hawk arrived not long ago, and it seems that the Royal Diatomist Dendro, as well as the king, have summoned Rowan to Tulium."

Chapter Ten
Promises and Broken Things

BLYTHE LAID ON HER BACK on the soft grass. She looked for pictures in the clouds as they leisurely floated across the sky.

"How long are they going to keep everyone waiting?" Bane's voice was sharp as he stood nearby. Blythe thought that if tones could cut, his vocalization would certainly slice through their reality.

"I know it's frustrating to not be hearing exactly what Cleric Jimson is saying right now, but it's probably best for Rowan to process the king's letter without so many people around."

Bane huffed into a seated position beside Blythe. "She can't go!"

Blythe turned her head to look at her friend. "Brooding about it isn't going to change anything." Under her breath, she added, "I should know."

He ran his hand through the front of his hair, the white catching the sunlight. "Did I tell you I picked up the necklace for Rowan?"

An excited squeal escaped Blythe as she pushed herself up to a seated position. "Do you have it now? Let me see!"

Bane pulled out a small bag of green cloth from his pants pocket. He untied the drawstring and slowly pulled out a sparkling, light pink gemstone with glints of orange embedded in a true-knot made of silver.

Blythe gasped and placed her hands overlapping one another over her heart. "It's even more gorgeous than I pictured. When are you going to give it to her? Oh, I can't wait until you two are officially courting!"

Bane sighed. "I was planning to give it to her yesterday, but . . ." His voice trailed off. He shrugged and put the necklace back in the cloth bag and returned the bag to his pocket. "Now she can't see colors, and she's been summoned to the king's castle in Tulium." Bane ran both of his hands through his hair as he let out a frustrated sigh that mimicked a growl. "But maybe it isn't the right time to ask her for me to be her suitor."

Blythe's nose wrinkled. "Are you scared she doesn't feel the same?"

His cheeks flushed. "I mean, I guess part of me is afraid she doesn't see us being more than friends. But it's more than that. How can I pour out my heart to her when she's about to travel across the country?" Bane shook his head, and his bangs shook, too. "I overheard my mother tell Pops that I'm too young to know what real love is. Maybe I am."

"Or maybe you're looking for a reason to make light of how you feel—like a shield in case you get hurt." Blythe watched as Bane's jaw clenched, and she cast her gaze down. "Maybe Rowan's right, and I have been talking with the clerics too much." She leaned back in the grass and sighed.

Bane fell into the grass beside Blythe. They both looked up at the sky. "Do you think Rowan will like the necklace, even though it's mostly pink?" Bane asked. "I wanted a completely orange stone because I know that's her favorite color, but it was a bit out of my price range. The girl in the jeweler's shop suggested this stone. There's a small blemish when you look closely, but I hope she doesn't mind. It kind of looks golden if you look at it directly—the blemish, I mean."

"I truly think she will love it. It's a beautiful necklace, and it's a gift from you."

The two sat in silence for several minutes. Blythe closed her eyes and soaked in the warm summer day.

Footsteps on the grass rustled the blades and drew the girl's attention. She sat up when she saw Rowan walking toward her and Bane.

"What did Cleric Jimson say?" Bane asked. He stood but then sat right back down as Rowan kneeled on the ground between him and her sister. She fanned her teal dress around her.

"It seems that King Isak is sending a chaperone and guards to pick me up and escort me to Tulium." Blythe watched as Rowan continuously smoothed the fabric of her dress without looking her sister or her friend in the face.

"Is that what you want?" Bane asked without pausing for a response. "If you don't want to go, there has to be something we can do."

"I want to see normally, and I want to get help for Blythe." Rowan rolled her shoulders back and looked at Bane directly. "After talking with Cleric Jimson, I think the best thing I can do is go to the king's court. The royal diatomist is the best option we have for fixing everything."

"What do you want us to do?" asked Blythe softly, placing a gentle hand on her sister's arm.

Rowan smiled, revealing the dimple on the left side of her face. "I need you both to promise to look after each other while I'm gone."

"Promise," Blythe said.

"Of course, I promise. I'll always look after you two. You're my family," Bane said with a serious expression, his mouth set in a firm line.

"I won't even make a condition for if the promise is broken because I know you two won't break it." Rowan extended her arms out and clasped a hand from both Blythe and Bane.

"Well, we need you to promise us something, too," Bane said before clearing his throat. Rowan raised an eyebrow in question, and he continued, "You have to promise that you aren't going to fall in love with city living and forget about us."

Rowan's giggles cut through the tense, heavy air. Blythe joined her sister, and the chuckles quickly grew into deep belly laughter. Even Bane began to laugh with them.

"I'm serious!" he added with a grin. "You might like living as royalty and decide to never come back home."

"Like you can get rid of me that easily." Rowan playfully pushed him. "I'll be back before you even have a chance to really miss me, and I'll have answers on how to repair everything that's broken."

Bane asked Rowan follow-up questions about how long it would be for her escort party to arrive from the castle, but Blythe's inner monologue drowned out their voices. She couldn't shake the hurt she felt at the perceived realization of Rowan's words. Her sister thought she was broken.

Chapter Eleven
Sleepless Night

A WARM TEAR ROLLED DOWN Blythe's cheek. She wiped it away with her hand, genuinely surprised she had any tears left. After Rowan left, Blythe had quietly wept on the loveseat until exhaustion took over. She blinked in the darkened room and came to the conclusion that her father must have put her to bed. She was still wearing her blue dress from earlier.

Blythe had never spent a single night without Rowan in her whole life. She stretched her arm out. The whole room, even the bed, felt too cold without her sister. A shiver went down Blythe's spine, despite the quilted blanket over her. She scanned the room, and her gaze landed on the window. The darkness of night encompassed the world outside, except for the shimmering stars above and a dim light in the distance. Baba must be up in the little barn in the backyard.

Her hips and knees protested, but she gritted her teeth. Though extremely stiff, she managed to put her feet flat on the floor beside the bed. Blythe's wooden cane leaned against its spot on the wall. Once it was in her grasp, she heavily leaned onto it in order to push herself to a standing position.

With each short step, she bit back whimpers. A small voice inside her head told her she didn't need to push herself now, or she would face even more pain in the future; but a louder voice told her being alone in that room any longer would be far worse.

Sweat beaded on Blythe's temples as she crossed the threshold of the back door in the small kitchen and walked outside. With small yet painful steps, she moved closer to her destination.

"Ow!" A howl escaped Blythe's lips as her bare foot hit a rock, and her instinct to jerk back sent a stabbing pain throughout her left knee. Blythe closed her eyes and focused on her breath.

"Do you want me to carry you, or do you want me to just walk beside you?" Baba's familiar tenor voice wrapped Blythe in a cocoon of comfort.

She inhaled deeply and let the breath go. "Will you carry me to the barn? I'm scared if I push myself, I won't have strength later. And"—her voice cracked—"I need to be strong."

"You and your sister can always count on me to be there when you don't feel strong enough and even when you do." Baba picked Blythe up with one brawny arm under her knees and the other behind her upper back. He kissed her forehead and crossed the yard in a few swift steps. Gingerly, he helped Blythe sit in a wooden chair near his workbench.

She quietly watched her father as he leaned over the wooden bench and grasped a carving knife in his hand. "What are you making?" she asked.

"Something I should have made for you a while back." Baba held up a piece of wood, shaven into a cylinder.

"A chair?" Blythe asked, her nose crinkling in confusion as she looked at the familiar-looking piece. She had watched her father and Mr. Oxeye build numerous items for their homesteads.

"A chair but with wheels. It'll be like your own cart to help you get around outside of the house."

Blythe straightened in her seat. "I could go to town? To worship? To get tea at Mrs. Bredon's shop? Oh! I could go to the library, too!" She blinked as warm tears fell down her face. Her heart swelled. She felt so seen through her father's actions, yet she still ached for her sister. "Maybe I can even move around the castle when we go visit Rowan in Tulium?"

Her father's jaw clenched briefly, but then he smiled. "I don't see why not."

Blythe ignored the tugging feeling that Baba was holding something back, reminding herself to focus on the doors the wheeled chair would open for her. Instead of talking for the sake of hearing words, she watched her father work, finding reassurance in his presence until she drifted to sleep at last.

Chapter Twelve
The Chaperone

ROWAN METHODICALLY TAPPED EACH FINGER to her thumb on both hands. Starting with her pinky, each fingertip took its turn. Once she touched the pointer finger to thumb she worked backward and then repeated the pattern.

A knock from the doorway caused Rowan to look up, but she stayed seated on her bed. Her fingers continued to fidget in the nearly compulsive calming technique. "Rowan, Bane is here and wants to see you. Do you feel like visiting for a bit before . . . " Rowan's mother's question trailed off.

With a quick nod, Rowan stood and smoothed her orange sundress; she only knew it was orange because of the wide bell sleeves and Blythe's earlier confirmation. Sighing subconsciously, Rowan walked into the small sitting area.

"Happy day, Rowan," Blythe greeted. She must have regretted the words because when they left her lips, Rowan saw her younger sister's face flush. "I'm finishing up a scarf for you. Tulium isn't close to the coast, so it's colder. I want to make sure you stay warm."

Rowan smiled at her sister but said nothing for a moment. She took a deep breath and cleared her throat, trying to hold back the tears brimming in her eyes.

"Do you want to go for a walk with me?" Bane asked.

"A walk? Sure, that sounds nice." Rowan's smile was thin. Once she and Bane were through the front door, she linked her arm through his elbow. They strolled at a relaxed pace down the dirt path.

"I can't believe I'm leaving today," Rowan said, her voice cracking. She looked at Bane who offered a genuine smile. Every feature was gray to Rowan, even his normally honey-brown eyes.

"I already miss you," Rowan whispered. Her gaze fell to his chest. She watched the waves of gray light and shadow ebb and flow.

"I feel like I haven't said the right words or done anything to help," Bane said, his pace slowing to a near stop.

"What? Don't—"

"I'm not saying that looking for you to make me feel better." Bane held Rowan's hand. "How much you think of others is one of the things I admire about you, and I was just saying I wish I was more like you, you know? You always know what to say and do to make me feel better, like everything is going to be okay. I want to do the same . . . " His voice trailed off, and then he cleared his throat. He pulled a little green pouch from his pocket. "Never mind what I was saying. Here, it's time for you to finally open your naming anniversary gift."

Rowan excitedly took the green bag. "I guess since you didn't forget, I won't make you take a bite of lemon, though technically that wasn't our deal." As she dropped the necklace into her palm,

Rowan gasped. "Bane!" Rowan pulled her hand close to her face to better inspect the jewelry.

There was a gemstone embedded in silver pieces that crossed over one another—a true-knot. Even though she couldn't tell what the exact color of the stone was, down the middle, she could see a faint line. The more she stared, the more Rowan felt like the line shone.

"It's pink. I know orange is your favorite color, and there are flecks of orange. But pink is good, too. Don't you think? You love pink daisies, so the color makes me think of you—bright and happy and full of hope and—"

Rowan threw her arms around Bane. "It's so beautiful, Bane. I've never had a necklace before, and I can't believe you. I want to say it's too much, but I just love it!" Rowan pulled away, turned around, and pulled her brown hair to the side. "Will you clasp it for me?"

"Of course."

"I'm so lucky that you're my best friend," Rowan said earnestly. "I—"

Up ahead, coming over a slightly hilly part of their path, a cart pulled by two black horses was moving in their direction. But it was different from typical carts found in Aconite as it had an enclosed covering. Behind the horses sat two men. One of them was Cleric Jimson.

"I thought I'd have a little more time," Rowan said, her voice soft.

"Me, too." Rowan and Bane stood side by side. The horses were moving quickly. "Before they get here, I need to tell you something." Bane shifted and turned to face Rowan. "But I'm not exactly sure how to say this—"

"Hello there," Cleric Jimson called out.

Rowan waved politely. Bane also waved with one hand while the other brushed through the side of his thick hair. They stepped off the dirt path to make room for the horses and covered cart.

"Happy day," said the man holding the horses' reins.

Bane and Rowan returned the greeting. "I've never seen a carriage like this before in person, sir," said Rowan. "It's like a scene from a book."

"The enclosure is much appreciated in the cooler weather of Tulium," said the man, politely. "And you can call me George."

"If you don't mind, Rowan, we will follow behind you to your house," Cleric Jimson said.

Rowan peered down the simple road. Behind the carriage were more horses and more men. The men wore simple garb; but looking closely, one could see chainmail poking at the edges of their shirts. Swords hung in the sheaths by their waists.

With a silent nod directed at Cleric Jimson, Rowan turned. She looped her arm around Bane's elbow like she typically did, but she felt his muscles grow taut under her touch.

He's worried about me leaving . . .

Then Rowan realized she was, too. She wanted to tell him everything was going to be just fine and comfort him like he said she always did. Instead, she fidgeted with her new necklace.

Quietly, Bane whispered, "You don't have to go."

"If it was just for my sake, I probably wouldn't. But it's for Blythe. I have to find a way to heal her."

Bane offered a weak smile. "I know you do."

The pair turned toward Rowan's front door, and the horses whinnied behind them. George stepped down and walked to the side of the carriage. Rowan examined the intricate silver design around the door as he opened it. A gloved hand took George's extended one. Out stepped a beautiful woman, roughly the age of Rowan's mother. Her light hair was pinned back in a braid with pearl pins adorning her head. She wore a cloak and simple traveling dress embroidered with a floral design around both the neck and hem.

"My goodness, George, it is warm out here, isn't it?" She removed her gloves and cloak and tossed them unceremoniously back into the carriage. "Let's get you and everyone in the convoy some water and some shade, yes?"

Rowan watched the woman with fascination. The woman turned toward Rowan and Bane. "Hello, Rowan, it's nice to meet you. I'm Lady Linnea, and I'll be your chaperone while you are a guest of the king in Tulium. Are your parents home?" She started walking toward the door.

With her words caught inside her throat, Rowan walked hurriedly to open the door for Lady Linnea. Her mother was sitting with Blythe.

"Happy day," Lady Linnea said with a big smile as she approached.

"Happy day. I am Maryam; please have a seat," Rowan's mother said, welcoming the guest.

Rowan's chaperone laughed. "I have been sitting in that carriage for nearly two days. If you don't find it rude, I would prefer to stretch my legs." The lady scanned the room, and her eyes landed on Blythe. "The cleric told me Rowan had a younger sister. Blythe, yes?"

Blythe set her knitting needles to the side. "Yes, milady." She looked at Rowan. "I don't think I'm going to have the scarf ready before you go," her voice choked on the final word.

"Don't fret, my dear," Lady Linnea said, walking over and sitting beside Blythe on the loveseat. "I have talked to Cleric Jimson. Rowan is free to use the hawks, as are you, to send letters back and forth. The hawks can travel much faster than we can. And I will take good care of her while she's under the castle's care."

Rowan watched her sister relax her shoulders a bit, and Blythe picked up her knitting again.

The visitor stood once again, stretching her back slightly. "As I told Rowan when I arrived, my name is Lady Linnea."

Rowan's mother gasped. "The *almost queen*? Why did you give up the throne?" She put a hand over her mouth. Red crept up her neck and blotched her cheeks. "I am so sorry. I shouldn't have asked that."

Rowan's eyes went wide as she realized exactly *who* stood in her house. Lady Linnea had been next in line to be the first queen of Wisteria, but her announcement as the official heir was postponed with her mother's second pregnancy.

Linnea rubbed the fabric of her cloak in between her fingers in a moment of quiet contemplation, her eyes looking out of the window. She returned to the loveseat and looked at Rowan's mother. "I have never publicly addressed that question, and I have seen no need to correct the people's whispers or assumptions."

"I shouldn't have . . . "

Linnea held up a hand, her face softening with a gentle smile. "No, I'm glad you did." She turned to meet Rowan's magenta eyes. "I was terrified of being queen, asking myself if I was capable by birthright alone. People questioning if a woman could rule independently as the reigning leader deepened my worries. I prayed ceaselessly for a sibling, for me to not have to carry such a heavy weight."

"Verimor answered your prayer. You have a brother," said Rowan.

"I do have a brother, and I love him very much. However, it isn't as simple as that, Rowan." She paused and took two steady breaths.

Rowan looked at her younger sister, her hands working diligently with the needles and yarn. She didn't remember meeting for the first time with only two years between them. Rowan felt she had always had her younger sister, a friend for life. Her eyes shifted back to Linnea and focused on the swirling gray and white in front of her chest. As her gaze lingered, she saw flashes of memories from Linnea's perspective.

"When my mother learned she was with child, my father didn't want to automatically change the succession if the baby were to be a boy. I begged and pleaded nearly every day. When my mother gave birth to Isak, my father told me the baby was a boy. He asked me if I was sure I wanted him to wear the crown. I said yes. As everyone knows, my father issued a decree that very afternoon. It wasn't until that evening that I met my new baby brother for the first time." Her eyes misted, and Rowan leaned forward as the shadows pulsated as if to say how much hurt this happy time concealed.

"My choice determined that innocent baby's future—a choice I made because of fear and stubborn ignorance that caused me to pull away from Verimor's teachings, rather . . . " Linnea stood abruptly and moved to stand in front of the lone window. "I'm becoming long-winded." There was another pause interrupted by a sniffle from Linnea and then a small cough. "The important thing is, I realized that I had skills within me that could help the kingdom. I had Divinely ordained talents to help my brother and help others take up their callings, to not try to run away. Am I making sense?"

Rowan parted her lips, but her mother spoke first. "You're a testimony that you can't run from Verimor's purpose."

"Even though you didn't become queen?" Rowan asked, her nose crinkling as her mind read between the lines of Linnea's story.

"I do not have the title of queen. However, though the king has ultimate authority, I am heavily involved in ruling behind the scenes, so to speak." Linnea turned once again to address Rowan and her mother face to face. "When we received word of Rowan's . . . *condition,* I took it upon myself to ensure her safe arrival and care while working with the diatomists to learn about the blessing. Maryam, I know Rowan will be far from home, but I will do everything in my power to protect her."

Rowan's eyes lingered longer than she intended, and the shadow and light in front of her mother revealed itself. As soon as the words "protect her" left Linnea's lips, the white grew in her mother.

Rowan watched Lady Linnea talk with both care and confidence. She could have been cold and bitter with the circumstances she had experienced, but she chose to continue to serve the crown and Verimor. She also seemed to show great respect to all people, even those who lacked royal rank. Rowan decided she rather liked the woman.

"Once we get settled at the castle, Rowan will be working with the royal diatomist's apprentice to see if she has been truly given the blessing of Sight." She paused. "I believe she does, indeed, have the blessing of a unicorn."

"What if she does?" Bane asked from near the doorway.

"Let's take it one step at a time. But"—Linnea looked directly at Rowan—"I want you to know that even when it feels too overwhelming, you have been born for this time. Remember that Verimor has a plan, and it includes you." The words left goosebumps on Rowan's arms.

Linnea clasped her hands together. "Maryam, is it possible to go ahead and get Rowan's things together? I apologize for sharing so much personal information, but I hope you do not think less of me."

Rowan's mother jumped to her feet. She reached for Linnea's hands as if she were an old friend. "Oh, not at all! I'm thankful you shared that part of your story with us. I will feel better about Rowan being so far away knowing you will help take care of her."

"It won't be for too long." Linnea pulled a folded piece of parchment from within her cloak.

Rowan's mother accepted it, pulled against the wax seal, and scanned the letter. Her eyebrows knitted together. "We are all invited to Tulium?"

Lady Linnea smiled. "George Ginty will be back in due time to escort you all. King Isak would love your whole family to attend his upcoming ball; it's held every year at the start of the Marigold Festival season."

"A royal ball? We're really invited?" Blythe asked in awe.

Rowan's pulse quickened as Blythe and Bane started asking questions. She didn't want to leave her family; but at the same time, the thought of traveling with Lady Linnea sent a shot of excitement through her. And her family would be joining her in a fortnight.

I think I can survive two weeks.

Chapter Thirteen
Blemish or Blessing?

THE CARRIAGE DOOR SLAMMED CLOSED. The loud thud helped the world come back into focus for Rowan. She peered out the small window. Though only a moment had passed since she had hugged her parents, Blythe, and Bane, she couldn't have recalled their last words exchanged if asked. She couldn't remember where Cleric Jimson had been since seeing him with George upon the convoy's arrival. In fact, it all felt like a strange dream.

"Your family loves you very much," said Linnea. She sat opposite Rowan in the small space.

Rowan's nose wrinkled as she considered the words, and she tilted her head to the side. "I get the sense you and your brother are very close with all you've been through, even with you being older." Rowan's cheeks blushed pink. "Not that you're old."

Linnea laughed gently. "Isak, my brother, is truly my best friend. You and your sister seem quite close, too."

"Blythe is the sweetest and most authentic soul I know. But she's sick. Sometimes, she can walk with the help of a cane; but other days, she's bedridden because of her pain," Rowan explained. "And I want the royal diatomist to help me in finding a way to cure her, even if it means my eyes don't go back to normal."

"Who says it has to be an either-or situation?" Linnea raised an eyebrow. "Sacrifice for love is a noble thing indeed, but senseless, self-induced suffering is not needed."

"I didn't cause my own vision to lose color," Rowan said defensively.

"We will find a way to help both you and Blythe." Linnea leaned closer to Rowan and pointed at her necklace, a glimmer catching her eye "Do you mind? That's really a lovely piece."

When Rowan nodded consent, Linnea held the true-knot encased gemstone in her fingers.

"My friend Bane gave it to me for my naming anniversary," Rowan whispered.

"Fascinating." Linnea tilted her head. "Did you notice this little line in the middle of the gem?"

Rowan glanced down as the older woman continued, "To the average spectator, it might appear to be a defect, an unwanted scar, a flaw. But can you feel that thrum within the stone?"

Rowan stared at the little rock in Linnea's fingers. She saw a thin, dark gray line through the light gray jewel. The longer she looked, the more it seemed to vibrate.

"It's not a blemish at all. In fact, with the slight gold shimmer, it seems to be a blessing from a—"

Rowan's scoff interrupted Linnea as she leaned back. "If blessings are like wishes, then they're nothing more than childish dreams."

Her chaperone dropped the necklace and sat up, too. Linnea frowned; but it slowly lessened, making her face appear more thoughtful than sad. "Blessings are far from fantasy or childish whimsies, my dear. You should keep that token of your courter with you always; one may never know when one needs a blessing of renewal."

"Wait . . . *courter*? Bane isn't . . . " Rowan's words became thick molasses in her mouth. She knew the meaning for that kind of jewelry. However, she hadn't allowed herself to say that was what it meant for her and Bane together. Is this what he had wanted to talk about before she left? Had he wanted them to be something more than friends? Did *she* want that for the two of them? Rowan shifted uncomfortably in her seat and wondered if Bane understood even the symbolism of the necklace. Maybe he hadn't even realized he had selected a gem with a true-knot.

"My apologies," Linnea said. "The true-knot is usually a sign of betrothal or courtship." She began to speak politely of the journey ahead, including when they would stop for an evening meal and a stretch. Rowan heard bits and pieces and nodded throughout. But her mind was elsewhere.

"I don't mean to make you uncomfortable. I know some people prefer silence over polite conversation." Linnea's voice broke through the fog in Rowan's mind like the morning sun brightening the sky at dawn.

Rowan's eyes widened, and her face flushed. "No, you have been lovely. Everything is a bit uncomfortable, I suppose. Traveling

away from home. Adjusting to a world without color. Accepting that my life now includes everyone saying I'm *unicorn-blessed*."

Linnea leaned forward and patted Rowan's knee. "I can't begin to understand Verimor's greater plan at work now. But take heart in knowing you were chosen to receive this blessing for a purpose."

The smile on Rowan's face did not reach her eyes, nor did it reveal her dimple. After a moment, she said, "I have to remind myself that my purpose is to help find a cure for my sister."

"I think that's a noble endeavor. But remember, Rowan, our goals as humans may not be attainable in the manner we imagine."

"Wouldn't Verimor want Blythe to get better?" Rowan's shoulders tensed, and her voice cracked as she tried to keep her volume in check. "Do you think He won't help heal her?"

Linnea looked at Rowan directly. "I learned a long time ago that what I think and what Verimor knows are two vastly different worlds. Would you like something to eat?"

Rowan watched as Linnea stood up and opened a small cabinet compartment above where she was sitting. She pulled out two bundles of wax paper, extending one to Rowan. "We'll have some warm soup when we stop for the night, but we still have a few hours to go. If you need a break sooner, let me know; and we can stop to stretch our legs earlier."

Rowan accepted the offer, hoping her nostrils were not noticeably flaring. She was upset at the thought that Blythe would never be pain-free. It also hurt that Linnea seemed to dismiss her by bringing out cheese, dried meat, and crackers.

After one nibble of a cracker, Rowan's stomach gurgled loudly. Linnea politely said nothing. Rowan focused on the food at hand, thankful that she had it; she hadn't even realized they had already spent several hours in the carriage. Rowan finished the food and happily accepted a waterskin Linnea offered to wash it down. Now that she was no longer hungry, her mood lifted. "It will take three days to get there?"

"Three days and two nights," explained Linnea. "We will stop a little before dusk today, as well as the next two days to set up camp and rest outside of the confines of the carriage. Then we should arrive in Tulium before the midday meal on day three of our journey."

Rowan closed her eyes, and she focused on the rocking motion. "The ride makes me think of the ocean. I love the coast and the water."

"You'll be back at the shore before you even really miss it."

Rowan ignored Linnea's attempt to provide comfort. "My favorite memories and even my favorite stories are all connected to the beach. My sister and I used to find jelly snails and keep gulls away while they made their way back to the water. Have you ever seen a jelly snail, Lady Linnea?"

"Not in person, but I have read of them."

"I think they might be my favorite animal. Along with goats, pigs, and cats."

"Personally, I adore cats. In fact, we have quite a number of cats that hang around the castle."

Rowan sat up. "Do you have any stories of the castle cats?"

Linnea laughed. "Castle cats? That's got a pleasant ring to it, doesn't it? Yes, I might have a story or two I could share. How about I share a story after you share one of your jelly snails?"

"Okay. Have you heard the story of the jelly snail who was taken far from the ocean?" When Linnea shook her head, Rowan launched into the tale.

"Once, on the sandy shores of Aconite, a blue jelly snail hatched. He looked and saw the ocean waves. He knew that's where he needed to go, but the water seemed an impossibly long distance away. Then he heard a squawking gull that made him tremble with fear and trepidation.

"Much closer to where he was, there was a woven basket. The jelly snail decided that it would serve as a suitable, temporary home. But shortly after crawling inside, his new abode began moving—a girl had run up and picked up the basket.

"The jelly snail looked over the edge carefully, his heart filling with more uncertainty as the ocean disappeared from view. After what seemed like an eternity, the basket was set down upon grass. Though the water was nowhere to be seen, the jelly snail felt the pull of the sea's call—it was where he was needed.

"But the jelly snail believed it would be easier to find a new calling. He reasoned that it was nearly impossible to reach the safety of the waters before, and being even further away sealed his fate.

"'Oh, you poor thing!' exclaimed the girl as her shadow covered the jelly snail in the basket. 'I'll return you to the beach—you creatures cannot live long without saltwater.'

"The jelly snail knew her words were true. Already, he was losing energy. Yet being left in the sand and having to trek through danger to reach the water nearly unnerved him. Even the rocking of the moving basket with each stride of the girl brought him no comfort.

"'You're home,' said the girl. She put the basket down, tipping it slightly. A splash of foam reached for the jelly snail. He looked at the girl and then at the waters calling him. Even though he had tried to run away, he was brought to fulfill his life's mission. The little jelly snail was thankful for the stranger who had helped him get where he needed to be."

"Rowan, you're quite a natural storyteller," said Lady Linnea, clapping her hands.

Rowan smiled earnestly. "Blythe and I love sharing stories. And Miss Thistle has asked me to lead story time at the library for the younger children a few times."

The carriage creaked to a stop, and male voices yelled back and forth outside. George opened the door and offered his hand to Lady Linnea and Rowan in turn. "Helene is setting up now, and your dinner will be served shortly," he said.

Rowan's gaze wandered over the activity of the evening's campsite. Men quickly assembled tents; one in the center stood much larger than the rest. Other people worked to start a fire under a large iron cauldron. Within minutes, scents of tomato and garlic wafted through the air.

With a warm soup bowl in her hands, Rowan sat on a short wooden stool. Guards rinsed their bowls in a communal bucket of water and then stacked them in another pail. Nearby, Mrs. Ginty cooked while Lady Linnea assisted her in packing up the dinner supplies and preparing for breakfast in the morning. Meanwhile, there were some men stationed at particular areas around the camp's perimeter, and a group of guards had set up an area to play cards near the fire.

Though far from boisterous, their strong voices carried through the night air.

"You think those purple eyes mean she is unicorn-blessed?" one soldier called to his companion.

"They aren't exactly purple," another man said.

A different guard protested. "Bert, the unnatural coloring and the fact a unicorn was talking with Lady Linnea to go get this girl prove she's been blessed! She is proof that prayers are answered, that Verimor has a plan, and that Wisteria can stop Obsilvia once and for all."

"What has Obsilvia really done, though, Cassian?" asked Bert. "There's been no acts of war."

The third guard harrumphed. "*No* acts of war? Then explain the Obsilvian sitting in the king's dungeon because of an assassination attempt, Bert. You're young, but I thought you were smarter than that."

"I am—there's been no declaration of war. How's that, Thaddeus?" snapped Bert. "Maybe Wisteria can learn some things from Obsilvia. Their kingdom is progressive; they have a vision for securing and ensuring prosperity for their people—"

"Yes, by killing our king and slaughtering any Wisterian who refuses to spurn Verimor. You better watch what you say, boy. Don't want to come off as an Obsilvian sympathizer."

"Maybe I just don't like the idea of getting killed on the battlefield." Bert laughed, and another man joined in.

Thaddeus slapped Bert on the shoulder. "Then let's hope this girl is legitimate."

"Hope? Thaddeus, I know you saw the unicorn, too, right?" urged Cassian.

"Enough talk." He shuffled a deck of cards in his hands. "Who wants to lose in a game of Weeping Willows?" Rowan watched the three men intently as their conversation shifted. She felt itchy being the topic of conversation without actually taking part in it. Her unease only grew as she looked at the swirling shadows in front of the three men. Cassian had the fewest shadows; the smoky orb on his chest was almost three-quarters light. Thaddeus had an almost equal balance of black and white tendrils. But Bert had little light. Rowan's eyes narrowed. She felt an expanding curiosity to know more about what her new eyes could do. If she could discern what caused the differences of light and shadows within the person and their memories' role in it all. Swirls moved and revealed the start of scene. There were flames and . . .

"Rowan, are you ready to get some sleep?" Linnea's voice pulled Rowan from the guard who doubted her and his card playing.

Rowan's shoulders fell slightly, but she offered the lady a polite nod. "Sleep sounds nice." She followed Lady Linnea into the large central tent.

Linnea let the opening fall and then pulled a rope in the center. "It's such a beautiful night. How about we let the stars watch over us as we rest?" As she pulled the rope, a small flap of canvas rolled up in the middle of the square roof.

Rowan sat on a cot with a down pillow and a thick quilt, and she looked up at the twinkling lights in the night sky. "Does the royal diatomist think I can prevent a war?"

Lady Linnea didn't respond immediately as she removed her outer frock. "I always fail to remember how warm it is closer to the coast. I think my underdress will serve just fine as a nightgown tonight."

Rowan continued to watch the stars, sure that Lady Linnea was ignoring her question.

"As you know, diatomy is made possible through faith and a connection that allows direct spiritual guidance from Verimor—it's how certain people can manipulate aspects of the natural world. But diatomists are not meant to have insurmountable power; instead, their abilities are meant to foster conviction and minister to people. I'm sure you have heard whispers among the guards already. Tensions are growing high with the kingdom of Obsilvia. Our diatomists, even Dendro, cannot stop men from enacting on misguided principles, nor can they stop violence from spilling into our borders."

Rowan propped herself on her elbow and turned toward Lady Linnea's cot, which rested a few feet from her own. "But they think *I* can?"

"Only Verimor has that power, but your Sight could prove useful in understanding the hearts of men. That could indeed help calm the boiling atmosphere." Lady Linnea stretched out, leaning her head onto her pillow. "I fear, at this time, war is inevitable. We'll talk more tomorrow. Let the stars lull you to sleep."

Rowan rolled onto her back and looked at the open sky once more. *Is Blythe looking at these same stars tonight?*

Chapter Fourteen
A New Friend

L OUD WHINNIES FROM HORSES AND shouting thundered nearby, but Rowan didn't want to open her eyes. She had struggled to sleep soundly during their overnight stops but had somehow managed to doze in the seat of the carriage.

"Rowan?" Linnea's voice was soft but commanding. "We are here."

"At the castle?" Groggily, Rowan pulled her feet off the seat and turned to face Linnea. She rotated her neck and shoulders to release the muscle tension her position had caused.

"Almost. We are in Tulium and are nearing the first gate to the castle. I thought you might want to see." With quick movements, Linnea pulled back a curtain that Rowan had mistaken as part of the carriage wall and revealed a much larger window than on the side with the door.

Rowan's eyes widened. Though she saw no color, the size of the buildings and the number of people filled her with awe. The carriage creaked to a halt, and she listened as men gruffly yelled at one another.

"Once we get through this gate," Linnea said, "we will only be a few minutes away from the main entryway. After arriving, we will get you settled quickly; so you can meet with Diatomist Dendro."

"Will King Isak be there?"

"You will meet him, too, yes."

Rowan didn't break her gaze from the window. Once on the cobbled street beyond the first gate, the amount of flowering plants on stone walls drew her in like she had fallen inside a painting.

"The castle is even bigger than I imagined," Rowan said. The carriage slowed and stopped for just a moment before jutting forward once more. She craned her neck to get a better view of the front of the castle, but her perspective was limited.

When the carriage stopped again, Linnea spoke. "Remember, whether we embrace the roles we are cast in or not, there is always an audience learning from our parts in the story of life. I pray that you know your blessing will bless others."

"But how do I use my blessing to help others?"

Before Linnea could answer Rowan's question, the door opened. George stood there. He extended his hand. Lady Linnea took it as she stepped out of the carriage. Rowan rolled her shoulders and accepted George's hand as she stepped down.

George said something, but Rowan didn't process the words. She gawked unabashedly at the towering door to the royal castle. Stone steps lead to an iron door tall enough for the giants Rowan read about in storybooks. But even more captivating to her was the thick wisteria-layered ivy around the entrance. The wisteria grew wildly across all the stone, creating a scene she might find in a storybook at the Magna Library.

"Miss?"

Rowan shook her head slightly and turned toward George. "I'm sorry, George. Can you repeat that?"

"Nora"—he gestured to a young girl who had walked over and now stood next to him—"will be your handmaid to assist you while you are a guest of the king and Lady Linnea."

"I don't need someone . . . " The shadow that seemed to cover Nora's pale, freckled face caused Rowan to bite back her words. Though Nora didn't look like Blythe, something about her demeanor reminded Rowan of her sister. In fact, she guessed that Nora was close to Blythe's age, even though the girl stood taller than both Rowan and her sister. "Thank you, Nora, for helping me while I'm here."

Nora flashed a wide grin. There was a slight gap between her two front teeth. "It's an honor, milady. George will work with Mrs. Ginty to get your personal belongings to your room. For now, I'm going to show you a quick tour of the wing you will be staying in and help you get freshened up to meet with the royal diatomist and his apprentice, Oren." Nora leaned in and smiled mischievously. "He's rather easy on the eyes—the apprentice, I mean."

Rowan couldn't help but join in with Nora's giggles. She felt completely thrown off by the girl's comment and surprised to find her not as similar to Blythe as she had first surmised.

"Hurry along, Nora," George said sternly, although his voice was not unkind. "Mrs. Ginty likes to keep to the planned schedule."

Nora bowed her covered head slightly and turned, motioning for Rowan to follow. Rowan clung to her cloak as the cold air of

Tulium chilled her; but as soon as they cleared the doorway, the biting wind was left behind.

"We'll get you a fleece-lined chemise to wear under your dresses," Nora said as Rowan took in the wide hallway leading to a foyer with two grand staircases ahead and to the right; the left opened into another hallway.

"The undergarment sounds wonderful. I'm not used to cold weather in Aconite."

"Lady Linnea sent for gloves and wool garments for you prior to her initial departure," Nora said cheerfully. "You're going to love all the beautiful colors. There's one yellow and green dress with the most intricate beadwork on the bodice. That's my favorite."

"Oh, I brought my other two dresses with me. There's really no need for everyone to go through so much trouble."

"You've been blessed by the unicorns!" Nora's volume caused several passersby to look. She cleared her throat and spoke more calmly. "What I mean is that you are an honored guest of the royal family. If it was me, I would be fully indulging in the hospitality of my hosts—especially since you don't know what they will ask you to do in the name of the kingdom."

Rowan's gait slowed. Nora didn't notice and kept her pace up the stairs to the right. Rowan jogged to catch up as the maid hurriedly moved away from the top of the staircase. "Do you know what the king plans to have me do?"

"I don't know specifics, but the staff have said you're going to help in a big way." Nora continued walking ahead of Rowan.

Rowan's breathing intensified. She felt like the castle was a giant maze, and Nora's long legs made Rowan feel she was racing

Bane. Her heart hammered in her chest. She already missed her home—and her friend—so much.

"Here we are," Nora said while opening a wooden door, which Rowan assumed was trimmed in brass, though it looked gray to her eyes. Nora turned and examined Rowan's flushed face.

"I apologize, milady," she said quickly. "I should have walked slower. I'm just excited to have someone like you here—I mean, someone close to my age, not the unicorn-blessed part. I mean . . . "

Rowan held a hand out to comfort the girl. "Just call me Rowan. Are there not a lot of young people in the castle?"

"There's not a lot of *kind* young people." Nora's pale face turned darker as she blushed. "I shouldn't have said that. It's just that the young ladies of the royal court, the daughters of the nobles and knights and others in the direct service of the king, don't like to associate themselves with someone like me." After a brief pause, she added, "But Oren the apprentice is really nice, and the ladies tend to keep their tongues in check when he's present." The girl let out a sigh as if caught up in her own daydream.

"Do you fancy Oren?" Rowan asked with her eyebrow raised. "If you don't mind me asking, that is."

"Oh, he would never have eyes for me, but wishful thinking can help the time pass." She coughed slightly, and Rowan inferred Nora was indicating her intention to drop the subject of the diatomist's apprentice. "First, we'll get you bathed, and I'll help style your hair and get you dressed. You will meet Diatomist Dendro in his study before joining Lady Linnea and the king for dinner."

"Is the king nice?" Rowan's words tripped over her tongue as if she had a mouth full of thick sticky bun icing. Despite numerous servants navigating the halls, it was strangely quiet as Nora led her to her meeting.

"Oh, King Isak is wonderful. He relies on Lady Linnea quite a bit. I think a part of him feels like he owes his sister—you know, since she was going to be the first queen of Wisteria before he came along. And then with their mother passing shortly after his birth, she basically raised him, even though she had only had seventeen naming anniversaries at the time."

"I'm glad family is important to him," Rowan said. "Maybe that will help me find a cure for Blythe."

"A cure? Is she okay?" Nora's mouth scrunched in concern. Rowan's stomach growled loudly, and Nora laughed. Her laugh was airy, and her amusement contagious. "Never mind right now. I'll grab you a bite to snack on once you're in the tub. I bet the traveling vittles weren't exactly satisfying."

"Actually, the tomato bisque was delicious, though I only had one small bowl." Rowan followed the quick steps of Nora into a small room. A clawed-foot bathtub was filled with steaming water. Rowan saw swirls within the water's surface and inhaled the scents of eucalyptus and mint.

"Do you want help getting undressed?"

"What? No, I can manage that myself." Rowan offered a smile, hoping she didn't offend Nora. "But I look forward to how you style my hair later."

Nora touched Rowan's hair. "Your hair is so thick yet smooth. It's going to be fun playing with it." Nora's hand dropped, and she turned. "I'll be back shortly," she said, pulling the door closed behind her.

When Rowan stepped into the bath water, she sighed audibly. It was the warmest bath she had ever taken. She leisurely watched the swirls of steam rise from the surface. She wondered what Nora's heart looked like and Lady Linnea's heart. She kept her gaze from lingering too long in the carriage, but maybe she should embrace the things the new gift revealed.

Is that what Linnea meant with her cryptic words when they first arrived?

After several minutes soaking, with her muscles fully relaxed, Rowan felt her eyelids growing heavy. A knock sounded at the door, and Nora entered.

"Milady—"

"Please, just call me Rowan."

"Rowan," Nora rolled her name on her tongue, drawing out each syllable. "I've got some fruits and nuts for you. Mrs. Ginty wouldn't let me bring anything heavier because she doesn't want you to spoil your dinner. Are you ready to get dressed? You can have your snack while I style your hair."

In mere minutes, Rowan was wearing a warm sham underneath a floor-length yellow velvet dress tinged with dark navy and orange, as described by Nora. Rowan sat on a stool in front of a large mirror by a window. Despite the cold autumn weather outside, the sun provided much light.

"You have really gorgeous hair," Nora said.

"You really think so? I usually keep at least half of it pulled back to keep it out of the way."

"I can do a half-up style, and I will add in a braid and some pearl pins. It will help you blend in with the current fashions, but maybe a familiar look will help you feel more at ease here."

Rowan smiled at the girl through the mirror. She let her eyes wander to Nora's reflection. Nora stood off to Rowan's side as she brushed her hair. Just as if she were looking directly at the girl, the reflection showed Rowan tendrils of light and gray shadow. Rowan felt conflicted but decided to look more closely at Nora as she talked to her. "Nora, are you happy here?"

The lights and shadows swirled together as Nora responded. "I suppose so. My life could be worse. Here I am warm, fed, and safe. Plus, I make good wages—enough to send back home to help look after my younger twin brothers."

Rowan watched as the light and shadows created moving images in grayscale. From Nora's perspective, she saw two freckled faces looking up at her. A young boy clamped around each of her long legs, laughing and encouraging her to walk around with them attached to her.

"Do you miss your brothers?"

The shadows moved slightly. Nora replied, "I miss them terribly."

Rowan watched as the images shifted to reveal the boys crying. A dark-haired man was pushing a small satchel into Nora's hands and shooing her down a dirt path. But then as quickly as the shadows increased, the light brightened, causing the darker grays to recede.

"But I get to visit them twice a year; and when they are here in Tulium, sometimes I see them when I run errands for Mrs. Ginty. And I know one day, I'll be able to use the skills I've learned here to find good work closer to my family."

"I miss my family, too. I'm not sure how long the king wants me here. And I'm not sure I can stay away from home for much longer."

Nora squeezed Rowan's shoulder. "Even when miles apart, the love of your family stays in your heart."

"That's lovely."

"My grandmother always says that," Nora said, seemingly with great pride as she straightened her shoulders. She moved around Rowan putting final touches on her hair, placing pins with thought-out precision.

"I don't know if Blythe or Bane would even recognize me!" Rowan said as she looked in the mirror.

"Are those your siblings?"

"Blythe's my sister, and Bane . . . well, he's my best friend." Rowan felt her cheeks grow warm.

Nora raised her eyebrows. She gestured to Rowan's necklace. "Did Bane give you that?"

When Rowan nodded, Nora grinned widely. "I think the girls at court will like you more since you're not a threat."

"A threat? Why would I be a threat?" Rowan absent-mindedly tapped her fingertips to her thumbs, trying to calm her rising nerves.

"Not only are you unicorn-blessed and *very* important to the king, but you're also beautiful. Even though all the girls want to be courted by Oren, he hasn't shown a particular interest in anyone." Nora shrugged. "Since you have a suitor back home, hopefully the girls won't see you as competition for his attention. Maybe they'll be nicer to you."

"I'm not really beautiful—at least, not in a threatening way. You keep saying I'm unicorn-blessed, but nobody knows that for sure.

And Bane did give me this necklace; but as far as I know, we're just friends." Rowan wrung her hands together. "Is it hot in here?"

"It's actually a little cooler since the fire has died down in the hearth. I think you're just worked up missing Bane." Nora winked. "And as far as nobody *knowing* if you're unicorn-blessed or not, I would bet my next pay that you have indeed been blessed by Cressida or another one of Verimor's messengers. I don't know what the blessing is going to do exactly, but I know you're going to help Wisteria in a big way."

Rowan tried to smile back at Nora as she stood beside the maidservant, but the bit of fruit and cashews in her stomach churned. She wondered how in the world anyone could expect her to help the kingdom when she hadn't even found a way to help her own sister.

Chapter Fifteen
Folktales and Findings

LINNEA WATCHED ROWAN AND NORA as the two girls made their way into the castle entrance. A sense of pride bloomed in her chest when Rowan didn't look back to find her. The girl seemed to possess a sense of confidence and surety she wasn't even aware of. It would be nice having her at the castle. Linnea felt she had a kindred spirit and that the girl was mature beyond her years.

A familiar voice pulled her from her reverie. "Lady Linnea, how was your trip?"

"Happy day, Oren. We made it back safely." Linnea's face donned a weak smile while her heart ached. Recalling the unicorn's words about the phoenix filled her with grief, both for her friend and for the world.

Oren, in his usual green robes, held a scroll in one hand and tapped it in the open palm of his other one. He tilted his head and narrowed his green eyes. "What's wrong?"

"Too much, I'm afraid." Linnea pulled her fur-lined coat tighter around her neck, clasping the top button in place. She motioned to the rolled parchment. "Do you have news from Diatomist Dendro?"

"The royal diatomist is currently readying to meet with the unicorn-blessed girl and asked not to be disturbed. However, contacts within the Dimidi Isles proved useful in uncovering some information." His steps slowed slightly as he looked around them as they walked down the main corridor toward the stairs. Servants worked throughout the space. "Perhaps you should look over this in private."

Linnea extended her hand to take the scroll. The weight in her hand informed her there were several pages rolled together. Excitement pumped through her veins and urged her feet to move swiftly. Rather than going upstairs to her quarters, she maneuvered through the castle staff on the first floor to get to the gardens.

More guards were present as was ordered since the parchment with the strange symbol and the dysfunction had been pinned to the tree. Linnea's gaze flickered to the tree; the sight of the arrow sent a chill down her back. The traitor had died while she was traveling to fetch Rowan, and no information had been gained from him. However, Linnea doubted he was the only traitor in the castle walls.

She shut the hazy, opaque glass door. Immediately, her fingers began undoing the string around the scroll. Linnea started to read as she sat on the stool by the round table.

Dear Royal Diatomist Dendro,

Here on the Dimidi Isles, there is a large, eclectic collection of people, histories, and stories. Therefore, I am happy to report that I have found the fictional Obsilvian tale I believe you are searching for. There are two versions—the original and one that is more recent. I will provide a note on the differences between the two at the end.

When the world was young, it was held by four men under four separate pillars. Their names were North, South, East, and West. They knew that if one of them failed in supporting his corner of the world, it would cause strain on the others. The greater the strain, the more challenging it would be to persevere.

Watching from the shadows, five snakes discussed North, South, East, and West.

The first snake hissed, "North upholds physical prowess. Without him, disease would run rampant. It would be easier to find prey."

The second snake rattled his tail. "South upholds purpose and meaning. Without him, people would no longer have faith in Verimor. It would be easier to manipulate hearts."

The third snake flicked his tongue. "East upholds emotional wellness. With no control of feelings, we could easily hunt the hurt and broken."

"But West," said the fourth snake, "upholds both resilience and alliances. If we got rid of him, the people would be too alone to stand together."

The four snakes argued which man they should attack first. After a long time, the fifth snake, who was the youngest, slid forward. "Why must we bother them? Can we not be content with our shadows here?"

The four snakes looked at the youngest and then at each other. They laughed, the sound like seeds being shaken in a container. "Ignorant snakeling. You're too young to know what you speak of."

The fifth snake quickly saw the error in his brothers' thinking, but he said nothing. He slid back into the shadows and watched as the oldest snake moved toward North.

"North," said the snake.

The man looked at the snake. Although his face was passive, he released his hold on his pillar and stepped away. The world rumbled slightly as the other men momentarily had to compensate for no health. The snake opened his mouth. North's mighty foot found the reptile's neck and split his head from his body.

North laughed with his hands on his hips. "That foolish snake thought he could best me, but no one is stronger than I am!"

He threw the snake's head and body, and both pieces landed together in the shadows. North stepped back onto the open space once again to form his pillar for the world.

The remaining snakes hissed angrily.

"I'll be smarter than our older brother," said the second snake. "I will not get too close too soon without making an offer." The second snake made his way slowly toward South. "South, do not be alarmed. I have only a question for you."

South turned his head and looked at the snake, but he did not step off his pillar.

"Do you not envy your brothers? They uphold something tangible each. But do you uphold anything if it cannot be seen?"

"Interesting theory," said South. He left his pillar and walked away.

The second snake rattled his tail in glee. "See, now it will be easier to manipulate the people of the world."

The third and fourth snakes cheered for their older brother.

"I wouldn't cheer yet," chided the fifth snake. He pointed with the end of his tail. His remaining brothers' eyes turned. "Why is South talking to West?"

South moved to East, and then to North. With great strides, South quickly returned to his pillar.

"Why are you back," the second snake questioned.

"Look out!" The fifth snake slunk back further into the shadows, as North came charging to the shadows' edge. His brothers still celebrated at the perimeter.

When the youngest snake turned around, all three of his brothers had been decapitated. North threw the pieces into the shadow. The heads landed next to the first brother, but the bodies were lost in the darkness.

The youngest snake was overwhelmed with grief to see all of his brothers killed by their exploits. He gathered leaves while he mourned. Hissing a melody of lament, he covered what was left of each brother together in the leaves.

The next day, alone, the fifth snake went to see his brothers' bodies. Under the leaves, there was movement! "Brothers?"

The youngest snake removed a large leaf with his mouth. His brothers were living—but not as four separate brothers. Instead, four heads shared one body.

"Brothers," said the fifth snake. "May you understand there are consequences for evil."

This is accepted as the original story, meant to teach readers that there are consequences as well as the importance of keeping oneself healthy in all areas including physically, spiritually, emotionally, and socially. However, there is another version in which the fifth brother does not provide a warning. Instead, he convinces his brothers to attempt to remove each brother individually, so he can build the four-headed serpent to take out all pillars of the world himself. This is the version that will interest you because of the origin.

I do not have documentation to send, only hearsay. Many people from different countries—primarily Wisteria and Obsilvia—have traveled to and from here, especially within the last decade. The later version of this story was told to me by an Obsilvian sailor. He had heard it from a cousin, who heard it from someone else, who swore the story was told by King Tramein in a meeting in which he asked them to join his assassination guild. If memory serves me well, he used the story to create a symbol for the members of his secret cohort. I believe the name is Order of . . . it was the name of the plant used in the alternate version of the tale—Sicarius, I think.

Though I cannot confirm or deny the truth of this, I can affirm that there is evidence of the image of a four headed snake being seen around the time of different significant deaths—including one here on the Isles eight years ago. It was determined an accident, but the circumstances were odd, to say the least.

But I digress. My hypothesis is that news of more sightings of the four-headed snake will be sent to you as more diatomists are able to respond. I do hope I am wrong, and no such sanctioned murder exists in Obsilvia. For if it does, only Verimor knows where evil ends in that kingdom.

Blessings,

Diatomist Neyon

Linnea laid the paper down on the table. Her fingers tapped rhythmically as her mind spun. A plan would be needed to determine who in the castle was aiding and abetting the Order of Sicarius. She stood up rapidly, the stool falling behind her. Linnea turned to right the stool and saw her gardening apron on the ground. Something underneath it kept the fabric from fully falling flush.

Pins and needles prickled the back of her neck, and goosebumps covered her arms. Linnea stepped closer to the garment. She pulled it back. Her shock was so intense, she made no sound. A butcher knife was stuck blade down in the dirt.

Linnea scolded herself for consistently refusing a guard, especially since it was now clear in her mind that the traitor was specifically targeting her. A faint cry pulled her down the aisle in the greenhouse.

"Oh no!" Linnea screamed.

Two prone cats, one gray and one calico, lay beside a saucer of milk—decorated with fine stroked painting of marigolds, just like the ones they put out for the cats outside of the kitchen.

"Smokey?" Tears poured from her eyes as Linnea lifted the gray cat and put her ear to his chest. She heard only shallow wheezes; but at least, he was breathing. "Cali?" Her hand stretched to the calico's stomach. The rise and fall there was weak and much too sporadic. Linnea reached for the milk. As she leaned over the dish, she noticed no abnormal scent from the milk. Her fingers hovered over the dish. A pale purple petal floated in the liquid.

Linnea got to her feet and scooped up each animal. She turned, and her heart threatened to leap out of her chest. Mud was smeared on the opaque glass door in the rough shape of a snake with four heads. Her feet pounded against the earth. The clinking of chainmail and sheathed swords alerted her that guards were trying to spring into action—someone called out to her, but she didn't have much time.

"Nanny Helene!" Her voice was hoarse. She brushed her hand across her tear-stained cheeks. "Nanny Helene," she called louder as she entered the house and moved full force toward the kitchens.

A young serving girl held the door open; and Linnea ran in, cradling the cats. Mrs. Ginty, standing behind the center counter, dropped her hands from her hips.

"I think they were given Somnum Crocus."

The lady's maid cleared the counter with a swoop of her arm, flour and dishes clinking and clanging every which way. She hurried to a window and started pulling from plants. "We need cilantro, goldenseal . . . " Mrs. Ginty ran into the hall, and Linnea put the cats on the cleared surface. "And crushed tomato."

Linnea grabbed a pestle and mortar and handed them to her former nanny. As Mrs. Ginty ground the herbs, Linnea wiped drool from each cat's tiny face in turn. "I don't know why they haven't killed me or Isak. Clearly, there is someone with access and means."

The red-headed woman said nothing as she mixed the newly made green mush and tomato juice. She pulled open a drawer and snatched out two spoons. Linnea accepted one, and they each force-fed the dying cats.

"Linnea, you need to go to your brother right now. Do not refuse a guard. Do not go anywhere else without protection."

"The cats . . . "

"If they survive or die, it'll happen with you here or with the king."

Linnea winced at the harsh words but knew that Mrs. Ginty was only speaking the truth. Cali started coughing, regurgitating her stomach contents—a good sign the antidote to the sleeping plant, a known toxic for animals, was working.

Adrenaline subsided, Linnea wanted to collapse. However, she moved almost as quickly to get to Isak's study in his wing as she did to get assistance for the cats. She was panting when she approached Isak's guard Linwood outside the wooden door.

"Milady?" Rather than demanding an answer, Linwood opened the door and announced Linnea.

Isak, alone at his writing desk, stood at attention, eyes wide with concern at Linnea's damp hairline and red, tear-streaked face.

"Did something happen to Rowan?" Isak asked.

"No, she's fine. It's . . . it's the traitor again. He's toying with me—he left a message in my garden house. Poisoned two of my cats." Linnea took a shaky breath. "We aren't safe in our own home."

Chapter Sixteen
Someone to Trust

"HELLO?" ROWAN'S VOICE SOUNDED TIMID even to her own ears outside a large wooden door.

A large green pendant marked the diatomist's study, the last room in the ornate hallway. Large, blue marbled vases filled with vibrant orange marigolds stood atop decorative white pillars between each door. Nora had shown Rowan where the royal diatomist was expecting her, but then she had promptly walked away. Rowan inhaled deeply, pushing down thought of retreating back to Aconite, and entered.

Her eyes roamed the room. Books lined three of the walls of the rectangular space. A large wooden desk with papers strewn across the surface sat in the middle of the opposite wall. To the right of the desk sat four armchairs curved around a stone hearth where a fire crackled.

Summoning all her might to try to make her voice audible, Rowan tried speaking again. "Hello, I'm looking for Diatomist Dendro?"

"Yes? Who's there?" called a gruff voice near the fireplace. She tentatively moved closer, rounding to see who spoke. A man with a long white beard and a wide-sleeved, green robe sat over a small wooden desk. His glasses perched precariously on the tip of his nose, and Rowan bit her lip to hold in the giggle that threatened to erupt when she imagined him sneezing and them flying from his face.

"George, is that you? I can't hear like I did in my youth. And these old bones of mine don't take as kindly to the cold as they once did; and there's been an influx of letters as of late coming in from the aviary, what with Linnea's search for that old Obsilvian fairy tale and everyone having questions about the girl blessed by Dinah and . . . "

Rowan cleared her throat, the action causing the elderly man to look up, his eyes hazy as if awaking from a deep slumber.

"You aren't George." His eyes narrowed and then promptly widened. He turned sharply, his knee hitting the desk with a thud.

"Are you all right?" Rowan asked, concern lacing her words.

The diatomist waved her worry away. He stood slowly, a hand on the small of his back as he stretched to his full height. "Yes, yes, yes! Rowan Tritonia, what a pleasure to meet you." Papers scattered onto the floor as he moved from between the chair and the desk. He grabbed Rowan's hand and adamantly shook it. "When Cleric Jimson wrote to me, I knew Verimor had answered our prayers."

A knot formed in Rowan's throat, preventing any words, as she knelt to gather the fallen parchments; but Diatomist Dendro did not pause to give her time to reply. "I would have met you earlier, but"—his hands motioned to the papers in Rowan's hands— "there's so much going on, I told Oren to make sure you knew to come here if I lost track of time. And time is of the essence, and we must make haste. Let's step into the library to confirm you are blessed and discuss what is expected of you for the sake of Wisteria. This way, please."

Rowan followed the royal diatomist, whose jovial whistle signaled ignorance to the weighty burden his words thrust upon her shoulders. Dendro shifted his feet toward the well-packed bookshelves. A wrinkled hand peeked out from the sleeve of his robe as he scanned a few book spines with his fingers. As he tipped a leather-bound book toward him, a loud thud sounded.

A small gasp escaped Rowan's lips as a doorway formed within the shelved wall.

The diatomist chuckled. "There's a real door to the library on the other side, but this way is simply much more fun." Dendro waved for Rowan to follow behind him. "My body might be old, but one can never outgrow secret passages, can they? Rumor has it, there's more than this."

Dendro continued to whistle a rendition of a familiar tune that Rowan couldn't quite name. She followed behind him; and after only a few steps, she found herself in a bright room, with windows overlooking the royal gardens. Like the study they had just left, books lined floor to ceiling shelves; but these books seemed much more inviting, reminding Rowan of the Magna Library. A pain shot through her chest as the thought reminded her of her increasing homesickness.

What is expected of you for the sake of Wisteria. The diatomist's words echoed in Rowan's mind.

"Let's have a look at the eyes Cleric Jimson wrote to me about, shall we?"

Rowan rapidly blinked her eyes as Dendro peered down, getting uncomfortably close to her face, his eyes staring into her own; but he did not touch her. After an awkward moment, he stood, a groan escaping his thin lips. He murmured something about the winter chill; and then, with surprisingly quick movement given his apparent back problems, Dendro selected a bound book from a small desk by one of the windows. His wrinkled and blue-veined hands placed it on a raised wooden lift designed to keep a book open while perusing the pages.

"Do you agree with everyone else that I am unicorn-blessed?" Rowan asked, her shoulders back, deciding she would do what was needed, whatever it took to help find a way to cure her sister.

"I'm quite certain that you are, indeed, but I'm going to ask a few questions to see if we can piece together how it happened." He picked up a quill and dipped it ready to write in the book. "I'm assuming your eyes have not always been magenta in color?"

"No, Diatomist Dendro. My eyes are actually brown."

He nodded and scribbled. "When the color change first occurred, did you experience any other symptoms?"

"I had a terrible headache. I even collapsed. After that, my friend told me my eyes were different. I couldn't see correctly. All the color was gone from my vision." Rowan's fingers tapped the tip of her thumb on both hands. She held them behind her to try to keep the nervous habit hidden.

"Prior to the episode, had you had any unusual encounters with anyone?"

Rowan's nose twitched as she thought. "No, not that I can think about."

"Met anyone new? Had a conversation with a stranger?"

"No. Bane, my best friend, and I were doing things in town in celebration of my naming anniversary. We stopped at the library, which is where I had a headache, and then went for tea and sticky buns. And before we even ate, the bad pain made me think I was going to pass out."

"And you didn't speak to any strangers or experience anything unusual before having your first bout of pain in the library?" Dendro raised a bushy eyebrow.

Rowan rubbed her forehead. "We stopped by Mr. Oxeye's fruit stand. He grows wonderful citrus fruits in addition to fishing with my father. But that's it, besides talking to Miss Thistle in the library and the flower merchant. But no, nothing out of the ordinary happened."

"Had you met the flower merchant before?"

"I don't think so. But I don't think getting a marigold flower crown counts as an unusual encounter." Rowan traced the perimeter of the window frame with her line of sight, focusing on the gray hedges and rose bushes in the garden below.

"Marigolds?" Dendro set the quill down and walked toward Rowan, resulting in her looking back at him. One corner of the man's lips curled upward slightly. "Did the merchant say anything when you took the marigolds? Did her words make you feel anything?"

"Something about the light and goodness of Verimor, maybe?" Rowan closed her eyes trying to recall the memory. "I think I felt a chill. I remember goosebumps on my arms, which I will admit is a little unusual for midday in Aconite."

"At least, we know that those saying you are unicorn-blessed are not mistaken." Dendro started muttering under his breath to himself and stroking his beard.

"What are you talking about?" Rowan's voice shook with exasperation. "What does buying a flower crown have to do with what's going on?"

"My dear, did you not know that marigolds are a symbol of Verimor's messengers, just as wisteria is a symbol of Verimor's encompassing presence and grace? That's why both plants are so popular across the nation. Why do you think the Marigold Festival season is so important?"

"But . . ." Rowan stopped her words as her thoughts caught up. "Are you saying I was blessed when I took the flower crown?"

A knowing smile spread across the old man's face. "Precisely."

"Why would a unicorn be selling flowers outside the library? Does this mean everyone she sold flowers to was blessed? If not, why did she choose to bless me?"

Dendro held up a hand. "Rowan, though I have devoted my life to studying our Maker and His teachings, I cannot answer all of your questions. However, I can wholeheartedly affirm that you are going to help us in winning a war that will threaten life as we know it for everyone in Wisteria and beyond." He clasped his hands in front of him, grinning ear to ear. His giddiness made him seem more like a schoolboy than an elderly man, even with his white beard and weathered skin.

Rowan swayed on her feet before leaning back against the glass panels of the window. "A war? I just need to know how to help Blythe," she whispered.

"Oren," Dendro called over his shoulder. "Please come here and escort Rowan to the dining hall. I'm going to meet the king beforehand. This news—it's what I expected—but we must work to ensure your training, once starting, is unhindered and that you are safe. Yes, yes, yes, safety is a top priority . . . " He continued talking, but his dropping volume made Rowan believe he was murmuring to himself as he gathered a few scrolls and books.

Dendro's forest-green robes rustled as he turned around a corner with his arms full of reading materials, indicating the library was bigger than Rowan's first impression. At the same moment, a young man of about Bane's height entered.

Rowan's mouth fell open. She could see his golden blond hair, icy green eyes, and sun-kissed skin wrapped in the lilac and sand-colored garments common among mages and clerics—she could see every bit of him in full-color.

Oren crossed his arms and sighed, seemingly annoyed. "Don't tell me you're going to be like every other girl here. I was hopeful your arrival would bring intelligent conversation—not shallow, unoriginal ogling."

Rowan's mouth snapped closed. She felt her nostrils flare and her cheeks heat as a rush of anger filled her veins. "My apologies if my initial shock at seeing you in full color after being able to see nothing but monotonous gray hues for *days* insinuated I'm unintelligent. But I can assure you, Oren, I do not—nor will I ever—have the desire to offer you *shallow, unoriginal ogling.*"

Oren dropped his arms and offered Rowan a wry smile. "Fair point. With vision like that, your staring would arguably be original after all."

Rowan crossed her arms. "If you do not want to show me how to get to the dining hall, I'll figure out how to find the king myself." She turned to walk through the hidden door when she first entered the library with Dendro; but to her growing frustration, the walkway was hidden again. With a huff, she turned and tried to quickly brush past Oren.

He extended his hand and clasped it around her elbow. "I never said I wouldn't help you. And you need my help, especially being unicorn-blessed. You need someone you can trust."

"You insult me and now tell me to trust you?" Though still irritated, Rowan felt the initial anger slip away as she let her gaze momentarily find Oren's green eyes. "Then tell me, why are you the only person that looks normal to me? And why can't I see light and shadows in front of your chest?"

"Your perspective is wrong," Oren said matter-of-factly. "You'll see sooner or later that I'm the one you need. Hopefully, for everyone's sake, it happens sooner." He turned and walked away with an arrogant stride.

Clenching her fists beside her and holding in a sigh of frustration, Rowan reluctantly followed. In the hallway, yelling echoed from another floor beneath them. Rowan's fingers tapped against the pad of her thumb in her systematic routine, and her pulse quickened.

She looked at Oren. He moved to the railing near the staircase up ahead, and Rowan followed.

A woman's voice cried out, "Nanny Helene!"

"Is a child hurt?" Rowan looked at Oren's profile, but his face remained passive.

"I'm sure it sounds worse than it is. Don't let it worry you."

Chapter Seventeen
Broken Wings

"I WISH ROWAN WAS HERE to travel to town with us. She would be so happy," Blythe said with an ache of longing.

"She *is* happy. I mean, she has you for a sister, and who wouldn't be happy to know me?" Bane said with a soft chuckle, pushing Blythe's chair on wheels from behind.

"You don't have to pretend. I know you miss her just as much as I do," Blythe said, her head turned to the side to ensure her friend heard her clearly. "I think we will both feel better after sending our letters. I'm thankful Cleric Jimson is allowing us to use the hawks at the cathedral."

Bane sighed. "I wish I was with her. Then I would know she was safe. Not that she's in danger," he added quickly. "The king's castle is probably extremely safe. I just mean I wish I had a reason to bring her home, if that's what she wants."

"Are you asking to be her escort to the ball? In your letter, I mean."

"No. I debated what to put," he stammered before quickly moving on. "But my letter's pretty short. I know she doesn't have much of a choice where the king summoned her, but I did tell her I was counting down the days until we reunite."

Conversation died down as the two of them hit the cobbled road near the edge of town. Blythe smiled and waved at everyone they passed as Bane navigated toward the cathedral which was a stone's throw away from the library.

The cathedral itself was about the same size as the Magna Library and also had walls of stone and stained-glass windows. But unlike the library, it had no stairs, and its roof tapered upward into a steeple.

Blythe shifted in her chair, barely able to contain her excitement as they neared the cathedral. Familiar faces of clergywomen, along with women from town, dotted the lawn for the mid-morning devotional hour. Several young mothers rocked small babies against their chests. Others quietly entertained small children while listening to the leading clergywoman.

Bane guided the chair toward the main entryway. Voices echoed from the front of the cathedral as retired men and women studied language. Instead of joining them, Bane and Blythe walked down a small hallway perpendicular to the group.

"Happy day, Blythe and Bane," Cleric Jimson greeted the pair of them with a smile as he looked up from a wooden desk. "Blythe, it is so wonderful to see you here. I pray you will be able to join your parents at our weekly congregation meeting."

"Oh, I would love that so much! I enjoy studying Vermior's teachings at home, but the community of the congregation helps you grow in ways you cannot in isolation."

Bane laughed but attempted to cover it with a cough. She looked at him, her head tilted in confusion.

"You sounded like a clergywoman. I, um, I didn't mean to . . ." Bane's voice trailed off as his face blushed red, and he looked down at his feet.

A bubbly laugh escaped Blythe. "Well, if Verimor grants me the opportunity, perhaps I will be a clergywoman one day."

"You would serve Verimor and all of His people within our congregation. Well, Blythe," said Cleric Jimson, "are you ready to visit the hawks to send your letters to Rowan?"

"We get to see the hawks?" Bane asked, his eyes growing wide. "I thought we were just giving you the letters."

"If you would rather . . ."

"No, let's go!" Bane walked away but then stopped and backtracked. "Aren't you excited, Blythe?"

Blythe echoed Bane's enthusiasm. "Who wouldn't want to be a falconer for a day?"

Cleric Jimson stood to their right in the wide hallway as they made their way to a door leading to the aviary which had both an enclosed and open area. Passing large cages, most of which appeared empty, the trio entered the outdoor portion.

"Happy day, Sid," called the clerk to a bearded man. He wore a thick, yellow glove on his wrist, upon which a hawk sat.

"Happy day, Jimson," replied the falconer. "I see we have some visitors today."

"Sid, this is Blythe, and this is Bane. They have permission to send letters to the king's castle. I thought they might like to see the hawks at work first-hand."

Using her cane which had been secured with a strap behind the chair, Blythe stood up. "I hope it doesn't come off as ungrateful or rude, but I think I'm going to hang back while you all send the letters."

"Do you feel bad?" Bane asked, his forehead creased with concern.

"To be completely honest, the hawk is terrifying," Blythe said, a little louder than she intended.

Sid laughed boisterously. "Nova here wouldn't hurt you on purpose unless you were a snake or small critter. But I know birds aren't everyone's favorite." The man made a quick motion with his free hand, and the hawk flew to a nearby post.

Bane looked back at Blythe with a questioning look. She waved him on. Then she turned and wandered through the opening back to the enclosed part of the aviary.

A woman with blonde hair piled in a large, braided bun on the top of her head and the traditional lilac dress of a Wisterian clergywomen knelt by one of the cages.

"Do you need any help?" Blythe asked. She held her cane for support but was able to put most of her weight on her own feet.

The clergywoman turned and offered Blythe a genuine smile. "I'm tending to this little fledgling. Her name is Demi. Her left wing never formed properly. Unfortunately, she'll never be able to fly with it, so she's not home here with the messenger hawks."

Blythe stepped closer hesitantly. "What will happen to her?"

"Sid will most likely release her. She's too old to get sustenance from her mother, and there isn't the means to care for her here."

"But is that safe? If she can't fly away from danger? Or look for food?"

The woman turned toward Blythe. She extended her arms where a small, fuzzy bird lay. Carefully, Blythe used her elbow to hold up her cane and accepted the feathered bundle. The baby bird nestled into Blythe's chest, unafraid to be handled by human hands.

Every trace of fear Blythe had upon first seeing Nova vanished as the fledgling inhaled and exhaled softly against her. Blythe looked up at the woman. "Are you new to the clergy? I thought I knew everyone here, but I don't believe we've met. I'm Blythe."

"It's a pleasure to meet you. Most people call me Ida. I'm just visiting Aconite for a bit. It looks like Demi likes you." She gestured to the bird.

"Do you think Sid will let me have her? I mean, maybe I can help her figure out a way to fly."

"Or maybe you can help each other realize one's reason for living isn't lost based on physical mobility. Purpose is found beyond limitations like a broken wing."

Blythe carefully stroked the young bird's head with her forefinger. "Most people might say she's lost her purpose. Being a bird who can't fly."

"It's limiting to think the only means of flying is with wings, don't you think?"

Blythe mulled over the woman's words. As she opened her mouth to respond, she heard the men and Bane enter from outside. She turned to smile at them. Briefly, she looked back to see Ida had left.

"What do you have there?" Bane asked, pushing the wheeled chair in front of him.

"It's a young hawk with a deformed wing. I was thinking maybe I could take her?" Blythe smiled hopefully at Cleric Jimson and Sid.

Sid ran a hand down his beard and nodded. "Demi doesn't have any hope here for happiness. I think you taking her is a fine idea."

Chapter Eighteen
A Dream, A Decision, and A Dress

"D EMI!" BANE CALLED, ENTICING THE little hawk with a thin slice of dried meat. Blythe laughed as Demi charged unexpectedly and Bane ran. He dropped the meat, and Demi happily enjoyed her snack.

"Who knew you had an attack bird?" Bane joked. Demi let out a small screech, turned, and made a beeline for Blythe's lap.

"She's really remarkable, isn't she?" Blythe gently stroked the hawk's head with two fingers.

"I'll say," Bane agreed. "I'm guessing Demi will be your date to the Marigold Ball?"

"I have a feeling Demi would not be a fan of formal gowns—too restricting." Blythe giggled when Demi squawked as if in agreement. Her smile faded as a thought occurred to her. "Do you think there will be any issues with Demi going to the castle with us?"

"I don't see why they would have a problem with Demi." Bane leaned forward, stroking the bird's neck lightly. "Plus, she'd probably fight anyone who tried to keep you two separated."

"I can't wait for Rowan to meet her."

"Can you believe it's almost been over a week without her?" Bane looked out toward the boats in the distance. The two friends and their avian companion sat in the thin grass above the start of the sandy beach of the shoreline. Blythe watched Bane as his jaw clenched. "Have you gotten a letter back?" He asked.

"No, but I'm sure there's a good reason." Blythe bit her lip.

Bane looked at his friend. Blythe's soft waves of brown hair flowed in the breeze. "What's wrong?"

"I had a strange dream last night. I know it was just a dream, but it keeps replaying in my mind like a memory of something real." Blythe shook her head as if to shake away her thoughts. "I'm worried about Rowan."

"Do you think the dream is because you miss her?"

"Maybe."

The two sat in silence, listening to the small sounds around them—wisps of grass rustling in the wind, gulls cawing in the distance, Demi picking at Blythe's dress to make a more comfortable temporary nest.

After a few minutes, Bane said, "Do you want to tell me about the dream?"

Blythe nodded slowly. "I'm running toward Rowan. But as I'm running, I think to myself, *How is this happening? When did I get better?* Right when I'm only a few steps from reaching Rowan, I find myself in my chair. Her eyes widen as she sees me, almost like she's in shock." Blythe paused, deciding to omit Rowan's words, *Let me fix you,* for fear her friend would agree she was something in need of repair.

"The ground cracks between us, and I start falling. I fall until blackness surrounds me. But then I stop at the bottom of a deep cavern, surrounded by flames. Water rushes in all around me. It douses the flames but also quickly fills the space. I thrash to keep afloat, but my legs don't cooperate. The water rises until it covers me. And then I woke up."

Bane rubbed the back of his neck. "Sounds like a nightmare."

Blythe nodded somberly. Demi nuzzled her head under Blythe's hand. Blythe, in turn, rubbed the bird's head.

"Ow!" Blythe drew back her hand as Demi looked at her, eyes large and alert.

"Are you okay?" Bane asked, jumping closer to her.

"Demi nipped me. It scared me more than anything." Blythe offered a weak laugh. "I shouldn't be surprised. She's meant to fly wild and free, but she's bound here with me."

"Don't do that." Bane's voice was unusually stern.

"What do you mean?"

"Don't make it sound like you are the one who clipped her wings. And don't assume you're such bad company." His brows furrowed as his words snapped.

Tears quickly filled Blythe's eyes. She took a deep breath to hold them back, but one rebellious drop rolled down her cheek.

Bane's expression softened. "I'm sorry. I didn't mean to—"

Blythe held a hand up, hushing him. "You don't need to apologize. Sometimes, it's easier to wallow in self-pity than it is to cling to hope." Blythe squared her shoulders.

"Well, I'm happy to remind you anytime how great a sister you are to Rowan—and even to me." Bane stood and offered his hands to Blythe. "Want help getting in your chair? It must be close to the evening meal, and your mother said she had a surprise for you."

Blythe sat with Demi in her lap as Bane pushed the chair. As they went, she rolled thought after thought through her mind. "Bane?"

"Yes?"

"Do you think I'll ever fall in love?" Blythe felt her chair jerk slightly as if Bane's steps faltered in hearing her question. She didn't give him a chance to respond immediately. "It's just that you and Rowan have grown up together. You were neighbors and schoolmates. I haven't been in school in so long. I'm not close with any boy my age; and even if I was, could someone love me like I am?"

Blythe bit her lip, only pausing for a second. "I know my worth doesn't depend on a boy's love, but it's still hard not to wonder if love and marriage are possibilities for me."

"It's easier said than done, but you can't worry about the future. Only Verimor knows what will happen." Bane laid a comforting hand on Blythe's shoulder as he pushed her chair. "Besides, anyone who spends any time with you Tritonia girls is sure to recognize how wonderful you both are."

"I thought we were going home." Blythe took in the approaching cobblestone street of the town's main square, forgetting her innermost worries momentarily.

"Your mother has a surprise for you, remember?"

Demi squawked as if reiterating Bane's question. Blythe leaned forward ever so slightly in her chair, cupping her hands around the bird. She took in every shop lining the side of the street, trying to figure out exactly where they were going.

"Are we getting tea and sticky buns before dinner?" Blythe asked as the pair approached Mrs. Bredon's tea shop.

Bane laughed. "I wish." He wheeled Blythe past Mrs. Bredon's and turned to enter the building next door.

"Mrs. Myrtle?" Blythe's nose twitched as she processed what was happening. *Why were they going to a seamstress?* A bell chimed as they entered the front door. "Mama?"

"Blythe, Bane, right on time." Blythe's mother smiled warmly. "Blythe, we are getting you a new dress for the Marigold Ball."

"What? That's too much." Blythe saw her mother's face fall slightly and dropped her voice lower. "Mama, you and Baba shouldn't spend that much money on me."

Her mother held up her hand. "I'm not able to do a lot of extra things for you and your sister. Please let me do this for you."

Blythe nodded hesitantly. But looking around the walls lined with new fabric rolls and seeing a seamstress approach her caused her stomach to flutter with excitement.

"If it's all the same to you, I'm going to leave you ladies to it," Bane said.

"Thank you for bringing Blythe," said her mother. "Tell your parents we look forward to dinner tomorrow."

"I will. Have fun, Blythe." Bane waved and exited the store.

"Welcome, welcome," sang an older woman, with snow white curly hair. "It's been a while since I've seen you, dear. You look well. Oh, how lucky you are to be attending the Marigold Ball in Tulium! I cannot believe the Tritonia family befriended the king—nothing this exciting has ever happened in our little coastal town." Blythe watched as Mrs. Myrtle's hand animatedly flew around her as she talked. "We must make sure you make a good impression. You will be representing my work, after all!

"Now, what are we thinking?" The seamstress put a hand to her cleft chin as her eyes examined Blythe from top to bottom.

"I know Tulium is much colder than here in Aconite, so maybe a warmer fabric," said Blythe. "Probably wool."

"Yes, we want to make sure you are comfortable. I can definitely do a wool surcoat underneath, but let's do something a bit more elegant for the main gown, hmm? Let's see, we could do velvet, but I've got more color options if we do silk or satin."

The woman clapped her hands above her head three times. "Maryam, we will need to get Blythe's measurements as well as yours. And I'll send a gown for Rowan, too. Do you know her measurements off hand?"

"Mrs. Myrtle, we'll just do a dress for Blythe. I can make do with what I have, and Lady Linnea has said that Rowan will be taken care of by her."

The old woman harrumphed. "No, my dear, I will be happy to do the three dresses. Though getting them ready before you all leave in a week will be quite a feat, it will get done. We'll make a trade—you take some of my designs and share my name with anyone and everyone. You three beauties in my dresses? I'll have girls coming from all over Wisteria to be dressed by me!

"Now"—Mrs. Myrtle turned to Blythe again, her short teal sleeves flapping in the breeze her movements created—"with your brown hair—hmmm, touch of auburn in it—and your brown eyes and your skin: beige with warm, golden undertones. You need something bold, something—ah!"

Demi jumped up from under Blythe's hands over her and perched on the girl's shoulder, surprising everyone.

"What in the name of the Admiral Ocean is that?" Mrs. Myrtle asked, adjusting her glasses and looking closer.

"This is Demi. She's a hawk. She was asleep. I'm so sorry." Blythe leaned over and scooped the feathered creature in her arms. Demi protested with small, squeaking trills.

Mrs. Myrtle laughed. "Lots of royals have pets, yes? Do you think your bird will wear a dress? Lots of those noble women might love to dress their cats or whatever in clothes. Don't you think so?"

Blythe couldn't hold back her laughter. "I think that's a lovely idea, but I don't know if Demi would like it."

The bird continued to squawk, seemingly in protest against the seamstress' idea.

"I'll put a pin in that idea. Anyway, I'm thinking deep pink—maybe even burgundy—for you, Blythe. And, Maryam, I'm thinking a shade of purple, possibly lavender for you. I'll go get some swatches; and once we pick the final fabrics, we'll move on to measurements." She turned her head to look at Demi more closely. "I've got some seeds. Maybe the bird can be bribed," she added to herself but still loud enough to be heard.

Blythe looked at her mother and smiled when the seamstress left them momentarily. "I can't believe this is really happening. We are getting fancy dresses to go meet Rowan at the king's castle. We're going to be princesses for the night."

Blythe's mother stepped closer and put her arm around her daughter. She pulled Blythe to her and kissed the top of her head. "I hope you know how special you are. I pray all of what is unfolding before us, opens doors for you that your father and I could have never imagined. But I also pray that you always know no matter how far away you fly from the nest, you can always come back home."

"I think Tulium will be as far as I fly." Blythe looked down forlornly at her legs. "But that's okay."

Her mother held her daughter's hands in her own. "If that's Verimor's plan, then that is what will happen. You have enough to overcome without adding more obstacles. Don't limit yourself just because your everyday life looks different than that of others."

Demi flapped her wing, and Blythe smiled.

"Let's try these," sang Mrs. Myrtle as she returned with an armload full of fabric. She held several swatches up to Blythe. Each piece of fabric generated the same pursed lips and small grunt from the woman. "I think doing a damask—see how there is a darker merlot in the velvet to make the pattern—is just gorgeous on you. What do you two think? Am I right, or am I right?"

Blythe looked behind Mrs. Myrtle where a floor-length three-sided mirror stood against the wall. She let her fingers trace the soft fabric as she looked at the rich red against her skin. "It's stunning."

"You really are," Blythe's mother whispered.

Blythe looked at her and saw her mother's eyes misty with tears.

"Can you stand, my dear?"

Blythe nodded, and her mother offered her an arm to help her. Blythe stepped on a short platform while Mrs. Myrtle used a measuring strip to get the numbers she needed. Blythe's mother stood nearby, with Demi held in her arms.

"Have either of you heard any updates from Rowan since she's been away?" the seamstress inquired as she scribbled on a slip of paper with a piece of chalk.

"We have sent her letters, and we hope to get at least one in return before we set out to meet her," explained Blythe.

"How is the king using her blessing? Mrs. Bredon next door told me the Sight changed her eyes from brown to magenta. Is that true? If so, I'll need to consider that when choosing her colors. Has she shared any updates on tensions with Obsilvia? I heard someone tried to kill the king!"

"What?" Blythe's face paled, and she shifted quickly to look at her mother. She had to hold her arms out to steady herself before falling. Her mother's face blanched.

"Oh, yes, tried to poison him, but Lady Linnea stopped him. I do say if we were to have a queen—and I'm not saying a woman should rule—she wouldn't be a bad leader for Wisteria. I do think it's good she's not in complete control, especially with the threat Obsilvia is making. And have you noticed the influx of boats at the dock? And the number of foreigners the ship crews have brought with them? I'm no conspirator, *but*"—Mrs. Myrtle dropped her voice as if someone in the empty shop may overhear her—"my cousin said she wouldn't put it past King Tramein to plan an ambush here on the coast. Apparently, a big piece of contention are those islands in the Admiral Ocean. And it makes sense, if you ask me, to crush Tulium from the coast and the mountains—you know, both sides—but I hope they don't ask me because, well, that won't serve Wisteria well, will it? All right, Blythe, you're all done for now. Maryam, up you go."

Blythe returned to her chair, taking Demi from her mother. She continued to listen to the old seamstress talk as if she were a watering can and Blythe and her mother were parched plants in a garden.

"Well, if my cousin is right, it will be good for you all to be in Tulium now won't it? But I do think my cousin is a few squares short of a finished quilt, if you know what I mean.

"King Isak is far too smart to let those Obsilvian supporters get the upper hand. Besides, Lady Linnea always has her brother's best interest at heart and will make sure nothing happens to Wisteria. Do you think he would have her back if she had been named the first queen instead of her coronation being put off until he was born? You know, for the world to see if he would be a boy and could be king?" Mrs. Myrtle laughed. "Like any of that matters now.

"All right, my Tritonia dears, plan to return in three days for the final fitting, so I can make adjustments as needed." She clapped her hands together. "Your beauty is sure to stop any conflict in its tracks—unless it's a debacle over who should be on my calendar and when, but that's a war we all want to see!" Mrs. Myrtle winked.

Blythe and her mother smiled politely.

"Thank you so much, Myrtle, for all that you're doing," said Blythe's mother.

The woman waved her hands. "I'm just grateful you came to me, my dear. Don't forget—three days!" The seamstress began moving folds of fabric to a worktable, paying no more mind to Blythe and Mrs. Tritonia.

"I want to try to walk a little bit," Blythe said, standing. She went to the back of the chair to grab her walking cane.

"Okay. But if you start to hurt, sit back down," instructed her mother.

Blythe put Demi on her shoulder. The small bird wasn't sure at first but then nestled in the nape of Blythe's neck, under her ear. Leaning on the cane, Blythe walked out of the shop. She held the door open for her mother, who pushed the chair.

"Do you think Rowan is safe?" Blythe asked as soon as they were beside each other.

Blythe's mother didn't answer immediately. "I think Cleric Jimson would have been one of the first people outside the castle to be alerted of any foul play. And if Rowan was in any danger, he would have told us. Don't let Myrtle's chatter worry you. She's very traditional in her thinking—to insinuate that a woman cannot be called to lead—but quite uninhibited with gossip."

Blythe nodded, but her heart was full of worry despite her mother's words.

Chapter Nineteen
The Dinner Party

"THE DINING ROOM IS UP ahead," Oren stated as he and Rowan walked down the hall. He nodded his head forward. "I know you're from the coast, and mannerisms vary across regions. To avoid embarrassing yourself, be sure to follow my lead. We won't sit until the king does. And once we do, you and I both will turn over the empty glass. This will alert servants that we will only be drinking water."

"I appreciate the advice, thank you," Rowan begrudgingly offered her gratitude. She found her eyes drawn to Oren, and it frustrated her. She didn't want to look at him, but he seemed like a ray of sunshine in a gray fog. Maybe, Rowan thought, he was the friend she needed, despite the poor first impression he gave.

The room was empty when they entered; but suddenly, a flushed Linnea stormed in, an entourage of men behind her.

"Rowan, thank Verimor you're okay!" Lady Linnea's voice was the familiar melodic tone from the carriage, but her words and appearance caused a heavy weight of guilt to settle over Rowan.

"Why wouldn't I be?" Rowan pressed one hand against her stomach and touched her necklace with the other.

"Rowan, there have been some developments," Linnea said.

"You are being assigned a guard to watch you at all times." The man directly behind Linnea stepped forward. He had multiple rings on each hand and a simple, blue tunic. Despite the jewelry, it was his confidence and air of authority that identified him as King Isak. He motioned a guard in the pale lilac shirt well-known to the king's men. "This is Cassian."

The man bowed as if Rowan was royal herself. "It is an honor to be of service to you, milady."

"Please don't do that," Rowan said. Her chest grew tight as she held back the desire to ask for details. What had happened that made her need a guard within the castle walls? Wasn't she supposed to be safe here?

"Rowan," the king said, waving his hand in a sweeping gesture in front of him, "I am sorry that your arrival to Tulium has coincided with the need to increase safety measures. But rest assured, we will protect you." He stepped to the head of the table and motioned for everyone to sit. "Diatomist Dendro has ascertained when he believes you encountered a unicorn in her human visage."

"Yes," Rowan said, a feeling of unease still creeping up her neck. Rowan sat to Isak's right next to Oren. Behind each person, a guard stood at silent attention up against the closest wall. To the king's left were Dendro and Linnea. "It does make one wonder if unicorns intermingle with us regularly or if they often watch over us in our daily lives."

The king smiled politely. He clapped his hands together and said something to a nearby servant in a hushed voice.

Servants placed bowls of tomato bisque topped with small cubes of bread in front of the members of the dinner party. It smelled as delicious as the broth they ate while traveling, but the bread made it seem even more appealing. Rowan watched as everyone sat still until the king took a sip of his soup. Once the other three guests picked up their spoons, Rowan did the same.

"Perhaps, Rowan, you will find a reason to stay in Tulium long-term," commented Dendro in between bites of his meal. "You and Oren are quite a handsome couple."

Rowan's face grew hot. She felt her nostrils flare from irritation at the audacious comment that surely was not appropriate, given the tension. Her hand grasped her necklace, and she rubbed the knotted jewel underneath the pad of her thumb. Her appetite was gone.

"Dendro, Rowan has someone waiting for her in Aconite," Linnea interjected, resulting in Rowan's blush deepening. Linnea set down her spoon, steepled her fingers together, and leaned her forehead against them. "Each person in here has an assigned guard. Commander Elias is interrogating all the staff again as we speak. Let's set aside all proclivities for polite conversation and share what needs to be known."

Rowan watched intently as the king sat back in his high-backed chair.

"Very well," said the king. "Rowan, to revisit your earlier statement, it's been ages since there has been a record of a unicorn walking among us; and if this is indeed the Sight referenced in the *Book of Verimor*, then we now have a way to counter King Tramein and Obsilvia. We can assert Wisteria's right as the primary ruling force in the world and keep our enemies in check."

Rowan placed her hands heavily in her lap under the table. The weight of King Isak's words felt like an impossible burden.

Dendro shuffled in his seat, and the movement pulled Rowan's attention to him. "Our faith is in Verimor," the diatomist said, "and He has called you forward for this task. You will learn how to use the Sight with help from both Oren and me."

Linnea affirmed Dendro's words with a firm nod. "Verimor knows what He is doing. You have been prepared for such a time as this, Rowan."

Tears welled in Rowan's eyes as she looked down at the orange-red soup in her bowl. She inhaled deeply and pulled her shoulders back as she raised her head. "I hope you do not think that I am greedy." She let her eyes dance between Linnea and the king. "But in exchange for my service to Wisteria, I request something in return."

The king sat straight in his chair. His eyebrows raised.

Dendro sputtered, "You were blessed by a unicorn, and you think you should be paid for your service to Verimor?"

Rowan internally cringed and bit her lip.

"Let her explain," Oren interjected, his hand raised placatingly. His eyes met Rowan's, and he offered her an encouraging smile. "Go ahead."

"My younger sister was struck over a year ago with an ailment that impacts her legs," Rowan explained in a single breath. "There was no fever or illness leading up to it, but she now lives with daily pain. Often, she cannot even walk. I've prayed for Verimor to heal her. Maybe He's given me this gift to help Wisteria but also find the answers to help my sister, too." Rowan tapped her fingers silently under the table.

Dendro exhaled loudly. Rowan did not know if it was a sigh of relief or a huff of frustration until he spoke. "He often works in mysterious ways, giving us answers when we least expect it."

"Beautiful things can be born from times of brokenness," Linnea added, softly. "Rowan, Diatomist Dendro—as well as the rest of us—will do what we can to have the answer on how to help your sister upon your return."

Tension melted from Rowan's shoulders. *Blythe, you're going to be healed. Verimor hasn't abandoned us.*

Chapter Twenty
What Is Normal?

MEOW.

The pitiful sound warmed Linnea's heart because it meant that the cat was alive. She gently pulled Smokey to her lap, Cali already on her chest as she sat on top of her bed. Linnea had not pulled the quilt back nor had she yet changed into her nightgown.

Mrs. Ginty rubbed the back of her hand, a nervous gesture that was out of character. "Are you sure you do not wish for me to stay with you tonight?"

"Cassian or his relief will be outside all night, Helene. You need to get rest yourself."

Linnea watched the woman as she paced by the foot of the bed. "Isak needs to cancel the Marigold Festival."

"No, we can't."

The bed shifted as Mrs. Ginty sat beside Linnea. She placed a hand on Linnea's knee. "Nothing is being done to keep you safe!" Mrs. Ginty dropped her raised voice. "Elias doesn't know who is working to torment you, and—as you said—who has opportunity to kill you or Isak."

Linnea put a hand on Mrs. Ginty's. Smokey did not protest to no longer being petted but simply remained asleep. "There has to be a reason the traitor hasn't taken it further. I believe it is because he can't do much more without giving his identity away."

"Someone close to the king?" The woman shook her head, causing red and gray strands to stick out every which way from her pulled-back hair. "It doesn't matter. More enemies could come in during the ball."

"If we stop the ball—halt the start of the most sacred season—those who oppose us and reject Verimor will use it as evidence that we don't have enough faith." Linnea squeezed Mrs. Ginty's hand. "Sir Elias knows those guarding us can be trusted. Thaddeus will be with me, and Rowan has Cassian."

"Elias isn't even here half the time! And what about the other members of the king's court? Their families? Who else might be targeted?"

"I believe my connection to Elodi is why the enemy sent the dysfunction and then went after two of my cats."

Mrs. Ginty pulled away, wringing her hands once again. "I just don't understand what is going on." She stood and resumed pacing. "The last prophet is killed, but Verimor sends a messenger to tell you her last prophecy. At the same time, you not only help the king navigate the start of a war but also have to watch your every step because someone dangerous is out to get you? What is serving Verimor achieving?"

Linnea bit her lip, blinking slowly.

"I didn't mean that. I'm just so angry."

"I know," Linnea replied softly. "As far as life here in the castle, we have to keep some sense of normalcy for everyone right now."

"What is normal now?" Mrs. Ginty stood, leaned over Linnea, and kissed her forehead in a motherly manner. "You're always so confident when trying to best protect others. I just need you to be protected, too."

"I think I know one way to do that."

"Yes?" said Mrs. Ginty, her forehead creased and eyes wide.

"I told you Elodi's last message. We need to figure out who is in it. The trapped rat has to be Hamlin in the dungeon. I need your help to figure out the rest. You're the only one outside of the council I wholly trust."

Chapter Twenty-One
Training and Tea

"I'M JEALOUS," NORA SAID AS she twisted a lock of Rowan's hair around an iron rod, heated by the fire in the room's hearth. "Your suitor back home would probably be jealous, too," she added with a teasing giggle.

"Bane's not my suitor." Rowan paused, her cheeks heating. "But I hope he will be once we have a chance to speak again in person." Rowan felt her chest grow warm, too. It was the first time she had admitted to herself that she had romantic feelings for Bane, and it made her light and happy. "But there's no need for anyone to be jealous. Oren is training me to help the king. And then Diatomist Dendro is going to help me find a cure for Blythe. That's it."

"Admit it. Oren is handsome."

Rowan closed her eyes as Nora pulled her curled hair into a simple updo. "I'll admit that Oren *knows* he's handsome. How he treats others based on the assumption that everyone is attracted to him because of how he looks is rather ugly." Rowan smoothed the front of her dress as she looked in the mirror.

Nora put her hands on Rowan's shoulders. "I never would have guessed you had some fight in you when I first saw you. That edge will be a good thing to have with members of the royal court."

Rowan followed Nora, unease building in her chest. "I don't want any edge," she blurted behind the tall maidservant. "That makes me think sharp and mean. I'm not mean, and I don't want to be."

Nora turned and offered a shy grin.

"It's the only way you'll survive here."

The sight of Cassian startled Rowan. She tried to keep her eyes from lingering on the scar that ran across his face. "Did you get any sleep?"

"I will be able to have a few hours later for rest. I am used to long waking hours, milady."

Nora urged Rowan forward. Rowan knew Cassian was following behind them a few paces.

The walk through the wing to the main staircase was silent, even when they passed Dendro's door, descended to the main floor, and exited a large door opposite the entrance when Rowan first arrived.

Cool air tickled Rowan's skin despite her long sleeves and thick sham under her dress. She wrapped her arms around herself while her eyes roamed over the lush world she'd entered. Several gardeners tended to flowering bushes, rows of marigolds, lavender, zinnias, and roses. Rowan stopped in her tracks as she saw a menagerie of large topiary bushes up ahead. One glance revealed a hawk, horse, and large cat spread over the immense garden.

"Happy day, Rowan," greeted a cheerful Dendro.

Rowan returned the old man's smile. "Happy day to you, too." She turned to thank Nora, but the girl was already walking away. Cassian stood at a respectable distance from her and the diatomist—near enough to keep watch but not so close that he could hear if they dropped their voices to a whisper.

Dendro started to stroll around the garden, a hum on his lips; and Rowan fell in stride with him. She felt comforted by the number of guards throughout the area. "Diatomist Dendro, will you tell me what wasn't said last night?"

"What do you mean?" His voice was steady, but his smile vanished.

"I could tell Lady Linnea was upset. Was she the woman who was yelling for a nanny yesterday before the evening meal?"

Dendro did not speak for several breaths. Rowan questioned if she had responded to him out loud or only in her mind. She opened her mouth to speak again but the diatomist pointed around the gardens. "A lot of preparation takes place here before the Marigold Festival. The royal grounds actually have a special itinerary each month leading up to the start of the holy season, which starts the day of the Marigold Ball."

"Back home in Aconite, we also have a celebration this time of year." Rowan smiled softly to herself, momentarily forgetting the stress of the expectation she would help win a war while recalling memories in the castle garden. "The dock workers string jars with candles along the pier leading all the way into the main street. There's a huge fair, a play with singing, and a special service led by Cleric Jimson."

"Jimson is a fine man of Verimor." Dendro nodded enthusiastically to his own comment. He slipped his hand into the front of his robe and removed two wax-sealed pieces of parchment. "Which reminds me, you have letters from home."

"Thank you, sir," said Rowan as she accepted the paper. She wanted to return to her earlier question, but Dendro motioned to the topiary bush a few feet in front of them.

"King Isak loves nature. He takes great pride in his topiaries here in the garden. Especially this one."

"A unicorn?" Rowan looked at the close-knit leaves trimmed into the shape of a horned horse.

"Yes. Of course, this shrub is in a unicorn's shifted form. But the role of Verimor's messengers in early history is important." He turned to Rowan. "And as one who has been blessed by a unicorn, your role in Wisteria's present—and future—is important. He closed his eyes and took a few deep breaths. "I like to begin each day with silence. The quiet allows me to open my heart and be ready to hear Verimor."

"Does He speak to you?" Rowan asked. "With words?"

"I've never heard Verimor's voice, but I have heard Him speak." Dendro turned to face Rowan. "It's been placed on my heart to tell you to stop doubting. To doubt yourself and this calling is to doubt your Maker."

Rowan bit her lip. "Sometimes, I do doubt. Like when Blythe got sick—and stayed sick and hurting." She inhaled. "But Mama says we can't lose our faith just because we don't understand."

"Your mother is a wise woman." Silence fell around Dendro, and he shifted his gaze to look at the topiary once again. "To answer your earlier question, Lady Linnea was the woman you heard last night. Her cats were sick, but they are okay now."

"I'm glad they're all right." Rowan sighed in relief knowing no child or animal were terribly injured.

"Tell me, what do you see when you look at me?" The old man's gray face turned to Rowan, expectantly waiting.

Rowan paused for a split-second, processing the sudden shift in conversation. "You, like everything else, have no color. When I look at your chest—where your heart is—there's a mix of light and shadow. If I don't look away, the light and shadow shift and form moving pictures."

"Don't avert your gaze. What do you see in the pictures?" He lightly held her wrist. She felt her own pulse under where his thumb was placed. Dendro's voice remained even; but Rowan could sense the anticipation within him in the slight manner in which his tone increased speed, and he leaned his head, with wide eyes waiting—even hoping—to witness something special.

Rowan hesitated for only a moment. She concentrated on the light. Her nose wrinkled as she processed what she saw. "It's like I'm seeing through your own eyes. You're dipping a quill into ink and writing a letter. To your mother. Telling her about your first week as a diatomist's apprentice." She looked up at Dendro's face. "I'm seeing memories, right?"

"The Sight is more than seeing someone's memories. It allows you to see the essence of a person's heart, their soul—the light and darkness within them. That's why the gift is so important. Not only can you see a person's past, but you can also see their emotions, even internal battles of morals. You can help sway people to make the right choices."

Rowan felt uneasy on her feet. "Tell people what to do?"

"You can encourage the light to grow and show it to people before they choose the darkness; you can help those who have strayed find their way back to Verimor." Dendro clapped his hands together. "You will begin your training with Oren immediately and then, after lunch, take the afternoon to rest." He sighed. "I would work with you myself but am being called away for another urgent matter, which—like your Sight—is a manner of life or death."

Life or death. Rowan's heartbeat quickened.

"But you are in good hands with Oren. He is a pious young man with a heart for truth. He reminds me of myself at his age." He spoke this last sentence in a lower tone, almost to himself. "I'll be back soon—with more good news, I pray—and you will be well on your way to mastering the blessing of Sight."

Rowan walked with Dendro back through the garden, following the path they initially took toward the topiaries. Her guard was always several paces behind. When they neared the entrance of the castle, Dendro turned and headed to a group of tables underneath a collection of willow trees. Several people, close to Rowan's age, sat in the shaded area. Rowan followed behind him.

"Ladies, let me introduce a guest of King Isak. This is Rowan Tritonia," Dendro said in a manner akin to grandfatherly pride.

Rowan smiled. "It's wonderful to meet you all."

"Likewise," said one dark-haired girl. "Please join us for tea." She waved to an empty chair. The girl picked up a small, porcelain bell. Upon ringing it, two servants emerged from a nearby canopied area with teacups and plates of finger foods.

"Thank you for your time today," Rowan said to Dendro.

He nodded and said, "Oren will be with you before too long." Then the royal diatomist walked away.

"What are . . ."

"Spending time with Oren?" the dark-haired girl asked curtly, cutting off Rowan's question.

"The royal diatomist's apprentice will be helping me with something as Diatomist Dendro requested." Rowan absentmindedly touched her necklace.

"Is that a true-knot? Are you betrothed?" another brunette sitting beside the first girl leaned in her seat, pointing to the stone around Rowan's neck.

"No, I think I'm a little young to be planning a wedding . . ."

"But you have a serious suitor," asked a blonde on the other side of the first girl.

"I think so," Rowan said. The first girl laughed, and her companions joined in even though Rowan didn't understand what was funny. "Oren doesn't have time for courting anyone, but it's nice to know you won't try to sway him from his virtuous work as a mage. Besides, even though you have a pretty face, I don't think you'd have much luck. Good for your *friend* back home. I'm Steffie, by the way."

"I'm Pearl, and that's Maude," the blonde girl offered before Rowan could fully process the backhanded compliments offered by Steffie.

"My mother is Sir Elias' sister and a close friend of Lady Linnea," said Maude.

"And my father is Sir Elias," said Steffie, sounding bored.

"He is the royal finance officer," explained Pearl.

"That means he deals with coin," Steffie said. "I know you're from some poor, rural town toward the coast. So if you need help understanding anything, please let me know." The girl smiled forcefully.

"Did I do something to offend you?" Rowan asked.

Steffie laughed and leaned back in her chair. "No, not at all. I just find it odd that a nobody would be *unicorn-blessed*. But what do I know?"

"Yes, what does the daughter of the court who spends her days ordering servants to fetch her tea and gossiping to her peers about anyone and everyone know about Verimor's will?" Every girl turned to find Oren emerging from under the servant canopy.

Steffie stood abruptly. "Oh, Oren. Would you like to join us? We were just getting to know *Rhonda*."

"No, thank you, *Sarah*. Rowan, are you ready to go?" Oren offered his elbow. Rowan stood and accepted it, happy to be leaving the dense tension with the noble girls.

Steffie laughed as the two walked away. "Oren, you're so funny. I'll catch up with you later," she called.

"That was odd," said Rowan as the two made their way back through the castle side entrance.

"Why didn't you say anything to defend yourself?" Oren's tone was sharp. "You can hold your own against me for stating the obvious but go mute when someone calls you a poor, idiotic nobody to your face?"

"Excuse me?" Rowan pulled away from Oren despite being on a staircase. "You didn't give me a chance to respond to them." As she pushed past Oren, Rowan fell forward on the steps. Before her face could collide with the stone edge, Oren's quick reflexes helped her regain her footing. Cassian, a few steps behind, yelled something that Rowan didn't comprehend.

"Are you all right?" Oren asked, his face close to her ear. She nodded, her face hot and her nostrils flaring slightly. He straightened and held out his hand.

Rowan's eyes found Cassian. He mouthed, "Be careful," and took a step back from the two.

Oren offered his elbow once more to Rowan. She hesitated, taking it for fear of falling again. "As you can see, Rowan, people here aren't always going to treat you fairly. Some members of the royal court will see you only for what you can potentially do for them as unicorn-blessed. Others still will see you as a threat to their power."

"And which of those two categories do you find yourself, Oren?"

"Oh, I'm not so shallow and unoriginal," he quipped, a smile tugging at the corners of his mouth. "I see who you are, Rowan—not for what you can do for me or even a kingdom but what you can do for yourself, what we can do together."

A shiver ran through Rowan as goosebumps covered her arms underneath her long sleeves. Unsure how to respond, she changed the subject as they neared the library. "We'll be training here?"

"Yes." He opened the door for Rowan. She entered, and Oren glanced back at Cassian before closing the door without a word. Presumably, the guard took his post on the other side.

Oren waved his arm toward their threshold. Rowan stepped in, immediately pulled to the windows overlooking the gardens they were at earlier. The broad-shouldered blond apprentice stepped a few inches behind her as Rowan's gaze landed on the girls still drinking tea. "They see you as a threat. It's up to you to confirm or deny their fears."

She turned to face him. Around him, the shelves and books were muffled in dull shades of gray. But Oren's entire being screamed in vivid color. Rowan's heart thumped in her chest—looking at his icy green eyes sent a thrill of adrenaline through her veins, a feeling she didn't like. "Tell me, why does my Sight see everything in black and white except *you*?"

Oren held his hands out in front of him, palms facing Rowan. He turned his hands slowly as he talked. "I'm the only thing unaffected by your Sight?"

"When I arrived, it seemed there was a hint of color around the wisteria on the castle walls; but yes, you are the only person that I see—I mean really see."

Oren nodded toward his right hand. "Define *see*."

Rowan's eyes settled on Oren's hand. Then her jaw hung open, unable to process what she was observing. The color slowly began retracting from Oren's fingertips until his entire hand nearly blended into the gray around him.

Chapter Twenty-Two
Shattered

"HOW?" THAT WAS THE ONLY word Rowan could say. She stared wide-eyed at Oren as all color retracted up his arm. In just as many seconds, vibrant color replaced the dull shades of gray.

"Your first lesson—initiative. If I tell you everything, how will you be able to handle true problems later down the line?" Oren cocked one eyebrow.

Rowan tapped her fingertips to her thumb one by one. "Are you controlling how I see you? Or is it the Sight itself?"

Oren barked a short laugh. "Who's to say it is simply one or the other?" He clasped his hands together. "Now, your second lesson is endurance."

Rowan watched Oren as he turned. He raised his right arm and moved his hand across the rows of books lining the shelved wall behind him. Oren selected a tome and dropped it on a table. Irritation built in Rowan's chest as she looked at the book's cover. *Words and Meanings.* You want me to study a dictionary?"

"Don't tell me we need a refresher on patience before moving forward. That's something you should have learned as a toddler at home," he deadpanned.

I have never met anyone so infuriating.

Rowan looked into Oren's green eyes. She saw a tug at the corner of his lips and sat in a wooden chair without further comment. Oren waved a hand, indicating he wanted Rowan to open the book. With a sigh, Rowan began searching for "endurance." When she found the scripted entry, Rowan cleared her throat.

"'Endurance, as used in the common vernacular known across the kingdom of Wisteria, means to engage in prolonged activity, physically and or mentally, often while withstanding great challenge, hardship, fatigue, and opposition.'"

Rowan leaned back in the chair slightly but then tensed. In the small window of time she was looking at the text, Oren had walked up behind her. He leaned one arm around Rowan and pointed to the words in front of them. "Which word is the most important in that definition?" His breath was warm on Rowan's neck, and he himself smelled of leather and coconut with a hint of pine.

Rowan felt her cheeks grow warm as Oren tapped his finger on the page, waiting for her answer. "Withstanding. If you cannot withstand forces against you, then endurance is not possible."

"Good girl. I shouldn't be surprised." Oren shifted, so he was to Rowan's right, leaning against the tabletop. "You will have opposition. Much of it will be from external forces, but you might even have internal opposition. Never let your own worries and fears stand in your way of greatness."

A shiver ran down Rowan's spine as Oren's fingers brushed against the fabric of her dress as he softly touched the true-knot around her neck. Then he took her hands and brought her to a standing position. "Let's put our lessons into practice, shall we?"

Oren stepped back. Rowan watched as the color he possessed slowly and steadily withdrew until he was as gray as the world around him. He pointed to his chest. "What do you see?"

Rowan struggled keeping her gaze on Oren. "I know that I can see memories. It feels like I'm invading a part of who you are."

"Invade, Rowan. This is important." Oren's voice was steady but gentle.

Pulling her shoulders straight, Rowan took in Oren's gray form. As her eyes settled on his chest, light and shadow swirled together. Rowan inhaled. "There's a lot of gray that looks almost like smoke. It's shifting. You're watching people walk past. From your point of view, you're young. No one looks directly at you. And . . ." Rowan's heart constricted. "You are overcome with confusion and grief."

Rowan wrapped her arms around herself as a chill crept down her spine. "You're cold. You look down at your hand. Oren . . . what is that? Is it blood? Whose hand is in yours? It's so cold."

Her magenta eyes snapped to Oren's face. His jaw tensed, but his expression overall was passive. Rowan's eyes swept back to the story in his soul.

"You turn your head. I can feel the tears on your cheek. This . . . this is your final memory of your mother, isn't it?" Rowan lurched forward, gasping. A pain ripped through her, leaving her momentarily feeling utterly broken.

Oren stepped toward Rowan, offering his arms as support for her to stand. "My father was a cruel man. He would go off for days at a time—months if we were lucky. One night, he came back. His mind was warped with too much wine, and he took his pain out on her. Like always, I couldn't stop him. I had my own slight shatterings before, but watching her take her last breath upon discarded refuse in the street when I should have been able to fight for her? That splinter will never heal."

Silent tears pooled in Rowan's eyes before cascading steadily down her round cheeks. "Is that what I felt? Your heart shattered?"

Oren touched Rowan's jawline, softly guiding her to look back down at his soul. "Rowan, you've never known the ill-awaited strike from one who is supposed to care for you. You've never battled hunger or the level of grief that comes with losing what you hold most dear. So it is no surprise you don't know the insurmountable amount of pain a heart endures in life. A heart shatters, like glass splintering, with every wrong thrust upon it. What you felt was a shadow of that first shattering my heart endured." Oren pulled away, putting space between them.

Rowan tried to blink back the refreshed rush of tears. She watched Oren's light and shadows as she looked into his soul. So many cracks, fissures, and shatterings met her gaze. Darkness—as black as ink—pooled within the crevices. She reached her hand forward, "Oren, how can I help? Tell me—"

Oren took one step back, throwing his hand up to stop Rowan mid-sentence. "I need you to understand that shatterings are almost like a never-ending plague. The pressure of a large shatter builds and creates smaller splinters. There is no stopping it once it is in motion. I've accepted my scars and what they are doing every day. There is no need to help me. But your ability to see shatterings, to feel another's heart and understand their soul? That's how you can help. You can influence the way in which the shatter splinters, and you can help refill the cracks."

Rowan closed her eyes. She opened them and looked in Oren's eyes then once again in his soul. She saw him—a young, scared child with nothing and no one. She felt her own fist clench as his own did in his memory. Rowan felt nearly consumed by his remembered emotion and the fire of so much anger.

She turned her gaze away once more, focusing on the floor. She felt Oren's touch on her arm and glanced up. He looked at her for a moment, then enveloped her in a hug.

"There's nothing to do for me. But my shatterings make it easy to influence how I want others to perceive me." Oren softly stroked Rowan's brown hair. "But I want to be honest with you, Rowan. You are clearly special, and I do not want to put a mask on anymore with you."

"You in full color? That was a mask?"

"Of sorts. But you've seen my heart and soul. Trying to hide from you still? Never. I want to stand with you on this journey."

Rowan placed a hand on Oren's chest, feeling awkward as he held her. She replayed in her mind how Oren had shared his deepest parts with her, had bared his soul.

The door pushed open, and Rowan pulled away. Cassian bowed slightly. "Milady, I did not want to leave without announcing my replacement for the afternoon. I will be back to resume my watch of you this evening."

Rowan saw the knight's eyes narrow as he looked at Oren before he left.

A familiar bearded face appeared in the doorway. "Bert, good to see you."

Oren's mention of his name allowed Rowan to identify where she recognized the new man. He was the Obsilvian sympathizer she'd overheard while traveling to the castle. Rowan took a small step closer to Oren.

"Rowan, I need you to meet someone. This person is important in showing us how to help your sister."

Emotions of apprehension and excitement swirled together in her chest. "We aren't going to leave the castle, are we?"

"No, of course not," Oren said, his eyebrows furrowed. "I would never do anything to put you at risk. We are just going to the gardens."

⁓

"I didn't realize how expansive the grounds were," Rowan said as she walked in tandem with Oren, past the topiary animals, and down a hedge-lined path that opened into a large field of marigolds. In the distance, Rowan could see a stone wall denoting the end of the gardens.

"Dendro and the other diatomists take great pride in the marigolds." Oren's nose twitched slightly upward.

"What about you?"

"No one can follow Verimor and not respect the symbolism in the flower." Oren waved with his arm and called out, "Dahlia!"

A woman kneeling within the rows turned toward them. She moved a woven basket filled with clipped flowers, stood, and wiped her hands on the apron around her waist.

"Happy day, Sir Oren. Sir Bert. Milady." She awkwardly curtsied after making eye contact with Rowan.

"Dahlia, Rowan is hoping to find a way to help her sister, who is sick. Of course, I thought of you and your Rosa. How is she?"

"My little girl is doing so much better, just like you promised." The skin crinkled around Dahlia's eyes as she smiled brightly. "She and my mother were going to have tea and cakes outside for lunch." Rowan watched her; the orb in front of Dahlia was fuzzy—almost as if Rowan's eyes were unfocused.

"I don't want to oppose, but is it possible for Rowan to meet Rosa?" Oren asked. "You can stay with her for the rest of the afternoon, and I'll make sure you get credit for a full day's work."

"You're too kind, Sir Oren." The woman bowed her head. "Since Rosa is doing so much better, she will be happy to have visitors." Dahlia turned and started walking in the direction of the far wall.

Rowan pinched the fabric of her dress by her knees to pull the hem off the ground as she followed Oren onto the dirt path. She couldn't help but wonder if anyone would be upset if she dirtied the dress and shoes too much.

Rowan saw several knights casually patrolling the top of the stone wall as they approached it after walking several yards. A short turret housed an iron-framed door that was attached to a pulley system.

Bert called up to the man. He glanced at the group, and the door started opening. Rowan placed a hand on Oren's shoulder in front of her. "I thought we weren't leaving the castle?"

Oren grinned ear-to-ear. He leaned over his arm toward her, his voice a low whisper. "We're leaving the inner castle wall, yes. But will you be in danger? No."

Rowan fiddled with the fabric of her dress, rubbing it between her fingers. She wanted to look at Dahlia's soul again to see if the woman could be trusted. Rowan looked at Oren. He hadn't given her cause to doubt him. In fact, he had been vulnerable with her when he didn't have to be. She resolved to trust Oren.

The area behind the stone wall opened into meadow. Outside the garden, the wind was noticeably colder without the diatomists' aid. Rowan forgot about her desire to keep the hem of her dress clean and wrapped her arms around herself.

"It won't be too far from here," said Oren. "Dahlia, like many of the laymen workers the castle employs, live close by here in Tulium, between the inner castle and the outer edge of the city."

There was no paved road, but a worn walking path was clearly marked. A few more knights were patrolling, and they greeted Bert as they passed.

Around a slight bend and over a small hill, rows of cottages greeted them. Unlike Aconite, which was full of small but separate homes, here Rowan found she was looking at a single, long building. However, the row of doors and windows of the front to the building indicated that there must have been separate rooms for different families inside.

"Mother!" A little girl, a younger version of Dahlia, stood and waved wildly. She coughed, and Dahlia sprinted forward. "Rosa?"

Rosa patted her own chest. "I'm okay, really, Mother, I am." When she smiled, Rowan noticed Rosa was missing her two front teeth.

"How old are you, Rosa?" Rowan asked.

"I have had six naming anniversaries. Do you want to have tea with me? Grandmother went to check on the kettle because I spilled a lot of the tea from earlier."

Rowan happily sat on the knit blanket after Rosa. Oren cleared his throat, still standing. "Rosa, can you tell my friend Rowan about when you were sick?"

Rosa handed Rowan an empty teacup. "I had a hard time staying awake. I was so tired, and everything hurt. But Oren and my mother helped me, and now I'm better. Would you like a sugar cube, milady?" the girl asked Rowan the question in an accented voice, like she was trying to sound all grown up.

"Yes, please," said Rowan. "Thank you." She moved the empty teacup to her face. "Yum! This tea is scrumptious. I wish I could drink it every day. What flavor is it?"

"It's just sugar water!" Rosa giggled.

"Only sugar water? You must have put your finger in it because not even sugar can be this sweet!"

"My hand in the tea? Ew!" Rosa's giggled erupted into belly laughter. She fell to her side as she started to settle.

Oren cleared his throat. "Use your ability to see what has helped to heal the girl—Dahlia almost lost her daughter before the cure."

Rosa pretended to pour tea with "finger" and "no finger" flavors for Rowan to drink. Rowan watched the little girl intently. At first, the orb appeared hazy—much like it had with Rosa's mother. Rowan leaned closer, putting all of her attention into her Sight.

The orb was completely black. Shadows crisscrossed over each other like a pretzel in Miss Bredon's tea shop. The darkness pulsated as it seemed to choke any light that tried to peek through.

Rowan sat back, her head snapping to Oren. He nodded as if answering an unspoken question. "It's only a bandage for now. She will need your power to stay cured indefinitely."

"Mother!" Rosa jumped to her feet as she heard her mother and grandmother exit their cottage, only a few feet from where the tea party was set up.

Rowan stood up, her gaze fixed on the girl, happy and whole with her family. Rosa coughed, her body shaking. Dahlia and her mother knelt in front of Rosa, concern in their matching pinched expressions. As rapidly as the coughing spell happened, Rosa was skipping circles around the women. "Is Rosa cured or not? I'm confused."

Oren grabbed Rowan's wrist and directed her to stand facing him. "Rosa is on the path to being cured. Only with your power can she be wholly cured. I can teach you how to cure her, and that will be how you cure your sister, too."

Rowan glanced over her shoulder, smiling as Rosa giggled when telling her mother and grandmother about her finger being sweeter than sugar. She squared her shoulders back, returning to face Oren. "I'm ready to learn."

Chapter Twenty-Three
Departure

BLYTHE OPENED THE WINDOW BEFORE sitting on the loveseat. She cracked the worn leather spine of her comfort read, which was a made-up story about a girl who befriended a wild horse. She dreamed of riding a horse again one day.

Demi chirped happily on the windowsill. The first time the window was opened, Blythe was afraid the small hawk would jump outside. But the little bird just liked the warmth of the sun on the wooden pane.

Blythe's eyes lazily scanned the words on the pages. She had read the book so many times, she could recite most of the text. A knock at the door pulled Blythe away from the fictional world. Her mother, setting aside her own book, got up from her chair in the room. "Cleric Jimson, happy day."

"Happy day, Maryam. Happy day, Blythe. Are you both doing well?"

"We are. Please come on in. Any news from Rowan?" Maryam asked.

The cleric put a hand inside his robe. "This letter arrived yesterday morning for Blythe. I apologize for not bringing it sooner."

"That's quite all right," offered Blythe as she sat up. She went to stand; but Cleric Jimson, with his long legs, was in front of her in two steps. Blythe's smile was so wide that her dimples showed. "Oh, I can tell it's multiple pages." She broke the wax seal and unfolded the parchment.

Her eyes eagerly soaked in the cursive writing. As she read, she paraphrased the letter for her mother and the cleric. "Rowan is exhausted but well. She says she's not had as much time to write as she would have hoped. The first few days were primarily spent meeting people and adjusting to life in the cold." Blythe looked up momentarily. "It's a good thing we got Mrs. Myrtle to do a wool surcoat." She giggled then continued with Rowan's note.

"She says that she likes the royal diatomist, but she isn't too sure of the apprentice. Her handmaid, Nora, thinks the apprentice, Oren, is very handsome, but Rowan thinks his personality hinders his appearance." Blythe snorted, then covered her flushing face. "She probably didn't mean for you to hear that part, Cleric Jimson."

Both the cleric and Blythe's mother laughed.

Maryam said, "Oh, I'm sure it's fine. You know your sister. Even though she sometimes overthinks and worries, she also is going to blurt out the first thing that comes to her mind—no matter whose company she's in." She laughed again softly.

"Apparently, he is an enigma of both help and annoyances. She says she doesn't know what to think of that." Blythe scrunched her face. "Um, let's see . . . she also writes that the diatomists have made it so that all sorts of flowers will be in bloom during the Marigold Ball. And she is counting down the minutes until she sees us."

"Is that all?" her mother asked, leaning forward in her chair.

Blythe flipped to the back of the second sheet to double check. "Yes, that's all. Other than her saying she loves and misses everyone. Nothing about attempted assassinations or any danger, so that's good."

"Attempted assassinations?" Cleric Jimson asked, one fair eyebrow raised.

Heat filled Blythe's cheeks once again. "I shouldn't have said that. I don't want to be a part of gossip." She looked down at her hands.

"We won't gossip. But . . . " Her mother sighed. "We do need to make sure any fear of Rowan being in danger is not founded. Cleric Jimson, we heard in town that there was an attempt on King Isak's life. There are also rumors about war coming from the sea into our own homes here on the coast. Are any of these claims true?"

Cleric Jimson sat back in the chair and steepled his fingers. "Obsilvia has become bolder in their actions, which *have* included an attack on King Isak's life."

Blythe's mother audibly gasped. Blythe made no sound but scrunched up fistfuls of her dress on either side on the loveseat cushion.

"The would-be assassin was caught and arrested before any harm befell the king or any other member of the king's inner court," the cleric continued. "There is no current threat to the castle, however; and despite rumors and whispered fears, I do not think either Aconite or Tulium are in immediate danger. We all

need to be vigilant in our prayers and aware of our interactions day to day, but we can't live in fear of what *might* happen."

Silence fell on the room for several minutes. Cleric Jimson cleared his throat. "With rising tensions, war might not be avoidable. But we must act in faith, trusting that we were born for this time and that we will be called to serve a greater purpose."

"Maryam? Are you here?" Blythe's father's voice called through the house as the back door slammed shut.

"Matthias, why are you back so early?" Blythe's mother stood and met her husband as he entered the front room from the hallway. Her facial features fell from pursed confusion to anxious concern seeing her husband.

His chest was rapidly moving up and down, as if he had just run from the dock. Sweat beaded his neck and pooled on the front of his gray shirt. The crow's feet around his hazel eyes were filled with salt and grime, emphasizing his weathered appearance. "What's happened?"

Blythe's father put both hands on his wife's shoulders. "We are leaving Aconite. Today. I need you to trust me. Pack up the essentials for you and Blythe. Grab anything that holds value for Rowan. We are meeting Oak, Rose, and Bane as soon as possible. Oak's hitching up the mules now."

"What's happened?" Cleric Jimson echoed the earlier question posed by Blythe's mother as he rose to his feet.

"It's no longer simple talk of enemies hidden among the dock workers."

"Baba? Is there fighting here?" Blythe asked. Her voice shook as tears pricked her eyes. How could there be danger here, right at home?

"The war is coming, and we need to move." Matthias' voice was calm but commanding. "Cleric Jimson, may Verimor keep you well in the days ahead."

The guest clasped hands with Matthias. "And you."

Chapter Twenty-Four
Patchwork and Barriers

"WERE GOING TO THE DUNGEONS?" Rowan took a step back, her hand over her own heart and her fingers wrapped around her necklace.

Oren laughed. "I'm not going to lock *you* up in the dark, damp, and forgotten recesses of the earth below. But in order to keep moving toward understanding and control of your Sight, this is a necessary step."

"Will it be dangerous?"

Stepping toward Rowan, Oren gently clasped her hand. He pulled it away from her true-knot necklace and turned her palm to his lips. He placed a light kiss, sending a flutter like butterfly wings in Rowan's stomach. It was nearly dizzying. But Rowan didn't pull away; she froze and watched Oren intently.

"The prisoner we will be seeing today is named Hamlin. He entered our kingdom under the guise of peaceful relations as a representative from Obsilvia. However, Hamlin soon shared his true intentions with an assassination attempt of the king."

Rowan's magenta eyes widened. "When did this happen?"

"Two days before the Court was alerted of your Sight. In fact, you are very much the reason he has not yet been sentenced to death for treason—which is what Elias wanted to do. However, I believe King Isak would prefer to use Hamlin as a pawn in negotiations rather than send Obsilvia a warning by killing him."

Rowan nodded her head but remained silent as she walked beside Oren. They descended carpeted stairs and turned down a long corridor two stories underneath the main floor. The air was warmer here and more humid than elsewhere in the castle, and Oren's earlier descriptor of damp was fitting. It smelled of musty dirt and ash. Every few feet of wall held sconces with fire-lit lanterns lighting the area.

At the end of the hallway was a soldier guarding another stairwell. He stepped to the side with a polite grunt. Oren nodded his head in greeting, and he placed a hand on the small of Rowan's back as they went down the steep, narrow stone steps. "Do not let Hamlin get into your head. You have the power to help him, Wisteria, and your sister."

The hair on the back of Rowan's neck stood on end. She didn't like being down here. But Rowan rolled her shoulders back in determination. She would stay there as long as it took if it meant it would help her save Blythe from continuing pain.

"Oren, Hamlin's been missing you," a cheerful and familiar voice called up ahead. "Asked if there were any more of your famous lemon tarts . . . "

The lantern light revealed a man wearing simple clothes, and an expression plastered on his face like a child caught in a mischievous act. Only the chainmail over his tunic and the sheathed sword at his side identified him as a soldier. He pulled an iron key ring off his belt, clearing his throat. "Your usual half an hour, or do you and the lady need more time today?"

"Normal time will be fine. Thank you, Bert," Oren said, teeth clenched.

Rowan looked from the guard to the apprentice. "You bake? For the prisoners?"

"Bert and I grew up together," Oren said, a forced chuckle. "I think that was his way of asking for the lemon tarts my grandmother used to make us. But the timing is inappropriate."

Bert opened the barred door and pulled a different key off the ring. He handed it to Oren. "He keeps mumbling something about reclamation and retribution? I don't know. Maybe you can make sense of his gibberish and earn some favor with Sir Elias." Bert winked. "See you two in a bit."

Rowan watched Bert as he sauntered to the entrance of the dungeon, whistling while he walked away from them. His whistling was different that Diatomist Dendro's jovial tune. She pushed down an urge to look into Oren's soul to learn more about his grandmother. Her apprehension grew, and she felt her palms moisten from sweat as she looked into the darkened cell.

"We don't have to go in too far." Oren moved forward, and Rowan stayed on his heels. The gray flickering lights offered shadows that made Rowan's feeling of unease increase. Despite the fairly warm earthen caverns around her and her long wool sleeves, goosebumps covered her flesh.

She bumped into Oren's back, watching the lantern light dance on the walls instead of looking ahead. "I'm sorry," she whispered.

Oren put the key into the iron lock and pushed the bars away from him. "Hamlin, make sure you're presentable. There's a lady with me today."

"Has Linnea decided to grace me today?" The voice was sharp and laced with disdain.

Rowan did not follow Oren into the cell but rather held back.

"No, I've brought Rowan—the unicorn-blessed."

A cold laugh reverberated through the small chamber. The laugh continued until the man started coughing and could barely catch his breath. His figure shifted in the darkness. A thud followed by a dragging sound echoed and repeated. Hamlin's face entered the light. His black hair was greasy and tousled and his black beard unkempt. His clothes were dusty and dirty. The most striking thing Rowan noticed, however, was his limp. Hamlin's left leg dragged behind him, and his left shoulder drooped. Still, he held himself as one of noble upbringing with his head in the air.

Scratching grated Rowan's ears as Oren pulled a chair from the corner. "Sit, Hamlin."

"You Wisterians will always fail. You know why? Because you cling to fairy tales. Fantasy stories. Unicorns, blessings, *Verimor*? Obsilvia will take back the Dimidi Isles and will take down your whole forsaken kingdom!"

"Silence!" Oren's booming voice made Rowan jump. He motioned her to his side without taking his eyes off Hamlin. "You're not going to make my guest uncomfortable with your ramblings. If you are cooperative, then, perhaps, I can provide something in return."

Hamlin snorted and crossed his arms over his chest. He leaned to the left in this chair, as if waiting for Oren's offer.

"Let Rowan do what she needs to do, and we'll see to your physical scars from your encounter with the *Pars Sicarius* nectar. Linnea's poisonous prick could have done much greater damage, but I know you would take your former stance over your current state."

Rowan watched Hamlin's eyes narrow. She felt the room's tension thicken even as the prisoner nodded his head forward, granting his agreement.

Oren walked behind Rowan. He placed a hand on her upper back. "Look, Rowan. For me. For yourself."

Rowan inhaled through her nose and released the breath through her mouth. She focused on Hamlin until the shadows and light in front of him began to shift.

"Your Sight will let you pull forward specific memories, specific emotions. Sift through until you find the soul's center— where the shatterings are visible to you."

An eerie cold creeped down Rowan's spine, but she pushed herself to look as Oren directed. Flashes of gray bombarded her as she saw faces from Hamlin's past. Her heartbeat quickened, and her instincts told her to run away. Faced with an avalanche of fear, heartbreak, and anger, Rowan's stomach flipped with rising nausea.

"Your brother was in the Dimidi Isles," Rowan said, trying to make sense of the swirling images before her. "He . . . he was killed by a Wisterian disease. You—" Rowan lurched forward as pain radiated through her own chest. She blinked through the blinding hurt as the clear shattering in Hamlin's soul made itself visible.

"Overthrowing a kingdom won't get your brother back," Rowan said, her throat dry and words hoarse.

"Rowan." Oren's voice sounded steady, powerful even. "I'm going to talk to Hamlin. I need you to pull forward the emotions and feed them into the shattered part. No matter what happens, do not stop until I say so."

Rowan nodded, keeping her vision locked into Hamlin's soul.

"Your brother's death clearly left a mark on you, Hamlin. But his death was not a secret. Whispers always find their way to me and my master. Even without the Sight of the unicorn-blessed, I knew your brother was the victim of the White Pox, a disease which natives of Obsilvia are not exposed to in childhood. But his death wasn't the first time you were abandoned, was it? You are a crusader against tradition and Verimor because time and time again, faith left you with nothing."

A whimper escaped Rowan as shadows poured out of Hamlin—shadows pulsating with disgust, disappointment, and rage. She watched as Oren lifted a hand out to the prisoner. With swift, subtle movements of his fingers, dark shadows were directed right back into the shatterings; and clouds of black, as dark and rich as ink, seemed to pool from Oren's fingertips and fill the cracks in Hamlin's heart.

Sweat dripped down Rowan's brow, and her body began to ache; but Oren didn't seem to notice her discomfort. "You always lived in your brother's shadow. Amil was the golden child and you, Hamlin, simply an afterthought who never measured up. And as the second son in a noble Obsilvian household, you were never meant to be titled. But you wanted that, didn't you? You constantly played Amil's keeper, cleaning up his messes. And you wanted him dead, out of your way. You deserved to hold the title of nobility for your house, not your lazy brother! But your prayers for change did nothing but fall on deaf ears. Until . . . your brother ran off to the Dimidi Isles and became ill. Then your prayers were answered."

"No!" Hamlin screamed. His voice was shaky. "I didn't want him to die. I didn't even know he had been stricken by the pox until I got the letter . . . I would trade places with Amil if I could."

"I believe that." Oren clicked his tongue. "Because your father refused to give you the title of duke. He refused to give you your inheritance and said you should have been with your brother. He blamed you for Amil's death. Then you, alone in the world for the first time in your life, built yourself anew. Without the weight of family ties. Without faith in false deities. By *yourself*."

The swirls of self-righteousness and wrath made the bile in Rowan's stomach rise to her throat. "Oren, I can't do this," she whispered to ears that acted deaf to her voice.

"Hamlin, you worked into the good graces of your nation's king. You earned respect on your own. But then your stupidity got you here: a dungeon awaiting death. To die with nothing. Just as your own father stripped you of everything years ago, you've ensured there's nothing of worth to your name. But—"

"Stop!" Rowan closed her eyes and turned. Her stomach heaved, and her throat throbbed from the force of her returned breakfast. Rowan wrapped her arms around herself. Sweat poured down her face and dampened her underarms and back; yet she was shivering and cold.

"What's going on?" Bert's voice called as the guard walked back up to the cell. "Oren, do you need more time?"

"No, we're done," Rowan announced through hiccups, tears streaming down her face. She pushed past the guard, still holding her own arms around her torso. The more space Rowan put between herself and Hamlin's cell, the harder she cried. By the time she was on the main floor, her breaths were shallow and inhibited by snot bubbles in her nose. Rowan couldn't remember ever feeling so broken. Was that how Hamlin always felt? Or had she caused the shattering to deepen to such an extent?

"Rowan?"

Rowan shook her head, tears still falling, as she pushed past Nora and into her room. She closed the door behind her and threw herself on the bed. She cried for Hamlin and his pain. She cried for home and her family. She cried for Blythe and for the uncertainty of maybe never being strong enough to help her sister heal.

A knock sounded at the door. After a moment, the knock came again but more forcefully. Rowan wasn't sure how long she had been in her room. She didn't turn her head at all when she heard the door creak open. "Lady Rowan, Oren is here and is saying he must see you at once. I can send him away if you would like."

"It's imperative that I speak with you, Rowan," Oren said over Nora's shoulder in the doorway. "It's news that will help your sister."

The small flutter of hope in Rowan's chest was enough. It gave her the energy to push herself to a sitting position on the edge of the bed. "You know how to heal Blythe?"

Rowan pulled back, hunching her shoulders as Oren entered the room. Hamlin, wearing manacles, was right on his heels.

The flood of emotions she experienced looking into his soul earlier threatened to drown her once again. "Why is *he* here?"

Oren walked up to Rowan. "Rowan, he's here because you need to see what power you are capable of."

"Won't you be in trouble for having a dangerous prisoner out of the dungeon?"

Oren patted her hand as if she were an inconsolable child. "Shh and be good. Bert is right outside. I knew having you brought back to the dungeon would be overwhelming, but I need you to finish what you started."

Rowan closed her eyes and shook her head. "I can't."

Oren placed a finger under her chin. "You can. Or you risk Rosa's health. Your sister's, too." He stepped back. "Hamlin, tell Rowan what you decided soon after she left."

"I am flawed and will only continue to fail in my endeavors on my own," Hamlin's voice was monotone, void of emotion. "It is clear that there are self-sabotaging and demeaning obstacles within me that will keep me from reaching my goals. I need help separating those parts within me."

"You see?" Oren asked.

Rowan stared at him with her mouth partially open.

Oren continued, "You have the power to help him. You can separate the shadows and the light within this man so that he can do what needs to be done."

Rowan rubbed both sides of her head as it suddenly filled with throbbing pain. "How does that help Blythe? Or the little girl Rosa?"

"Without your Sight, he would not have seen what to do. You will go in and barricade the shadows from the light. This will allow him to access great power but continue to be malleable. It will allow us to be victorious in the war. But the same process will allow you to heal Blythe. Watch. When you succeed, his physical ailments will be rectified."

Rowan looked at Oren and then to Hamlin. Her eyes scanned the room around her, and she hoped to find Nora. But the girl wasn't there.

"You did so much already, patching the shattering. But the next step is erecting a barrier. You need to create the barrier in his soul."

"Maybe . . . maybe we should wait for Diatomist Dendro," Rowan said.

"We could," replied Oren. "But if we wait too long, you will have to start over with the patchwork. Do you think you can do that again?"

Rowan absentmindedly tapped her fingers. "I just need some time. I need to sit and ask Verimor if this is truly what I'm meant to do with the Sight."

Oren's jaw tightened, and a flash of something crossed his face. Before Rowan could process it, his expression softened. He leaned his forehead forward until it touched her own. "Don't you trust me?"

Slowly, Rowan nodded.

"Good girl." Oren pulled back, looking into Rowan's eyes. "I'm not going to lead you astray. Do this, and you'll know how to use your new power to save Blythe—and anyone else who needs help."

Rowan stood and looked at Hamlin once again. "Oren, how do I make the barrier?"

"Look into his soul, go to his shatterings."

Rowan's breathing sped up. "Okay, I see the shatterings and the splinters off of them." She felt she was looking into a broken mirror with the sharp, jagged edges looking back at her. There were more plumes of pitch black than ever before. The shatterings and splinters were completely dark, and only bits of light peeked around the perimeter of Hamlin's soul.

"Earlier, you pulled forth shadows to fill the shatterings. Now, you need to locate the main shatter. When you do, I will be able to stretch the shatterings to create the barrier to use the shadows to fully engulf the light."

Rowan bored into Hamlin's soul, focusing everything on the shadowed fractures. She tried to drown out the sound of her own heartbeat in her ears and the inner voice begging her to stop. She mentally latched onto the primary shattering.

"It burns," she mumbled.

"Keep going. You don't want to come so close just to walk away before being able to heal Blythe. Think of everything she endures. Think how happy she will be that you can help her be pain-free again."

Rowan grit her teeth, pushing past the burning pain tearing at her muscles, the racing anxiety slashing through her veins, and the bile rising once again in her throat. She pulled with all of her might.

Oren raised his hand once again, and the shadows morphed. They grew. Hamlin's soul was so dark, it was nearly consumed completely by blackness.

Rowan fell to her knees, gasping for air. She wanted to cry, but she was too exhausted to shed any more tears. She looked up when she heard a man cry out. It was Hamlin. He, too, had fallen forward.

Hamlin rolled his spine up and stood. His face was passive.

"Rowan," said Oren, his voice confident and commanding. "You will do so much good. *We* will, together."

Oren's smile was wide. Rowan shook her head slightly. Oren's face was wrong, like he had more teeth than a person should. She watched him walk out of her room, Hamlin behind him.

And the prisoner walked without any trace of a limp or slump in his shoulder.

Chapter Twenty-Five
Detour

BLYTHE'S JOINTS WERE STIFF AND achy as she moved; but today, the pain was minimal, allowing her to bear her own weight. She placed Demi on the now-bare bed. The hawk twittered as Blythe folded her nightgown and two dresses to wear during the day.

She threw two of her favorite books, a small copy of the *Book of Verimor*, and the letters from Rowan on top of the pile. Blythe's eyes moved from the now empty chest-of-drawers over to the bed she shared with her sister, then back again. Atop the set of drawers, there was a knit doll and a glass figurine. Blythe ran her finger over the yellow yarn hair of the doll. She briefly considered taking it, but she hadn't played with the doll for months.

The glass figurine was sapphire blue and shaped like a jelly snail. She and Rowan had saved coins for over two years to get that. She picked it up and wrapped it in a pair of socks before placing it in between her dresses. Blythe pulled the corners of a thin quilt together to form a makeshift bag with the few belongings. As she pulled the knot tight, her father walked into the room.

"I've got your chair in the cart, and your mother has packed up food for the journey to Tulium. Are you ready?"

The cold numbness Blythe felt in gathering her belongings quickly thawed, revealing a despotic sense of fear. "Baba, will we ever get to come back home?"

Her father wrapped his arms around her. "I don't know." He pulled back. "But the most important thing right now is that you and your mother will be safe."

Baba stood straight and grabbed Blythe's blanket pack. "Get Demi."

Blythe scooped up her pet and hooked her cane on her arm. It wouldn't have hurt to use it, but she was capable of moving without it at the moment. And even though she had some pain and resistance in her legs, choosing to push through and succeeding gave her a sense of control when everything around her was complete chaos.

"This isn't right! Mr. Tritonia, tell my father running away is cowardly." Bane's uncharacteristically raised voice caused Blythe to blink rapidly. It was more difficult for her to process Bane yelling at their parents than the danger of impending violence.

"Be reasonable." Mr. Oxeye held the bridge of his nose. "The dam is starting to break, and we need to leave before we are caught in the flooding."

"That's why we need to wait. We need to make sure everyone knows it isn't safe!" Bane looked at Blythe and each adult in turn. His face was ashen, his eyes red and shiny as if tears threatened to fall. "We can't abandon all the people here."

Blythe intertwined her fingers into her mother's hand, watching as Bane's mother wrapped her arms around him. She held onto him, even when he did not return her embrace. "Son, do you smell that? It's our family orchards ablaze. Obsilvia operatives, and maybe even some sympathizers, have set countless acres on fire—"

"We need to work together to quench it—"

Bane's plea was cut off as Blythe's father finished Mrs. Oxeye's explanation. "Fighting started in the fish market. The all-out brawling was contained, but one obnoxious soul declared an entire fleet is arriving tonight. There's no means for anyone to protect themselves."

"Everyone deserves a chance to evacuate," Bane pushed on, while returning his mother's hug.

"Son, between the spreading smoke and everyone who was at the docks earlier, people will know. And each family will have to make their own choice." Mr. Oxeye placed a hand on Bane's shoulder behind him.

"Cleric Jimson was here when Oak came in. He still holds out hope that the brunt of battle will not touch Aconite," Maryam offered. "He and the clerics at the cathedral will be the helpers for those who choose to stay."

"But . . . " Bane's voice was a whisper, an echo of his earlier demeanor.

"But we can still be helpers on the road to Tulium," Blythe declared, the confidence in her tone surprising to her own ears. "And once we get to Rowan, we can make sure she's safe, and make sure the king knows how volatile things are here."

"Volatile?" Bane chuckled. "Let's get you in the cart, Miss Reads-A-Lot Blythe." He pulled away from his mother and offered a hug to his father and his hand to Blythe's father in turn. "I'm sorry I—"

Mr. Oxeye waved his hand as if the motion would send his son's words away in the wind. "Let's load up. It's going to be a long journey to reach the castle."

Blythe accepted Bane's help climbing into the back of the open, wooden cart. Blankets had been layered down on the floorboards. Blythe settled into the front corner, opposite her chair and the few belongings the two families had packed. She pulled one of the blankets to her lap and stroked Demi. The bird was oddly quiet, almost like she, too, was feeling weighed down by the departure.

Blythe reached into the apron pocket of her dress and silently fed Demi some sunflower seeds. Her mother and Mrs. Oxeye climbed in, too. Bane sat on the end of the wagon, letting his feet dangle over the end. His father glanced over his shoulder once; and with Blythe's baba beside him, he urged the mules forward.

"Mrs. Myrtle will be upset we didn't get to show her handiwork off at the Marigold Ball." Blythe attempted to break the tension in the wagon but immediately regretted her words. Her mother closed her eyes and bit her bottom lip. She visibly swallowed grief as a single rogue tear slipped down her face.

"I'll make it up to you. I know the dress—"

Blythe reached over and took her mother's hand. "Mama, no, I don't care about the dress. I mean, it was exciting, but I would forsake all of the glittering gowns fit for royalty to have us all safe and together."

Her mother raised their intertwined hands to her mouth, and she kissed the back of Blythe's hand. Silence resumed.

The few minutes they had spent talking before setting off was enough time for the smoke to become even more noticeable, yet not suffocatingly thick. No flames appeared in Blythe's line of sight; but she knew the fire had consumed crops, livelihoods, and day-to-day plans. Blythe closed her eyes. She focused on the steady motion of the wagon and the *click-clack* of the two mules' hooves on the dirt road.

"Cleric Jimson didn't think there was any immediate threat. How could he be so wrong? I mean, he's a representative of the royal diatomist. Shouldn't he have known?" Blythe's voice quavered.

Maryam wrapped her arm around Blythe's shoulders and pulled her daughter's head to rest on her chest. She calmly stroked Blythe's hair.

"Do you need some help?" Blythe lifted her head upon hearing her father's strong voice call out as the wagon slowed to a stop.

"You wouldn't happen to be carrying some carpenter's tools, would you?" a husky voice replied. "The wheel broke on our wagon, and I don't know how to get my family far away from here."

"You and your family are welcome to join us on our journey to Tulium."

"Thank you kindly. My wife, Juniper, has some family in Abelium about a day's ride outside of Tulium. You and yours are welcome to rest and refresh when we get there."

Blythe watched as her father and Mr. Oxeye got down to help the stranger get his donkey hitched in front of their mules. Bane jumped down to help the stranger's wife, Juniper, into the wagon.

A small boy clung to his mother's dress, and Juniper's belly was round. Blythe's heart jumped in her chest. She loved children and babies, and having a young child and his pregnant mother join them was a bit of sunshine in today's clouded sky.

"Happy day, little one. I'm Blythe."

The small boy turned his face into his mother's shoulder. Juniper smiled. "This is Ash. He acts shy now; but when he warms up to you, you'll wish he was still shy."

"It's nice to meet you, Ash. I have a pet hawk. I call her Demi." Blythe lifted the feathered bird up. The boy peered with one eye at Blythe, the rest of his face still up against his mother. "She loves listening to stories. So I'm going to tell her some. She says she hopes you like listening, too." The bird let out a timid squawk.

"Tell the story about the jelly snail who had to find his way back to the water." Bane had turned around and was now facing the other occupants of the wagon.

"That's a good one." Blythe took a deep breath and began the story. "Once, on the sandy shores of Aconite, a blue jelly snail hatched . . ."

Chapter Twenty-Six
True Colors

"ROWAN? YOU DIDN'T EAT DINNER last night, and now you've missed the morning meal and lunch. Are you not well?" Nora's usual sunny temperament was clouded with concern.

"I'm just exhausted," Rowan said, her voice monotone. "Maybe I'm getting homesick."

"Mrs. Ginty has sent up a bread roll with a slice of cheese. She's right; you need to eat something. And it's such a lovely day. Why not walk around the gardens while the sun is out after?" Nora offered an encouraging smile.

Rowan took one bite of the bread and then picked away crumbs and stacked them on the plate rather than eating them.

Nora threw open the thick velvet curtains. Rowan shielded her eyes with her hand. "I've got the perfect pale green dress for you to wear. It'll be great for your walk and for dinner with Lady Linnea and Diatomist Dendro."

Half-heartedly, Rowan went through the motions while Nora tried to make small talk, but her voice blended with grays that made up the world around Rowan.

"I'll walk you down to the gardens." Nora put a hand around Rowan's shoulder and ushered her through the door, letting it shut firmly behind them.

Rowan hazily walked with Nora through the wing, down the main staircase, and along the hall to get to the gardens. "I have to go help Mrs. Ginty prepare for tonight's meal, but promise me you will at least do one lap along the garden path before returning indoors?"

With a weak smile, Rowan nodded. "I will, Nora. Thank you . . . for all of your kindness."

Nora quickly wrapped Rowan into a tight hug before turning back into the castle.

Sighing as the rays of the sun warmed her despite the cool temperature, Rowan casually strolled along the main garden path. Around a natural curve in the stone walkway, Rowan saw a girl sitting on a bench with a book in hand.

"Happy day, Steffie," Rowan called, attempting to sound cheerful.

"Happy day," Steffie replied, looking up briefly before closing her book. "You look awful. Are you well?"

Rowan's bottom lip trembled, and a rogue tear slipped down her face. "I'm fine."

Steffie scoffed. "I didn't know dishonesty was a character trait of yours, but I've found I cannot trust anyone. So I should be far from surprised."

"Where are Pearl and Maude?" Rowan asked, her eyes glancing over the vicinity.

"They made their own plans." Under her breath, she added, "Everyone eventually leaves me behind."

"It seems your mood is as poor as mine." Rowan motioned to the bench. "May I join you?"

Shrugging, Steffie asked, "How helpful will a pity party for two be? But I have heard misery loves company—quite cliché, no?"

"Are you miserable?"

"Are *you*? You sure look like you are."

Rowan sighed loudly. "It's been really difficult adjusting to life in Tulium, in the castle. I want to go home, back to before my sixteenth naming anniversary. Then I could stay home and not get the marigold crown and avoid this whole blessing business. Maybe actually get a somni melon with at least one seed."

"I had one seed in my somni melon, and my wish was a waste. So at least you didn't have any false hope." Steffie leaned back on the back of the bench with a sharp exhale of air.

"I was once told that wishes and prayers are different. But often we pray for things our hearts wish for, right? Does not getting an immediate answer to a prayer mean our faith is hopeless?" Rowan turned to the girl beside her. "I feel more cursed to carry a heavy and unwanted burden than I feel blessed with a gift from Verimor. But I can't say believing is just false hope because I know. I just *know*."

Steffie tilted her head as if contemplating. "Use whatever semantics you would like—wishes, prayers, dreams. They're all a fantasy. My father will never be proud of me, and he will marry me off to whomever he deems the most beneficial partner to himself, regardless of my feelings. I'll never have a real friendship or relationship of any sort that is genuine. What would be the point of waiting for something that will never happen?" She shook her head slowly. "But you're 'unicorn-blessed.' You'll serve the king and earn love from all across the kingdom. You'll have your choice of suitors and a say in your future. Perhaps that is why I was so petty in our first meeting. I'm jealous of you, Rowan."

"I don't think my plight is anything to be jealous of, Steffie. I used my Sight—this *blessing*—yesterday. And now I feel so broken."

Steffie's hazel eyes found Rowan's, her gaze intent and one eyebrow slightly raised. "If you used the Sight in Verimor's name, then you would feel the opposite—especially after your whole miniature lecture on faith and hope. Did you use it correctly?"

Rowan stiffened, and indignation flashed in her chest. "I did exactly what Oren said to do," she snapped.

"If you say so." Steffie stood up, smoothing her yellow chiffon skirt. "I don't feel like spoiling my afternoon being yelled at; therefore, it is time for me to take my leave."

"Wait." Rowan touched Steffie's arm. "I'm sorry . . . maybe we can help each other?"

Steffie's stiff posture relaxed slightly. "I'm listening."

"You may be right in that I'm not using the Sight correctly. I can practice with you; and hopefully, it will help you be less miserable?" Rowan waited, eyes wide and pleading.

"I suppose the worst outcome is no change at all . . . yes, I'll help you practice."

Rowan excitedly grabbed Steffie's hand as she rose to her feet. "Wonderful! So, you stand here, and I'll stand across from you. Like this."

"And you stare at me?" Steffie's voice was laced with uncertainty.

"I'm not looking at you exactly—it's your soul."

"What does my soul look like?" The girl's voice sounded more intrigued.

"Like everyone's I look at, it's made up of swirls of different shades of gray and wisps of white. As I look, there are ripples; and then I can see memories. And things that have hurt you, that have left scars—they're called shattering."

Steffie visibly shivered. In a whisper, she asked, "You can see all of that?"

Rowan's lips pursed, mirroring the furrowing of her eyebrows. "Now, I can see you. You're looking up at a man, arms outstretched. But he yells for someone. A nursemaid scoops you up in her arms and carries you away, ignoring your cries."

Steffie closed her eyes tightly. "Please . . . I can't bear to go through every memory of my father dismissing me."

As Rowan watched the gray light and shadows move, she tapped each fingertip to the pad of her thumb on both hands simultaneously. "Your strained relationship with your father— that's caused a shattering within you."

Steffie clenched her fists in front of her torso, and a tear slipped down her cheek. "When do I start feeling better?" Her attempt at a laugh was stilted by shaky breathing and trembling knees.

Rowan's eyes jumped from the dark to the light in front of Steffie. She prayed silently for guidance. "Tell me, where do you feel safe?"

The girl scrunched her face up. "Safe? In the stables or riding my horse, Firefly."

"Describe riding Firefly. Tell me, what do you see? Smell? Feel?"

Still quivering, Steffie spoke. "I see his white coat bespeckled with black. I run my hand over his neck, and I can feel the warmth of his breath on my cheek." As she talked, her voice steadied. Rowan watched as the white shimmered within her soul.

"I don't sit side-saddle. No, I have a pair of breeches I borrowed from my brother. I have my hands on the smooth leather reins, and I can feel his wild, white mane blowing in my face as I lean closer. Firefly starts at a trot; but soon, the green grass of the countryside is blurred. I'm free from obligation, shallow routines, and feeling like I'm never good enough . . . free from who I am as the unwanted daughter of Sir Elias."

"Firefly makes you feel free and wanted." Rowan felt a warmth in her own chest as the light continued to sparkle within Steffie. "And you are wanted, Steffie."

Steffie's mouth opened, but no words were uttered. Her bottom lip trembled.

"Even when you feel alone, Verimor is there. And even when you think you've been abandoned, He is there. And He has placed, and will place, people in your life to help you on your journey through this world." Rowan reached out her hand and soundlessly urged the light to grow and fill the shattered places.

The movement of the white plumes was a crawl compared to the rushing of the black ink spill with Hamlin. But Rowan didn't hurt. She felt both herself and Steffie enveloped in a comforting, unexplainable, healing warmth as the white swirls shifted to a threadlike thinness and started to stitch the crevices caused by so much hurt and longing.

Steffie lifted her arms and stepped forward, suddenly wrapping Rowan in a hug. Rowan embraced her new friend back.

"This is unexpected." Oren's voice carried down the garden path. Rowan let Steffie break her hold first, and she looked directly at the approaching mage. "I didn't think you two liked each other much."

"First impressions aren't everything," Steffie said, dabbing at her eyes with a gloved hand. "There's a reason Rowan is here and why she was called forward by Verimor. Take care of her." Steffie turned, offering a smile and small curtsy to Rowan before walking back toward the castle.

"Do you want to tell me what all that was about?" Oren asked.

Rowan clasped her hands together. "Steffie was helping me practice with the Sight and—"

"Why were you practicing by yourself? Rowan, don't you know how dangerous that is? You could have hurt yourself or Steffie! Remember how sick you were yesterday? You don't understand the power you have."

Feeling her nostrils flare, Rowan crossed her arms over her chest. "I didn't get sick today. The answer is the light . . ."

"Stop." Oren held up his hands, palms facing Rowan. "There isn't time for you to act like an insolent child. You can't tell me that there are no unseen repercussions at work for misusing the Sight, which you clearly did. You feel good now, but do you know what damage is being done right now because of your selfishness? Not to you but to that poor girl?"

"No." Rowan shook her head, but the conviction wavered in her now quiet voice. "There can't be."

Oren grabbed Rowan's shoulders. "We aren't going to tell Dendro, or anyone, about this. At dinner, just let me explain how your training is going, all right? I need you to trust me."

Rowan blew air out of her nose forcefully. "And I need you to get away from me. Just give me some time to think." She turned and walked toward the castle. To her relief, there were no footsteps behind her.

"If you don't trust me, you won't be able to save your sister." Oren's voice was ominous and caused Rowan to pause mid-step. "Or Rosa or anyone else," he added. Rowan waited until she heard Oren's shoes on the stone path behind her before continuing.

Chapter Twenty-Seven
Miracle

"I'VE NEVER SEEN A CHAIR with wheels before," Ash chatted, sitting between his mother and Blythe. He turned his neck from the chair to Blythe. "You use the wheels 'cause your legs won't walk?"

"Ash, don't pry," his mother scolded, her eyes closed and hands on her swollen stomach.

"It's fine, truly," said Blythe. "Yes, my legs don't always work like they're supposed to, so the chair helps me get around."

Ash nodded in a fashion that seemed much too mature for his five years. He leaned into Blythe. "Baba says it's brave to not give up. So that means you're brave for having walking wheels instead of giving up when your legs don't want to let you go."

Bane laughed. "I agree with him, Blythe; you are brave. Also, Ash should name everything. Walking wheels? That's great."

Blythe smiled, and her cheeks flushed slightly. "Sounds like you have a good baba. I do, too."

"I love my baba. And my mama! Mama, did you hear me? I love you," Ash called out in a sing-song fashion.

Juniper's eyes were still closed. She inhaled deeply through her nose and released it through her mouth. "I love you, too, baby boy." The cart hit a rough patch, and Ash's mother made a sound that was a mix of a grunt and a cry.

"How long have you been having contractions?" Blythe's mother asked, one hand on Juniper's arm.

The woman released another breath, and the muscles in her face relaxed. "It's not time. I had false alarms for weeks before Ash arrived. It's nothing."

"Here," said Mrs. Oxeye. "Chew on this sprig of mint. It can help ease the intensity of the pains."

"Thank you." Juniper reached her hand out but then dropped it. She gritted her teeth and released a sharp exhale.

"My dear, this doesn't seem to be a false alarm," asserted Blythe's mother. She raised her voice to be heard over the rumbling of the wagon wheels. "Oak, how far are we from Abelium?"

"Caleb says we are about two miles or so away. Is everything okay?"

"Juniper is in labor," replied Maryam.

"What if some of us left the wagon, so there's not so much weight on the mules and they can get her to town faster?" offered Blythe.

Mrs. Oxeye nodded. "Stop the cart!" Before the wheels completely stopped turning, Bane had jumped to the ground. He jogged to the side and started to lift Blythe's chair down.

"Rose," Maryam said to Bane's mother. "You stay with Juniper and Ash. Matthias and I will walk with Blythe and Bane, and we will find you once we get to town."

Blythe held on to her cane and Demi. She carefully crawled past Juniper, and her mother helped her down.

"Happy day!" yelled Ash in delight. "Your legs are working, Blythe. But you're still brave."

Blythe touched the boy's hair. "And you're brave, too; you be good for your mama. Soon you'll have a new brother or sister."

"You'll tell us *both* more stories later?"

"Promise." Blythe kissed her index finger and held it up. "Verimor, wrap Juniper and her baby-to-be in your arms." The rest of her family beside her made the same gesture.

Dust rolled in the air around them as the cart pulled away, mules braying. Blythe rested her head on her mother's shoulder. "Do you think the baby will be born by the time we catch up to them?"

"It's hard to say. Even when I went into labor, I didn't think Rowan was ever going to come out."

Baba laughed. "That stubborn streak of hers comes from you."

Blythe sat in her chair, and her baba grabbed the handles at the top to push.

"I was expecting hours and hours of labor again with you, but you were ready to meet us. Rowan talked to my belly all day, every day. I think you were ready to meet her most of all."

"We are so close to seeing Rowan again in person." Blythe smiled, her shoulders lifting. "I can't wait to wrap her in a hug, let her and Demi meet, and tell her all about Ash and the new baby."

"I'm sure she will have a lot to tell us about her time in the castle, too," Bane said.

The group made small talk as they continued moving forward on the dirt road. Blythe noticed other bands of travelers on foot and in wagons. One, pulled by a horse, slowed next to them after over ten minutes.

"You all leaving Aconite or Navigum?" asked the man with the reins. A woman, presumably his wife, sat next to him.

"Aconite," Blythe's father responded, moving to place himself between the wagon and his family. "And yourself?"

"Navigum. Figured further inland would be best in case the navy battle moves onto the coast," said the man. "I have a lame foot, so I wouldn't be worth much when it comes to fighting. But my boy—he'll be near the fighting when it happens."

"Keep him in prayer, will you?" asked the woman, her hands clasped in her lap. "Our Bert is a royal guard in the castle, so I'm not sure where he will be sent with everything happening."

"Of course, we will pray for his safety, as we will for all men entering combat," replied Maryam.

The woman on the wagon smiled, her brown eyes brightening. "Would you like a ride the rest of the way to Tulium—if that's where you all are headed? We have room in the back."

"We are stopping in Abelium first to see some family," explained Matthias.

"We can drop you off, can't we, Adam?" Adam pulled on the reins, and the horses stopped their leisurely walk.

"Should be room for you all and that chair. Mighty nice carpentry work. My brother's a carpenter himself."

"We are thankful to you both for your kindness," said Blythe.

With Bane's help, Baba got her chair loaded; and then they climbed into the wagon, which was larger than their own. However, the couple had loaded much of it with personal belongings, including a table and chairs; so the family had little more room than before.

Adam's wife, Lorraine, turned and talked with Maryam. Blythe stroked her pet hawk's feathers as the wagon moved forward at a much faster pace than the mules.

Blythe looked over the side of the wagon and watched as the forest lining the road began to thin. After half an hour, the forest faded away. She turned her neck and saw buildings coming into view.

"You can let us off here before you finish your journey," said Maryam. "You have been such a blessing to speak with, Lorraine."

The woman leaned over the front seat and clasped Maryam's hands. "You as well. I can never express how much our meeting has meant. Sometimes, we all need an unexpected friend, no?"

Unloaded and with a wave of farewell, Blythe and her companions watched Adam and Lorraine continue through the town. There were people, horses, and mules galore.

"More people left their homes than I first thought," said Bane.

Blythe's father walked up to a young man selling apples out of a bag. "We're looking for the family of Caleb and Juniper?"

"The Breen family," Blythe's mother added. "Those are her parents."

"Ah, yeah, Mr. and Mrs. Breen. Miss Juniper just came through by wagon not too long ago; she didn't look too good. Red in the face and all. If you go through the center of the square, take the second left. Their homestead is at the end of that road, past all the cottage clusters."

"Thank you," Matthias shook the boy's hand. Bane pushed Blythe's chair and fell in line behind Maryam, who followed her husband.

Blythe shivered. Though it was only midafternoon, the weather was much cooler than on the coast. She kept her eyes on the back of her mother's head, feeling nervous with people staring at her, even though she tried to tell herself that it was the chair drawing attention.

As they approached the cottages near the Breen home, a distant yell sounded.

"Do you think it's safe here?" Blythe questioned, pulling Demi close to her chest.

Her mom chuckled. "Sounds like we are getting close to Juniper. And she's close to meeting her child."

In their single-file line, Blythe's father knocked on the door of the last house. After a few minutes, Oak opened the door. "You made good time. Rose is with Juniper in the bedroom. Juniper's father will be home this evening, and her mother has Ash occupied in the backyard. Caleb and I are waiting in here." He stood back to let Matthias and the others enter.

Blythe took in the roomy space with wooden beams visible throughout the front room and kitchen.

"I'm going to see if Rose needs anything," said Maryam.

Blythe stood. "I want to help, too." She handed Demi to Bane, and he gave her the cane that was hanging on the back of her wheeled chair. Blythe followed her mother, who easily located the room based on Juniper's cries.

Maryam pulled open the door, and Rose looked up immediately. "Here, Blythe, you use this cloth and water to wipe her forehead, try to keep her cool. Maryam, have these linens ready. The baby will be here after a few more pushes."

Blythe sat on the large down bed next to Juniper. She dipped the cloth in a bowl of water, wrung it out, and gently wiped Juniper's face. The mother's lips were pursed, her forehead furrowed; and a vein in her temple stood out.

"Remember to breathe, Juniper. When you exhale, you're going to push," directed Bane's mother.

"It hurts. Even more than with Ash. I . . . I can't do this. I can't!" Juniper's breath was quick and erratic.

"You can, and you will," Maryam said authoritatively but not unkindly.

Blythe stilled the damp cloth on Juniper's head. She used her other hand to unfold Juniper's clenched fist and hold it in hers. "You can do this. Ash is waiting for you and his new sibling. Isn't he going to be such a wonderful big brother?" Juniper nodded. "And you will be a wonderful mother to them both," continued Blythe. "Breathe in. Good. Let it out and push."

As Blythe sat there, Juniper squeezed her hand until Blythe felt pins and needles in her skin; and then a baby began to cry.

"Congratulations, Juniper. It's a boy," said Rose. She wrapped the wailing infant in linen, and Maryam handed the bundle to his mother.

"He's beautiful, Juniper," said Blythe softly with tears in her eyes.

Juniper kissed her baby boy's head. She turned to Blythe. "Thank you for what you said. For not letting me give up."

"Somewhere along the way, I've learned that focusing on all the pain can be terrifying. Hurting can be debilitating in more ways than one. But even when the pain is the worst, it doesn't mean there isn't goodness in life, too."

"So wise for such a young girl," said Juniper. She turned to her boy. "Children are truly a reward."

"Blythe, why don't you go announce the good news and then check on Ash?" her mom suggested.

Blythe nodded. "I can do that." She stood, grabbing her cane that was leaning against a nearby table. "Does the baby have a name?"

"Nathaniel—our gift from Verimor."

"That he is." Blythe left the room, her legs cooperating with her fairly well. "Baby Nathaniel is here, and his mother is doing well," she announced, walking into the main living area.

Juniper's husband relaxed his shoulders, and the other men shook his hand in turn. Blythe navigated to the back door using her cane.

"Blythe! Grandma, I know her," yelled an excited Ash. He ran up to Blythe but stopped abruptly in front of her, eyeing her cane. "No walking wheels because you have the extra wooden leg?"

Blythe giggled. "Today, that's all I need."

Ash carefully grabbed Blythe's free hand. "I'll let you use my legs, too. That's one . . . two . . . three . . . four . . . five! Five legs. Grandma, we're walking with *five* legs!"

An older woman with streaks of gray in her golden blonde hair laughed. "I see your five legs coming at me. It's so kind of you both to be working together." She stood from a wide, wooden swing. "Ash has gone on and on about you, dear. He says you are a good storyteller."

"Not *good*. She's great! Blythe, show Grandma how great you are at stories," Ash demanded, gently tugging Blythe's arm.

Both Blythe and Grandma laughed. "You best wash up for dinner. Maybe your new friend will be up for sharing a story after we eat."

Ash's eyes brightened, and he jumped up and down. "I can't wait." Then the boy turned and ran toward the house.

"He's the sweetest," Blythe said.

"He is. But he's also the cause of half of this gray hair." The woman laughed. "Do you want to help me in the kitchen?"

"Yes, Miss . . . "

"Oh, just call me Grandma."

Blythe walked with Grandma into the house and followed the woman to her kitchen. They walked in, only to find the kitchen already full of willing hands and wonderful aromas.

"What in the name of Admiral Ocean is this?" asked Grandma.

"It seemed everyone had their hands full, so we decided to finish dinner," explained Caleb. "I found your pie crusts, so we went ahead and made meat pies." Blythe watched as her baba lifted a lid over the iron dish on a rack over the hearth warm with orange flames. Mr. Oxeye and his son were rolling out dough.

"And we are doing tangerine tarts for dessert," Mr. Oxeye said.

"Sweet as sugar, you three. Blythe and I will get the table set." Grandma opened a cabinet and pulled out a stack of clay-fired plates. She carried them to the wooden table, then placed a pile of forks on top. "Dear, you set the places. And we'll need to add a few more chairs here. Bane? Can you lend me your young muscles, please?"

Bane laughed, wiping his hands on a cloth. "It would be my pleasure."

Blythe sat in a chair after the table was set, and Ash climbed into the seat to her right. The door opened, and a new, gravelly voice called out, "My, my, I didn't know we were having a party, Gale."

Grandma went up to the man and kissed his cheek. "Why wouldn't we? You've got a second grandson, Harold."

"Juniper is here?" His eyes found Caleb. He clapped his back while embracing him. "Congratulations on your son."

"Caleb and his friends cooked tonight; so if you don't like it, blame them." She winked. "I'm going to take Juniper a plate, and I'll eat with her. Ash, you behave, and maybe Blythe will tell you a story."

Blythe's baba handed a tray with two plates with steaming slices of the pie, potatoes, carrots, and meat sliding out in a delightfully savory aroma to Grandma. She took it and left the room. Shortly after, Blythe and Mrs. Oxeye entered the kitchen.

"Father, this is Maryam and Rose. They helped Nathaniel enter this world safely," introduced Caleb.

"Happy day to you both." Harold sat back in his chair. "It's been some time since this little house had so many smiling faces. An old man can get used to this." Everyone picked a seat around the crowded table. Harold closed his eyes. "Verimor, thank You for Your provisions of new life and new friends."

Caleb served the pie.

"Smells better than Gale's, but you didn't hear that from me." Harold chuckled and slapped the corner of the table good-naturedly.

"Grandpa, Blythe told me a story earlier about a jelly snail. Have you ever seen a jelly snail? She also told a story about a girl who loved a horse and another story about a hawk who saved a boy from a snake. And did you know, Grandpa, that she has an extra wooden leg and walking wheels to move around?"

"Take a breath every once in a while, Ash," Caleb said before laughing broke out among everyone.

"Blythe, you seem to have made an impression on the little one," commented Mrs. Oxeye.

Blythe looked at Ash. "He's definitely made one on me. I miss telling stories to the children at the library."

"Well, I, for one, am looking forward to hearing a story from you. I'm probably more excited than Ash is," said Harold, his wrinkled eyes twinkling.

Blythe set down her fork. Even though she still had half a slice of pie on her plate, she was already full. "I can tell one now, if everyone would like to listen?"

"Yes!" Ash exclaimed. "Wait, where's your bird? She's got to listen, too. And Mama and the baby!"

"I think your mother and new brother are too tired to listen," said Bane. "But you should listen really well, so you can tell them the story tomorrow." He stood and walked to the front room, returning a few moments later with Demi in a small blanket.

"Can your bird sit in my lap?" asked Ash, moving to the floor by Blythe's feet.

"I think she will enjoy that," said Blythe. "Now, what tale shall I tell tonight?" She paused, though she had already selected the story in her mind earlier.

"Many years ago, there was a young woman named Dinah. Dinah helped her father and four brothers on their farm. But a period of drought resulted in difficult times.

"'Girl, what are you lazing around for?' snapped Dinah's father.

"'Baba, I just put a loaf of bread over the fire,' explained Dinah.

"'And I suppose you think because you got it going, you're going to eat it all yourself?' The man grunted. 'You're lucky I haven't kicked you out. I would save more coins if I didn't have to feed you. And I'm getting too old to look after someone who refuses to grow up. You're nobody, and nothing can change that.'

"Dinah bowed her head, saying nothing. She didn't want to provoke her father any further. Instead, she went to the well and refilled the water jugs before returning to the kitchen to remove the bread and let it cool.

"Hours later, Dinah walked through the nearby forest. Her stomach was gurgling in protest of only having a small, rationed piece of bread to eat. She was always exploring the woods and kept an eye out for edible berries or wild mushrooms she could take back home.

"One day, Dinah ventured further than she ever had before. To her delight, she found a bush filled with blueberries. She happily ate her fill while piling blueberries in her empty basket; and still the bush seemed untouched, so full it was with fruit.

"Hopeful that there was more fruit to find, Dinah continued to move deeper into the woods. To her surprise, the trees thinned. Her heart nearly leaped out of her chest when she saw a meadow full of orange marigolds. Tears brimmed her eyes at the sight; and without a moment of hesitation, Dinah walked into the field. She sat among the marigolds and soaked in their natural beauty, trying not to blink for fear the flowers would disappear.

"Wind picked up from nowhere, and orange and golden petals swirled into a thick cloud. Dinah held her arm over her eyes to brace against the forceful gale. When the sporadic gust settled, she put her arm down and found herself looking at a woman with a horn.

"'Dinah, I've been waiting for you,' said the woman.

"'Are you . . . a unicorn?' Dinah asked as her mouth fell open in surprise.

"The woman nodded. 'I am Cressida, a unicorn in service of the maker Verimor. He sends you a gift through a blessing to help King Liam and his son preserve their kingdom in his name.'

"'Me? But I'm just a . . . a *nobody*. Why would Verimor want to bless me?' Dinah was filled with disbelief. She pinched her arm to wake from the dream she momentarily wondered she was having.

"'You're a child of Verimor, and all of His children have purpose. You are *somebody* because you belong to Him.' Cressida picked up a marigold and brushed it over Dinah's face.

"Dinah blinked and found the world had changed. Everything was void of color. 'You have been blessed with Sight. It will allow you to see the true hearts of men and help steer Liam and Cillian in the path they need.'

"Dinah watched intently as Cressida picked a dozen or so marigolds. She pulled a ribbon from the bottom of her own braid and wrapped the stems together. 'Go to the king; and for three days, you each will steep one marigold. And for three days, you will each drink the tea before sunrise. This will strengthen the Sight to allow you to fully see into men's hearts, and it will grant Liam three dreams and the ability to interpret those dreams.'

"Dinah accepted the bouquet and Cressida's extended hand. Once on her feet, Dinah bowed her head. 'I'll give my all in serving Verimor.' She lifted her face and found herself alone in the meadow once again.

"Walking with the marigolds in hand, Dinah left the field. She walked past the flourishing blueberry bush and then found her well-worn walking path. Once on the main patch of dirt path outside of the woods, Dinah looked toward her home. She inhaled deeply. While exhaling, she turned the opposite direction— toward the home of the king.

"What happens next is another tale, but Dinah followed her calling and proved to herself she was indeed somebody. May her story remind you all that you are all somebody because you belong to Verimor."

Applause broke out. "How did you find all that out about Dinah and Sight?" asked Bane. "I didn't think the *Book of Verimor* was very detailed about that."

"The day we were in the cathedral and I got Demi, remember I went into the library while you continued to help in the aviary?" Blythe explained. "I went through some archives and pieced together some information, but I will admit I took some creative liberties like adding in the blueberry bush, drinking the tea, and some of the conversation. But I think some of that dialogue could have really happened."

Ash's head bobbed sleepily. "One more story, please?"

His father laughed. "I think it's time for bed for you, son. And you need to let Blythe get some rest, too."

Ash stood up, rubbing his eyes with one hand, Demi grasped in his other arm. "Blythe, you can sleep in my bed."

"I'll get you all some blankets. We've got enough to make pallets on the floor in the front room, but you young'uns may be more comfortable in the hayloft in the barn," said Harold, standing up and stretching his back.

Soon, Blythe found herself in a small bed next to a window. There were no curtains, so the stars smiled through. Placing Demi on the windowsill with a small piece of linen, Blythe leaned back on the down pillow. Ash crawled beside her, abandoning his blankets on the floor, without a word.

Gingerly rubbing the boy's arm, Blythe soon listened to his deeper breaths while he slept. She closed her eyes.

Beams of sunlight warmed Blythe's face and woke her. She turned her head and found small toes beside her on the pillow. Carefully, Blythe moved to a sitting position, but the movement woke Ash.

"Happy day, Blythe." He sat up and yawned. "Do you smell that? I think Grandma is making cranberry muffins!"

Blythe slowly moved to the side of the bed and stood. Her knees were achy, but she was overwhelmed with gratitude for having had a bed as opposed to the wooden wagon, the ground, or the hayloft. Ash quickly changed and washed his face in the room's water basin. He handed a cloth to Blythe before bouncing out of the room.

Blythe washed her face, rinsed her mouth, and used a comb sitting beside the bowl to brush through her tangled brown hair.

With her cane, she walked to the kitchen. Fresh muffins rested in the center of the table, but only Grandma could be seen as she scrubbed a pan.

"Happy day," greeted Blythe.

"Happy day, dear," replied Grandma. "Your folks are loading your wagon now; your father says you all are going to Tulium to see your sister. I think Rose and Oak are going to stay here. We don't have a local midwife or a healer, so she can do a lot of good. And Harold can always use more hands at the blacksmith shop. I hear Oak is a fast learner."

Blythe's nose crinkled. "Do you know if Bane is staying, too?"

"I think he talked with them about going on with you. Said he can't wait any longer than necessary to see Rowan."

Blythe nodded. "They're going to get married one day," she said matter-of-factly. "Rowan is going to be so happy to see him; and truthfully, it would be a bit strange for him not to finish the journey with us."

Grandma grunted a reply to Blythe's comment. "Go ahead and eat up. I've packed some food already; but if you'd like, I can throw in some more muffins."

Blythe bit into the buttery pastry. The cranberries were tart, but surprise chunks of chocolate balanced it with a sweeter taste. "I see why Ash was looking forward to breakfast today."

Grandma laughed. "That rascal grabbed one and ran directly outside to his grandpa. He likes helping with the goats when they visit." She sighed, wiping down a small counter. "All right, are you ready?"

Blythe went back and gently picked up Demi, feeding her some leftover berries and seeds that Grandma had. "We'll get you some dried meat soon, okay?" Using her cane, she joined everyone outside.

Her mother and Mrs. Oxeye were embraced in a tearful hug. Baba was shaking hands with Harold and Caleb in turn; the former held Ash on his hip.

"You will have to come back and visit Ash," said Juniper, walking up to Blythe. "He told me his version of your story from last night. I know someone drank tea made from a flower, and someone had very good eyes; but that's about all I could catch from his tale." Juniper laughed, rocking her small infant against her chest.

"I hope we won't be long in Tulium," Blythe said.

After rounds of goodbyes, Bane helped Blythe and Demi into the back of the wagon. Blythe's mother sat in the front beside her husband. The mules pulled forward, jerking the riders slightly. Blythe waved at Ash; and he waved back, until she could no longer see him on the horizon.

She looked at Bane who sat across from her. His face was impassive, and his shoulders were tense. "Do you want to talk about anything or just sit?"

The corner of Bane's mouth quirked up for a moment. "Meeting the Breens was great, but it's just strange—leaving my parents in a new town, going to the castle to see Rowan. So much has changed so fast."

Blythe nodded, her eyes moving to Demi as the bird hopped around the wagon investigating the space. "It feels strange, too. We left when we did to escape the outbreak of violence; but other

than passing other people fleeing, too, the last day feels like an unnatural reprieve. With war comes death. In a way, life as we knew it perished. But we witnessed a miracle with Nathaniel's birth, and Ash and the whole family just showed how much goodness there is in this world—even when wickedness rears its ugly head."

Bane lightly tapped his foot to Blythe's and smiled. "Maybe I would be as wise as you if I read more. Rowan would like that, I think."

"Rowan likes you just like you are." Blythe offered a smile in return.

Though the air was cool, the rays of the sun acted like a warm blanket. Blythe closed her eyes.

A sudden jolt woke her back up. She blinked. It was already dark, with stars out. Her stomach growled. She was lying on burlap sacks as a pillow.

"I didn't know if you were ever going to stop sleeping," Bane said. "I was about ready to find a frog to kiss you to wake you up."

Blythe giggled. "That's not how the stories go, and don't you dare put a frog anywhere near my face, please and thank you."

Bane handed Blythe a bundle wrapped in cheesecloth. "You wouldn't even budge for the midday meal. You've got to be hungry."

Blythe, stomach still growling, unwrapped the parcel and happily ate the cranberry muffin. There was also salted ham and cubes of cheese. She looked and saw a gate in front of the stopped wagon.

A guard with the Wisterian seal on his chest and sword on his hip yelled, "Open the gate."

The iron bars lifted up, and the wagon pulled forward once again.

Eating her food and sharing some with the small hawk, Blythe watched the road. The castle was large and looming. The closer they got, the more overwhelmed Blythe felt by the building's size.

They stopped at a second gate, narrower than the first. "Business?" asked a guard. Blythe's baba handed the invitation from Linnea over. "The Marigold Ball isn't for two more days."

"Yes, but our daughter is currently in Lady Linnea's care. Her name is Rowan," offered Blythe's mother.

The guard walked over to another guard, who turned to someone else. The third man, thin and gangly, took off running toward the castle. After several minutes, he returned, his chest heaving. He simply nodded to the other guards before bending over on his knees, trying to catch his breath. The iron grated as the gate was lifted.

Blythe was in true awe as she examined every inch of the view. Along a stone wall along the perimeter of the castle, there were hooked posts where lit lanterns hung. The light from the flames made the purple and pinks of the wisteria covering the wall sing with vibrance.

"It's beautiful," Blythe whispered. Her heart swelled with the sight. Soon she would have her arms around her sister.

Chapter Twenty-Eight
Revelation

"Happy day, Rowan." welcomed lady Linnea, already sitting at the dining table. "And to you, Oren."

"Happy day," they both said in unison as they took their seats.

Boisterous voices echoed through the room as King Isak and Diatomist Dendro entered through the wide entryway side by side.

"Greetings to all of you. Rowan, I trust your training with Oren has been constructive?" asked the diatomist as he pulled out his chair.

"Indeed, it has, sir," Oren replied. "Rowan is a quick learner, and it is apparent that she will play a central role in all of our futures."

While Oren spoke, Dendro's brow furrowed slightly, causing two distinct vertical lines in his forehead to appear. Rowan, aware the diatomist was watching her intently, offered, "Oren has devoted much time to helping me understand the Sight."

King Isak waved to a nearby servant, and several attendants served the first course of beef and cabbage stew. "Thanks to

Verimor for His unicorns, His blessings, and His provisions," said the king. "Mage Oren, I understand you have a demonstration of sorts you wish to present?"

"Are you dabbling in the theater in your free time?" quipped Lady Linnea.

Rowan's lips curved up in response.

Oren laughed. "I'm afraid I am a terrible actor. No, rather than distract with unnecessary entertainment, I will show you how powerful Rowan is. Then you can determine for yourselves how to move forward." He turned to a young boy holding a water pitcher. "Tell Bert to enter."

The boy disappeared into the servants' entry, and Bert stepped forward. Behind him was Hamlin, still in manacles.

Rowan saw both Dendro and Linnea visibly stiffen.

"I can't decide if this is going to be a comedy or a tragedy," Linnea said, tight-lipped.

"King Isak, did you approve this?" asked the diatomist.

The king nodded before taking a large drink from his goblet. Setting down the cup, he said, "The mage assures the change within our enemy is one we must witness firsthand. Plus, the man is shackled and guarded. And we all know Linnea can hold her own if chaos ensues."

Rowan looked at Hamlin, who moved easily from a straight posture to bended knee. There was no sign of physical pain or long-term ramifications from being poisoned. Between Hamlin and King Isak, Bert stood with his hand hovering over the hilt of the sword, eyes never wavering from his prisoner.

"Get on with it then," Dendro ordered. Rowan felt his eyes land on her. She glanced at him and immediately looked at the bowed head of Hamlin. Dendro's gaze felt cold, so unlike during their previous interactions.

Oren stood and began pacing behind his chair. "As previously theorized, the power of Sight—"

"*Blessing*," Dendro's raspy voice interjected.

"One and the same." Oren waved his hands as he spoke. "This *blessing* allows the target to be swayed. As you can see, Hamlin, former Obsilvian assassin, has now pledged his allegiance to the crown of Wisteria."

"Has he taken you for a fool?" asked Linnea. "Words of loyalty mean nothing without action, and his actions have not proved fidelity." Dendro grunted his agreement.

Oren clucked his tongue. "As you will see, these are not just pretty words of empty promise. He has information that will affect the tides of the brewing storm."

Rowan watched Oren's face alight as the king leaned forward in his seat. "Hamlin, share what you know."

"King Tramein of Obsilvia has two operations in motion to overthrow Wisteria without resistance. These were to move into motion whether or not the attempt on King Isak's life was successful. First, there are simultaneous assaults planned for both the mountainside and coast of your nation."

"Aconite," blurted Rowan. She turned, face ashen, to Lady Linnea. "Is my family safe?"

"Word arrived two days ago that some violence has broken out among the docks with rumors of a naval fleet arriving," the king shared in an even tone. Then his jaw clenched. "According to the local cleric, several Aconite citizens—including your family—left. Sir Elias has already issued armed troops to march and is working to get our own ships dispatched, but Aconite is most likely not the primary target."

"Correct, Tramein's general has targeted a city to Aconite's north," explained Hamlin, still in a monotone.

"The port housing our kingdom's armada is where we expected for Tramein to aim, and Wisteria has been making preparations in case he chose to act cowardly instead of first declaring war," said Linnea. "Like the king explained, we already know battle is knocking on our entryway. Sharing old news does not validate the mage's claim you are loyal to Wisteria."

Rowan's finger tapping did not help her think. Rather, she felt her chest tighten. The words surrounding the barely touched bowls of soup on the table made everything feel too real.

"In addition to the military campaigns, the Obsilvia court has issued a proclamation that any individual who can retrieve the unicorn-blessed girl and present her to the king will be titled and heavily financially compensated." Rowan's head spun as she registered Hamlin's words. She pushed back her chair, her steps unsteady.

"Fetch Thaddeus at once! Cassian, both of you will be Rowan's personal guards moving forward." The king's voice sounded distant as Rowan felt her blood rushing in her ears.

Oren put his hands on Hamlin's rounded shoulders and then motioned for him to stand. "Hamlin is no longer protecting Obsilvia's interests but is looking out for you, King Isak."

Dendro sputtered, "Or is he looking out for his own self-interest? Boy," he said to Oren, "you look at him. Use your training—does the darkness emanating from him not worry you?"

"What concerns me," Linnea interposed, her voice cold and cutting, "is that Hamlin knows of an Obsilvia proclamation, though he has been a prisoner since Rowan's blessing was known. Pray tell, how did Tramein learn of her Sight, and how did *you* learn of his desire to kidnap Rowan?"

"Not all in your castle are loyal," Hamlin said.

"Oren, do you know of this?" Dendro stood.

"I need names now," the king ordered.

Hamlin took a breath; his eyes flitted to Bert. The guard drew his sword; and he held it over his head, ready to strike. Rowan's scream intermixed with other voices.

Bert swung; but instead of hitting flesh, he hit the iron chain of Hamlin's shackles as the prisoner tried to shield himself.

"Ahh," roared a deep voice, and a flash of silver knocked Bert's blade from his hands. "I knew you were not to be trusted," Thaddeus said before pricking the skin of Bert's neck with his own rapier.

"Rowan, return to your room at once," Linnea ordered. Rowan immediately stood and tore away from the chaos, tripping over her own feet as she used the door opposite the main entryway and the servant's door.

She walked down the hall, turned, and continued to the main staircase. As she crossed the last step of the first flight, her breathing became erratic. Rowan slipped to the ground, one hand on her chest and the other on a wooden guardrail.

"Rowan? It's okay." Oren's strong voice did nothing to soothe Rowan. He knelt beside her. "I would have warned you. No, I would have kept you from that dinner entirely if I had known what was going to happen." He pushed a fallen lock of hair behind her ear. Goosebumps flooded Rowan's arms despite feeling too warm for comfort.

She closed her eyes and pictured her mother. Breathing in through her nose and out through her mouth, Rowan steadied herself. Tears pooled. "The idea of violence, of war . . . it all feels like a foreign concept. But to see that . . . Bert's betrayal? Swords meant to maim or *kill*?" She shuddered.

Oren took her hands and helped her to her feet. "I understand it's difficult to have witnessed that, but you are so strong. And I'll help you stay strong because this will get more chaotic before it gets better."

Rowan shook her head, clenching her fists. "Oren, those inky shadows . . . "

"Together, we can determine how history will one day be written. Your Sight, my shadows. Together we will defeat all enemies and have unconquerable power."

"I don't want power." Rowan bit her quivering bottom lip.

"The power will help you save Blythe. Didn't you see Hamlin was physically cured? *You* did that." Oren kissed the back of her hand.

"The black shadows in the shatterings—that can't be the answer. I—"

"Shh." Oren intertwined his fingers with Rowan's. "Your power is new. Don't let doubt overwhelm your senses and lead you astray."

He stepped behind her, pulling what hair was left down in her half-up style off of her neck. "I'm giving you this gift as a symbol of my commitment to us and all that we can have."

Rowan blinked, and a new necklace was layered over her piece from Bane. "Oren . . . "

"I can see you're overwhelmed, and I understand. But I'm looking forward to announcing our betrothal at the Marigold Ball and for what our future holds." He leaned forward.

Rowan quickly turned her head. "No, Oren," she stated firmly. "My heart belongs to another."

Oren's lips landed on her cheek before she could move away.

His pale green eyes shone menacingly as he smirked. "You'll realize your true feelings soon enough."

Rowan was frozen as she processed the disregard Oren had for her autonomy—her ability to decide and declare what she felt, what she wanted—as the apprentice went down the stairs.

A monsoon of tears escaped Rowan. She went up the final level of stairs before turning to the wing which held her room. Once her door was closed, she leaned all of her body weight against it. Rowan saw her gray reflection in the large vanity mirror. The gemstone on Oren's true-knot shimmered frosty green like the mage's eyes.

Her head pounded. She grasped Oren's necklace and pulled. The chain easily snapped, and she let it fall to the floor.

The throbbing pain in her head was so deafening, it felt as though she could actually hear it.

"Rowan?" Linnea's familiar voice called from the hall. "Are you all right?"

Inhaling shakily, one hand on her temple, Rowan opened the door. The lady handed Rowan a steaming cup. "Drink this. I thought a hot tea with cinnamon and honey would be welcome. I'll get Nora to bring some ginger tea later." She motioned to Rowan's hand on her head. "May I come in for a moment?"

Rowan nodded and stepped into the room. A small crunch caused her to turn around. Lady Linnea had stepped on the necklace she dropped. "I do apologize," she said, bending down. "But it does appear only slightly scuffed."

"I don't want it," Rowan crossed her arms over her waist. She sat on a velvet chair in front of the room's fireplace.

Linnea sat in the other chair, a small side table between them. "A true-knot. I'm assuming an unwanted suitor?"

Rowan twisted her jewel from Bane as it hung on her neck. "He just assumed I wanted to say yes to his proposal. He doesn't care about what I think or who I really am. He thinks he can mince words and make me into who he wants me to be." She took a deep breath, choking on a sob. "What if I don't get the chance to see Bane again and tell him how I truly feel about him? And what if the war prevents me from saving Blythe—let alone seeing her one last time?"

Rowan's shoulders hunched, and her face fell into her palms. She shook with each and every wail that escaped her.

Lady Linnea sat on the arm of Rowan's chair and stroked her back. When Rowan's sobs softened, Linnea asked, "Is Oren the one who gave you the necklace?"

Rowan lifted her head, the skin around her eyes already swollen, and nodded.

"I think you are wise to recognize how his treatment toward you is not acceptable. And I must confess, after all that transpired at dinner, I question the apprentice's own loyalty. I fear Bert is not the only betrayer still in our midst."

Rowan's tears halted. Her nose crinkled in thought. "You think Oren would betray Wisteria? He's a mage, the royal diatomist's apprentice. And he must be a follower of Verimor, or else he couldn't perform diatomy."

Rowan heard the sharp inhale of Linnea's breath. "Dendro has had a fondness of Oren for years, even before he took the boy as his apprentice. But even he is wary after the show with Hamlin." She shook her head. "Thaddeus and Cassian will be outside your room and will escort you around the castle moving forward. Until I can determine all parties' loyalty, you will not be alone with Oren again. Understood?"

With a nod, Rowan wrapped her arms around Lady Linnea, who returned the hug.

A knock sounded at the door. "Rowan? I know it's late, but you have guests. I didn't think you would want to wait." Nora opened the door as Rowan stood.

Speechless, Rowan ran to the hallway to embrace Blythe and her parents.

Chapter Twenty-Nine
Hearts Unveiled

BLYTHE DIDN'T WANT THE HUG to break but did not protest when Rowan pulled away. Blythe's chest constricted seeing Rowan's puffy face and red, swollen eyelids. She surmised her older sister had been crying for some time.

"I don't have the words to say how happy I am to see you all," said Rowan.

"Rowan," said Nora. "If your parents would like, I can show them their rooms. Then I can help your friend. Your sister is welcome to stay with you, or—"

"Yes!" Blythe and Rowan blurted simultaneously before laughter bubbled over, the sort of laughter that is intensified by fatigue.

"You have to tell me all about your journey. And that chair. And that bird!" said Rowan, her voice overcoming giggles. Blythe's parents gave her and Rowan a kiss on the cheek and a hug in turn.

"And I will take my leave as well for your reunion," said Lady Linnea with a polite curtsy. Blythe rolled herself into the room and tried to give Rowan and the loitering Bane some space, too.

Blythe watched as Rowan played with her true-knot necklace. "I'm glad you are here, Bane."

The muscle in Bane's jaw clenched. "You don't have to wear the necklace I gave you. I saw you with the diatomist on the stairs. You two seem . . . close."

Blythe bit her bottom lip and let her eyes focus on the fire across from her rather than look at Bane and Rowan.

"What? No, that . . . we're not. I mean he tried to kiss me, but . . ."

Despite her best efforts to give the two of them privacy, Blythe couldn't help looking over her shoulder. Bane had taken a step back as if physically pushed. Rowan stepped after him and wrapped her arms around his neck, sobbing into his shoulder. Bane didn't hesitate to return Rowan's embrace. He gently rubbed his hand up and down her back between her shoulders.

"I . . . " Rowan hiccuped between words. "I don't want to be pursued by any suitor but you, Bane Oxeye. Oren, the mage, showed me what I don't want, what I don't need. I need someone who makes me better, who flames the light in me, not tries to darken it."

Bane put a hand under Rowan's chin. He kissed her forehead. "As long as you'll have me, I'm yours. You and your sister get some rest, and I'll see you first thing in the morning."

Rowan hugged him tightly once more and then stepped away. Nora cleared her throat, standing in the hallway behind Bane. He looked once more at Rowan before turning and following the maidservant.

Blythe watched as Rowan leaned out of the doorway and watched the pair walk away for a moment before closing the door. Blythe smiled at her sister, who walked over to her. "Nora will be back, and she'll want to run you a bath. You will love it with the hot water and all the lovely oils and soaps. But while we wait, do you want some tea? Lady Linnea had a kettle and cups brought up. It's cinnamon and honey."

"That sounds lovely." Blythe stood out of her chair and walked the few steps to one of the chairs directly in front of the fireplace. Demi squawked, and Blythe put her down.

"Oh, there are castle cats, so watch out for them roaming around." Rowan's nose crinkled slightly.

"Thank you for the warning. Demi can't fly, so I'll definitely have to be vigilant." Blythe's voice held a bit of shaky worry.

"The cats are usually outside unless they wander into Lady Linnea's wing." Rowan sighed contentedly after taking a sip of tea. "I've learned that the Sight allows me to see people's souls and what's in their hearts—their emotions, memories, and what makes them who they are. Oren, the royal diatomist's apprentice . . . " Her voice caught. "He wants me to pool darkness into the shattering— the broken parts within people. He said that the only way to heal you was to use my Sight and his power together. I feel torn because I've seen the shadows heal a little girl. You deserve to be healed, too. I'm going to do whatever it takes, Blythe."

"Rowan, it's all right—"

"It's not fair for you to keep hurting and suffering. You deserve a chance to live like everyone else," Rowan continued.

Blythe's hands tightened on her teacup. "But—"

"I know I failed you to not have a cure right now to give you. I promise, I'm not giving up on you. I will find a way to fix you, fix everything—"

"Do you see me as so broken that I'm not worthy to have a life, even if it looks different than most?" Blythe felt her nostrils flare, and hot tears rolled down her face. The tears amplified when she caught sight of her sister's own tears pooling.

"Blythe, I'm doing this for you. Why are you getting so mad?" Rowan clenched her hands into fists. "Don't you want life to be normal again?"

"I think you mean me. Just say you want *me* to be normal, Rowan!"

Rowan stood and placed her hands on her hips as her voice raised. "What's wrong with that, hmm? I'll do anything for you. Don't you see that? I can go back to Oren, figure out where I've gone wrong, so you can walk and be like you were before."

"Stop! You're becoming obsessed—like finding a cure is the only thing that matters anymore!" The teacup and saucer shattered on the floor as Blythe threw them beside her.

The door flew open. "Are you two all right?" Thaddeus and Cassian barged in the room.

Blythe rubbed her sleeve across her nose. "Can one of you help me find my parents?" Hiccupping through sobs, Blythe pushed against the wooden wheels and propelled herself to the doorway. Without looking at her sister, Blythe said, "I . . . I didn't know you loved me with conditions."

Chapter Thirty
The Marigold Ball

"I DON'T THINK I COULD be royalty. All this fuss is overwhelming," Blythe said, as one maidservant rubbed scented oils into her hand, another pinned pearls into her hair, and a different woman made final touches on the hem of her gown. "Not that I'm not appreciative of you all," she quickly added, her face reddening.

Nora, who was adding silver pins that looked like sprigs of baby's breath to Rowan's hair, laughed. "No offense taken, but I have to disagree. I would love all the fuss and to be pampered and attend the Marigold Ball as a guest." She sighed, seemingly lost to a daydream.

"I'm thrilled to be going to the ball, but Blythe's right. All of this is very different from what we are used to," explained Rowan. Her shoulders were tense. She and Blythe hadn't spoken about their argument.

Rowan stood, glancing at her reflection in the full-length mirror opposite. Everything was gray, but that didn't take away from how Rowan felt. "It is something to look like a princess," she said, pulling her shoulders back and reaching up to lightly touch the curls on her shoulder.

Blythe looked at Rowan. "You truly look like a beautiful princess." Without asking, she described the dress. "Your dress is a deep, burned orange down the middle, with the color widening as it touches the hemline. The outer portion, including the bell sleeves and cinched waist, is golden yellow with swirls of sparkling satin that mimics the stars. The bottom is flared and rounded from the small hoop and tulle underneath, but you can see that."

With assistance from one of the maidservants, Blythe stood beside her sister. "My dress is a burgundy damask in the center with a black petticoat that has lightweight flowing sleeves." She smoothed the front with her hands. She did not wear a hoop or extra tulle; so the fabric gracefully hung straight, the hem a handbreadth from the floor. "I think Mrs. Myrtle would approve of this, other than the fact it isn't hers."

"Myrtle of Aconite?" asked Nora. "She sent these for you two. We have good seamstresses but only so many hours in a day. We wouldn't have been able to get your dress finished in time, Blythe. And truthfully, though Lady Linnea put in a request for Rowan, her dress wasn't finished in time either."

"How in the world did Mama and Baba afford these?" Rowan asked, her fingertips hitting her thumbs in quick succession.

Blythe put a hand to her heart. "How in the whole Admiral Ocean did she get these finished and sent here with everything going on?" She turned to her sister. "Mrs. Myrtle was giving us the dresses to wear to the Marigold Ball in exchange for letting everyone know she was the seamstress who designed and sewed them."

"That is so generous of her." Rowan's face fell.

"What's wrong?"

"What you said. There's so much going on, so much brewing within the kingdom—within the *castle,* even. But we're about to go to a ball in these extravagant—though admittedly beautiful—gowns? Is it not strange to attend a celebratory event when war knocks?"

Blythe reached for her sister but then dropped her hand back to her side. "Diatomist Dendro said last night that threats of darkness do not cancel the light of this holy season."

"Besides," Nora interjected, "what's the point of sulking around when there's nothing we can do about the fighting?"

"I heard the enemy was pushed back from the coast and has retreated to the Dimidi Isles in the sea," added another maidservant. "That's one reason to celebrate tonight."

Rowan audibly exhaled, and her shoulders relaxed some.

"I like the royal diatomist," Blythe added. "I can't thank Diatomist Dendro enough for finding Demi a safe place in the royal aviary for tonight. Though it is a little strange. I've had her for just a short time, but it feels like I'm missing a part of me not having her right here with me."

Nora opened the door for the girls to exit one behind the other. Before Rowan crossed the threshold, she went over and picked Oren's necklace off the tabletop by the fireplace. She held it firmly in one fist as she turned around.

"Oh!" Rowan clutched her chest, her palm resting on her necklace from Bane around her neck. Her heart thumped rapidly in her chest. "Sir Thaddeus, I apologize. Even after all this time with Cassian and now you always in the room or outside the door, I have not grown used to having guards."

The knight's eyes crinkled, revealing many smile lines. "I don't know that Lady Linnea will be too happy if I give you a heart attack when I'm trying to keep you safe." His laugh was jubilant as he upturned his head and slapped at a raised knee.

Rowan giggled at the man who reminded her much of Bane's father. The thought of Bane did not slow down her racing heart, and butterflies fluttered in her stomach.

Thaddeus fell behind as the girls walked to the main stairs. At the top, Rowan turned. The guard extended a gloved hand to Blythe. "Would you like me to carry you down?"

Blythe blushed, but she nodded. "Yes, if it's not too much trouble." Rowan said nothing, but her gaze flickered to the ceiling. Annoyance crept along her heart because Blythe didn't want her help to be better.

Within minutes, the trio were on the main floor. Bane stood with Blythe's chair. His eyes widened. Rowan soaked every visible part of him in her vision. Even though his hair was slicked back with oil, the white streak which ran through the bangs of his black hair was still visible. He had a dark doublet with an intricate pattern behind buttons that shone.

Bane walked up to Rowan, and her pounding heart froze. "You're an image from a fairy tale."

Rowan playfully pushed his shoulder. "Did you read that book?"

Bane smiled. "Admittedly? No. You're too distracting for me to focus on fiction." He cleared his throat. "The gold design on my shirt matches the pattern in your dress."

"Hopefully, everyone knows we're a pair," Rowan said, interloping her hand through Bane's arm. She moved the necklace she was holding into her other palm.

"What's that?"

"Something I need to return."

Bane nodded.

Blythe rolled herself forward. "Are you two lovebirds ready?"

"Let's go to our first royal ball," Rowan declared.

Bane went to push Blythe's chair, but she waved a hand. "I want to enter myself, but I will be sure to let you know if I need help later."

Marigolds and flowers of all kinds covered the hallway from the front entrance to the stairs and to every corner that could be seen. Servants carried trays of appetizing, bite-sized morsels to be enjoyed before dinner. People in colorful gowns and doublets were scattered around.

Crossing into the entry for the ballroom, the sight—even in grayscale—was awe-inspiring. Wisteria vines wrapped around the rails of the staircase on the opposite side of the room, leading to a second tier where some guests mingled near the orchestra.

People were everywhere. Some stood by tables partaking in refreshments, while others were on the dance floor enjoying a line dance. The noise of multiple conversations and music was almost overwhelming for Rowan. She felt her chest constricting. Bane held her hand, leading her from the threshold to an open space against the wall where the dance floor could be easily observed.

"Everyone seems to be enjoying themselves," Blythe said as she joined them. Her light voice calmed Rowan somewhat. She thought absently how even when angry with her sister, Rowan knew Blythe was always there for her.

Rowan's eyes scanned the crowd of people. It did not take long before she found the green eyes of Oren, his colored form attracting her attention like a moth to a flame. She looked up at Bane. "Will you stay near me while I return this?" She motioned to her hand with a nod of her head.

Bane placed a gentle hand on the small of her back. As Rowan got closer to Oren, Bane's touch fell away.

"Oren, I'm glad to see you," Rowan said, extending her enclosed fist forward.

"I'm surprised because it seems you've been avoiding me." Oren went to hold her hand, but Rowan deposited the green-gemmed betrothal necklace in his palm. He clenched his fingers around the jewel and chain, and his jawline grew taut and his shoulders stiff. "You're making a mistake. More than one," he added, his gaze flitting briefly behind her.

Rowan offered a small smile. "I'm not. I hope one day, you see that." She turned and linked elbows with Bane, who stood only a few paces away.

"Are you okay?" he asked.

She looked back at Oren. All his color receded. She started to let questions run through her mind but shook her head. Rowan looked at Bane, her grin reaching her magenta eyes and revealing the dimple on the left side of her face. "I will be once you ask me to dance."

"You better not step on my toes," Bane teased, his eyebrows wiggling.

"I'll be leading; so as long as you follow, it shouldn't be a problem."

"If my toes you do break, then . . . "

Rowan stood on her tiptoes and planted a kiss on Bane's cheek. "No bitter teas or gross tomatoes or thoughts of broken promises." She giggled, adding, "Or toes."

Bane's entire face turned scarlet, while a giant grin spread across his face. He nodded and took Rowan to join the *carole*—the circle dance—on the ballroom floor.

As they caught their breath after the song concluded, a new chord began on a viola. The music was slower paced this time, and Rowan put her hands on Bane's shoulders while he gingerly put his hands on her waist.

"Is it strange my eyes are different than before?" Rowan asked.

"The color is different, but I wouldn't say it's strange. Behind your eyes, I still see you."

Rowan's gaze dropped to Bane's chest; the grayscale swirls were so vivid and close. She let her eyes wander once again; and she landed on Blythe, who was talking to Steffie and another girl Rowan didn't recognize. "Do you think Blythe wants to dance?"

"She seems content," Bane observed. "But you'll have to ask her how she's feeling."

"Let's go find out." Pulling Bane behind her, Rowan left the dance floor and walked over to her sister and friend. "Happy day, Steffie. I see you've met my sister, Blythe."

"Rowan, you didn't tell me how delightful your sister is. She's read more than me, and I think we could talk about books for hours," said Steffie. "This is my sister, Rose."

"Nice to meet you." Rowan gave a small curtsy.

"The pleasure is mine," said Rose, returning the gesture.

"Blythe, would like to dance with me?" Rowan asked.

Blythe's brown eyes widened, and her lips quirked. "I would love to, but I don't think I'll be able to keep up with my knees today. But I'll still have a good time here, watching."

"What if you didn't have to leave your chair?" Rowan raised one eyebrow.

"I . . . I don't know how that would work." Her younger sister tilted her head and wrinkled her nose, contemplating. "It's an intriguing idea, but I don't know how I will steer myself to keep up with the music."

"I'll lead. I'm great at it; just ask Bane!" Rowan pushed Blythe's chair to the dance floor as the slow tempo song faded out.

Several people stared, and quite a few retreated from the arena. After a seemingly long pause with no music, Rowan began stepping to a quicker paced dance. Bane stepped forward as if he was Blythe's next partner in a circle dance.

The orchestra started playing, and people on the perimeter began to clap. Others joined in the dance. Rowan's smile beamed as she saw Blythe being spun around on the backs of her chairs' wheels all while laughing. Rowan imagined Blythe had a shimmering light around her; she exuded so much happiness.

A sharp outro with flutes and cellos signaled the end of the dance. Applause erupted, and Rowan found Bane near Blythe. A small group had stopped and were talking to Blythe about her chair.

"I'll go get some water for you and Blythe," said Bane.

"Thank you," Rowan replied, her cheeks flushed from the fast-paced dancing. She moved up to her sister as the group departed.

"What a delight, that girl!" said a middle-aged woman as she passed Rowan. "And that chair. I think Tululah's boy would benefit from one, don't you, Albert?"

"Oh, Rowan, that was the most fun I've had in such a long time!" Blythe said, extending her hands to hold her sister's.

"I'm so glad." Rowan kissed her sister's hands and then helped guide the chair to a spot near the wall. She couldn't help adding, "And just think how much fun you will have when you never have to use that chair again."

"What . . . " Blythe snatched her hands away from Rowan.

A loud clang echoed through the large ballroom, causing conversations to fall silent. Rowan looked and saw a large cymbal on the balcony near the orchestra. "Presenting King Isak, leader of Wisteria with Verimor's blessing," announced the man next to the cymbal.

Rowan joined in the round of applause as the king, with a simple gold crown on his head, waved from the center of the second floor, a balcony on either side of him. Lady Linnea, Diatomist Dendro, Oren, and a guard stood in the background behind him. "Welcome, guests from near and far as we begin this festival season tonight. Though times have been tense, let us soak in the warmth of the marigolds and wisteria around us. And let each petal remind us of both unicorns and their guarding guidance, as well as Verimor's promise of continued grace. Let's raise our glasses to thank our Maker for providing us with means to be victorious over our enemy, and—"

A woman's scream drowned out the king's words. Sounds of iron clashing against itself rang out as the scuffling ensued, and it took Rowan several seconds to comprehend the scene around her.

A silver tray oscillated on the floor in front of the staircase, and shards of broken crystal lay on the floor. Rowan's gaze moved up the stairs. Hamlin stood in the balcony on the opposite side of the orchestra. But he was not the same man she had previously seen. Dark shadows swam across the whites of his eyes; black veins bulged across the skin of his neck and face as he held a knife to Lady Linnea's throat.

Two men in attire of Wisterian knights held swords pointed toward where the king and his entourage stood. Like Hamlin, shadows infiltrated both their eyes and their veins. Across the ballroom, knights turned on their fellow Wisterian brothers-in-arms, revealing how deeply rooted the treachery within the castle was.

"Unhand the lady at once," the king demanded. He turned on Oren, his growling voice carrying over the silent ballroom. "You said he is a simple pawn. Control him!"

Oren stepped forward. One of the armed guards still by the king moved against Oren, his blade raised for an attack. At the same time, Oren used swift movements to remove his opponent's weapon and then jabbed it into the man's stomach.

Rowan covered her mouth with her hand as bile bubbled in her stomach. Screams echoed around the ballroom as the guests stampeded toward the exit. Additional knights tried to make their way through the chaos to climb the stairs but were pushed back. She watched as Dendro put his hands to the floor. The ground rumbled; and the stones below cracked, throwing occupants on the balcony off balance.

"We should leave," Bane called to her. His voice seemed to come from a long way away as though he were speaking underwater.

"No! We have to do something." If Bane replied, Rowan didn't hear. She watched, mouth agape, as Oren fell into the grasp of the other traitorous guard next to the king. Dendro, on the ground, could be seen gasping for air, a sword hilt sticking out of his chest.

Hamlin let out a guttural growl. "Long live King Tramein of Obsilvia! If you want your sister returned alive, you'll meet his demands, *King* Isak." He spat on the ground.

Rowan fell to her knees and threw her arms over her head as stained glass fell like rain—Hamlin, Lady Linnea, Oren, and the traitor were all gone. Cold winter wind howled through the newly broken window. Only the darkness of the night looked in the ballroom.

The bitter chill broke her from her state of immobility. She rushed forward and raced up the stairs. She knelt over Dendro, his face pale and sweaty. "Hold on, we'll get you a healer."

"Rowan," the old man's words came out grated and shaky. "The . . . Sight. Find their . . . souls . . . find them." He wheezed.

"Don't talk," Rowan whispered. She turned slightly and yelled over her shoulder, "A healer! Get a healer, now!" When she faced Dendro again, she noticed that his breaths were shallower.

"Listen . . . " he rasped. "Souls . . . unique . . . only way." His mouth went slack, and his chest ceased to rise and fall.

Rowan wrapped her arms around herself. In the distance, she could make out the yells from the king, the Wisterian soldiers, and the crowd. She sat motionless. The world blurred as tears filled her eyes.

"Unicorn-blessed!" Hearing those words, Rowan stood and fumbled to the top of the staircase. She shrieked when she saw Blythe held in the air by her upper arm. A knight she did not recognize had her younger sister in his grip, not caring that the girl was trembling and sobbing in terror. "I know you don't want your sister harmed. Surrender yourself and come willingly to Obsilvia, or"—he pulled his sword from his sheath—"she dies."

"No," Rowan rushed forward. In her hurry, she tripped and rolled down several steps. She stopped after the fifth step down as she slammed into two fighting knights. Pain throbbed in her jaw and chest from hitting the marble steps. Rowan fought to catch her breath. She pushed herself up, although her legs were unsteady and her heart raced at an uncontrollable speed. "Don't hurt her! You can have me!" Habitually, her fingers found her necklace, and she rubbed the gem inside the true-knot. The stone felt cracked, but she didn't look at it.

Most of the guests had evacuated, but some had joined the fighting. Even the violent chaos was thinning with guards falling maimed or killed. The dwindling numbers surrounding the man who held a sword too close to Blythe's neck made Rowan believe several of the traitorous knights working against Wisteria had retreated.

Rowan didn't pull her eyes away from the knight or her sister. "Let her go."

A smirk graced the man's face as he pushed his helmet open. He threw Blythe hard on the floor between him and Rowan.

"Blythe!" Rowan rushed forward. She reached for her sister, but the knight's heavy hand grabbed her. "Let me make sure she's okay."

"She won't be." Dragging Rowan as if she were a doll, the man raised his sword. "Where is your Verimor now?"

Rowan fought with all her strength to get in front of the man. Something warm splashed across her face. She screamed, only to find herself staring at Cassian. He stood behind the man who'd tried to capture her. The enemy knight's head sagged sideways at an awkward angle. His grip loosened, and he slumped to the ground. Rowan rubbed her arm across her cheek. She felt a nauseous knot in her stomach as she saw the dark stain on the fabric of her sleeve. Was that . . . *blood*? Ignoring the fear continuing to fester inside her, Rowan turned to face her sister.

"Watch out!" Blythe yelled.

Cassian turned and blocked a sword behind him.

Rowan took advantage of the moment to sprint over to her sister. "Are you okay?"

"Yes. Have you seen Bane?" Blythe accepted Rowan's help to stand. Rowan shook her head. "Oh, there he is!"

Rowan followed Blythe's finger. Bane joined Cassian in fending off an enemy. "We need to get out . . . "

The ground shook. Fire seemed to explode from everywhere. Rowan's ears rang. Smoke filled her lungs as she pushed herself up to a seated position. She wondered if there were any diatomists who had joined the knights who betrayed Wisteria. Exactly how deep did the poisonous treachery reach?

"Blythe?" Rowan saw her sister lying unmoving a few paces from her. "What did you do? No, no, no!" Rowan crawled to Blythe's side, rolling her sister onto her back. "Blythe? Blythe, do you hear me?"

Blythe did not respond, and an ashy pallor spread over her features. Rowan choked on her sobs. "I should have told you I'm sorry. I don't love you with conditions." She stammered, "B . . . Blythe?" She wrapped her arms around her sister's prone form, burying herself into Blythe's neck. "How am I supposed to live without you?"

"You . . . you don't have to." Blythe coughed, and her eyes fluttered open.

Rowan's hands flew to her mouth as she suppressed the impulse to reach out and hug her sister tightly and never let her go. But she didn't want to hurt her sister if Blythe was injured. Instead, she released her grip on Blythe and knelt, touching her cheek gently, careful to avoid a burn on her sister's forehead. "Are you really okay?"

"Let's go!" Bane emerged from the smoke-filled atmosphere with Cassian behind him. "You all need to stay here for now. We need to make sure there's not an active threat elsewhere on the grounds."

He joined Rowan in helping support Blythe as she rose shakily to her feet. She hissed, sucking in her breath and collapsing into Rowan's arms. "My leg hurts so bad," Blythe said.

"It's going to be okay . . ." Rowan's attempt at comfort trailed off as she looked down at her sister's leg. Severe burns ran across the lower half of Blythe's calf. A sob constricted Rowan's throat, and she cradled her younger sister's head against her shoulder. Tears fell from both girls, mingling together and leaving splattered spots on Rowan's dress. One of her tears hit the cracked gem within her true-knot. A curious warm sensation spread across her chest. With one arm still around Blythe, Rowan stole a glance at the true-knot necklace dangling around her neck. It vibrated and glowed as she wrapped her fingers around it. Her hand grew warm as she clutched the necklace tighter. A golden light seeped through her fingers. A sound, like a bird's call, echoed high above their heads.

Rowan opened her hand, letting the necklace fall back against her dress. A flash of light burst from the broken gemstone and encompassed Blythe's burns. Blythe gasped. Rowan's eye widened. The skin, though marked by ash, was unmarked when the light dissipated. Rowan reached out her hand as her gaze moved to her sister's face. "Blythe . . . your hair . . . "

Blythe turned from Rowan to Bane. "What? What's wrong?"

Bane's eyes grew large like Rowan's. "It's . . . different now. It's bright red."

Rowan touched a strand of hair that framed Blythe's face. "Except for this piece."

Bane tilted his head. "Does that mean you've been blessed, too, Blythe?"

Blythe slowly reached up to brush the lighter piece of hair behind her ear. She dropped her arm, and white flames fanned from her fingers toward her sister. She jerked back, pulling away from Rowan. "I didn't hurt you, did I?"

Although Rowan was just as startled as Blythe, she was quick to reassure her sister. Shaking her head, she said, "No . . . and it seems that we have our answer."

"Please listen," Rowan pleaded as the king leaned with clenched fists over a table. On it lay a map of the kingdom.

"Diatomist Dendro told me—"

King Isak slammed his palms against the table, pushing it back an inch or so. "Dendro is dead, and I don't have time to listen to a child with half of a plan." Rowan visibly bristled at the king's harsh words. "I'm your king, and I order you to leave at once."

Rowan fled the room. Thaddeus went to follow, but the king's voice made him stop. "You're with me for now, Thaddeus. Cassian, watch her."

"He won't listen," said Rowan to Bane and Blythe, who were outside the room. "I know my Sight can help in some way." She pulled her palms down her face. "But I don't know how to use it to find them."

"The Sight allows you to see a person's heart, right?" questioned Blythe as she leaned on her cane for support. When her sister nodded, she continued. "Does everyone's soul look the same?"

Rowan's nose scrunched up. "Everyone's soul is a mix of gray and white." She put her hand to her chin, looking from Blythe to Bane and back again. "But now that I'm thinking about it, each one I've looked at is different—distinctive to each person. And Dendro . . . his final words to me were that I needed to find them and that they were unique."

Blythe's brightened face reflected Rowan's. "So that means there's a way for you to find a person based on knowing what their soul looks like. Try closing your eyes and searching for Lady Linnea's soul."

Rowan chewed on her bottom lip. Closing her eyes, she focused her mind to recall that first training session. She envisioned the gray and the black shadows with minimal swirls of white. A strange sensation of rushing wind settled over her limbs as her mind flashed past dozens and dozens of people's grayscale hearts, then mostly darkness as she looked beyond manmade roads into the western mountains.

Rowan inhaled sharply as her mental journey entered a cave to find silhouetted figures over Oren's soul. He lay on the stone floor, while the shadowed figures beat him with their fists and kicking him repeatedly. Lady Linnea, her arms bound with a rope, was sobbing in a chair.

"Lady Linnea and Oren are being held inside the Celaris Mountain," Rowan whispered, her eyes opening. "We need to find Nora." She quickly moved toward bustling servants. "Have you seen Nora?" she asked repeatedly.

"I think she's helping Mrs. Ginty in the kitchen," said one boy.

Rowan hurried to the kitchen, nearly crashing into Nora.

"I need your help," she said to the maidservant. Rowan dropped her voice. "Can you get me a horse and a way out of the castle grounds?"

"Me, too," said Bane, causing Rowan to jump. "I know what you're thinking, and you're not going alone."

"I'm going, too," Blythe said, moving slowly into the crowded kitchen.

"Blythe—"

"No, I decided I'm not going to let my physical limitations define me, and you shouldn't either."

"Oh, Blythe," Rowan threw her arms around her sister. "I'm so sorry I got so caught up in finding a cure, a way to make things like they were before you got sick, that I didn't realize that my goal to help stop your pain was becoming nearly an obsession—one that was making you feel less than you really are. Can you forgive me?"

Blythe held her sister, nodding her head. "I may never go back to pain-free days or complete use of my legs. I just want you to still love me as I am—not what I used to be."

Rowan squeezed her sister tighter. "I do." She pulled away and found Nora watching, her eyes glossy with tears. "Nora, can you help us?"

"I can help you; but with everything going on, I don't think that's safe," said Nora, her gaze falling to the floor.

"Please, Nora?" Blythe asked.

"I would listen to the girl," the deep voice of Cassian thundered from outside of the kitchen door. He pushed his form in as best he could. "It isn't safe. But I am sworn to protect you."

Rowan grinned as the knight attempted to bow, but the limited space prevented much movement.

Nora sighed but whispered theatrically, her face full of mischievous glee, "Meet me by the servants' entrance in your room in a quarter of an hour. One of the stable hands owes me a favor."

Acknowledgments

WORDS ALONE WILL NOT ADEQUATELY express my gratitude for those who championed me throughout this novel adventure, but I would be foolish not to try.

Thank You, God, for placing stories on my heart and for placing such wonderful people on the path of my own life's story.

Thank you to my amazing husband, Matthew. When I started this project endeavor years ago, our daughter was but a whispered prayer; now, she is here to celebrate this achievement with us. My wonderful father, Cliff, has since transitioned to his eternal home—I wonder if there are audiobooks in Heaven? I hope you're proud of me for seeing this through, Daddy.

Thank you, Mama, for always believing in me even when I am full of doubts and for encouraging me to trust that my creativity is a gift from our Creator. Thank you to Kari, Tyler, my grandparents, and extended family for always supporting me.

Thank you to the team at my publishing house for believing in this book, the messages within the narrative, and that *The Goodness of Unicorns* can and will share the goodness of God with readers. Thank you also to my amazing editor, Sydney, for helping polish Rowan and Blythe's story for it to shine at its fullest potential. And thank you to all alpha readers, beta readers, and launch team members who helped encourage me and helped to spread the word about this book.

And thank you, dear reader, for being a part of this journey. May you embrace the light and the gifts placed within your heart by the King of kings and always remember His goodness is reflected in you.

About the Author

KAYLA E. GREEN IS AN author, poet, and queso aficionado. When she isn't writing, reading, or spending time with her family, she loves singing loudly and off-key to KLove Radio and pretending she's a unicorn. She has written an award-winning YA fantasy novella, *Aivan: The One Truth*, and an inspirational poetry collection, *Metamorphosis*. Kayla also has stories and poems featured in various anthologies, contest-winning stories published with *Clean Fiction Magazine* and online with *WOW! Women on Writing*, and several flash fiction stories available online through Havok Publishing. Connect with her at theunicornwriter.com and on Instagram @theunicornwriter93.

Abandoned as infants, Tovi and her twin brother were raised by an eclectic tribe of warm, kind people in a treehouse village in the valley. After her brother's sudden disappearance Tovi questions her life and her faith in an invisible King. Ignoring her best friend Silas' advice, she decides to search for her brother in the kingdom on top of the mountain. Amidst the glamour of the kingdom above the cloud Tovi is torn between her own dark desires and unanswered questions.

Seventeen-year-old Adaliah is the warrior and Lady of Targe, but when she wakes up in the Kest River, presumed dead by the world, she has lost her memory and is being hunted by unknown forces. Injured and alone, she must put together the pieces of her broken past and shattered kingdom.

Artka, once a nobleman's son, is now a Carnalian soldier fighting a war against Ecclessa, which is said to be ruled by a ruthless Magician. Lost in the forest while escaping tophets, Artka is pierced by an Ecclessite's kingsman sword—but the sword does not immediately harm nor kill. To survive the piercing and heal his heart's wound, Artka must seek Logon. As, invisible enemies lurk around him, only the runes on his Ecclessite sword can lead him to safety . . . if he can survive the journey.